LIGHT IT UP

LIGHT IT UP

IT UP

KEKLA MAGOON

HENRY HOLT AND COMPANY · NEW YORK

Henry Holt and Company, *Publishers since 1866*
Henry Holt® is a registered trademark of Macmillan Publishing Group, LLC
120 Broadway, New York, NY 10271 • fiercereads.com

Library of Congress Cataloging-in-Publication Data

Names: Magoon, Kekla, author.
Title: Light it up / Kekla Magoon.
Description: First edition. | New York : Henry Holt and Company, 2019. |
    Summary: Told from multiple viewpoints, Shae Tatum, an unarmed
    thirteen-year-old black girl, is shot by a white police officer, throwing
    their community into upheaval and making it a target of demonstrators.
Identifiers: LCCN 2019002033 | ISBN 978-1-250-12889-8 (hardcover) |
    ISBN 978-1-250-12890-4 (ebook)
Subjects: | CYAC: Death—Fiction. | Police shootings—Fiction. | Race
    relations—Fiction. | African Americans—Fiction.
Classification: LCC PZ7.M2739 Lit 2019 | DDC [Fic]—dc23
LC record available at https://lccn.loc.gov/2019002033

Our books may be purchased in bulk for promotional, educational, or business use.
Please contact your local bookseller or the Macmillan Corporate
and Premium Sales Department at (800) 221-7945 ext. 5442
or by email at MacmillanSpecialMarkets@macmillan.com.

First edition, 2019 / Designed by Sophie Erb

Printed in the United States of America

1 3 5 7 9 10 8 6 4 2

For Noa & Kate

THE INCIDENT

At the end of the day, a girl is dead. Maybe it's winter. Maybe she had a black ski hat on. Maybe she was running and didn't stop when he ordered her to. Maybe because she had headphones in, so she didn't hear him shouting. Maybe she was late for something. Or maybe she was running simply because it was cold and dark and she was nervous to be alone on the street. It was dusky already at four-thirty p.m. When the lights flashed behind her, maybe it didn't seem unusual. Maybe she never imagined it was about her. She was tall for her age, bundled in her warmest coat. She looked bigger than she was. Thicker. More like a man, an adult. But still thirteen years old.

DAY ONE: THE INCIDENT

PEACH STREET

No one saw anything.

In the aftermath, the curb is dewy with blood. The man crouches by the girl's body. They are both now smaller than they were.

"No, no, no, no, no." He is on his knees. On his lips, a litany of sorrows.

He shoves away the iPod lying on the sidewalk. It jerks back, tied to the body by headphones. The sound of low talking blossoms into the silence.

He is supposed to press the walkie-talkie button, call again for backup.

Instead, he reaches around her puffy coat collar, presses fingers to her neck. "No, no, no, no, no."

What he sees—it's impossible. He prides himself on being a good shot. Prides himself on his instincts.

WITNESS

You don't expect it. Ever. Walking home, like usual, the last thing you expect is to witness a murder. Shootings happen around this neighborhood, of course they do, but somehow you still never expect it. You worry about it, in a ghost way. A sliver of thought in a dusty back corner of the brain. A curl of gray matter that gets woken up once in a blue moon, given an electric shock to remind it never to fade.

You expect to cross the street, avoid the hoopla, like always. There's no call to get involved. No one wants to be a witness. To put yourself out there like that, against some gangbanger you maybe went to high school with? Hells no. Not this cat.

The squad car, lights flashing, is at the other end of the block. A traffic stop, maybe. Or a domestic thing, checking up on some hipster's noise complaint about the sound of fighting next door.

It's a whole block away. You figure you have time to get around whatever's going on. There's no crime scene tape. But then suddenly you're upon them. The cop and the child. You can tell it's a child, somehow. Maybe you know the world all too well.

When you're first on the scene, here's what you find:

The body looks unreal. Some punk-ass King, or whatever, rendered inert. Black coat, like a marshmallow. Strange kicks, for a gangbanger. Is pink the new red?

The sirens are blaring. Response time was slow. One cop in the area, got to the scene first.

"What happened?"

"He's dead. He's dead," the officer says. "He had a gun."

The world inverts. This is a whole different thing. You can't help it, you blurt out, "You shot him?"

The officer lunges to his feet. His weapon rises up. "Step back."

You freeze, then slowly spread your hands wide. "Whoa, man. I ain't do nothing. I ain't see nothing."

Heart pounding, skin pounding, the pulse pumps firmly in your chest, your knees, your eyes. You pray. *Keep pumping. I ain't gotta die today.*

That corner of your brain, that worried corner, is much bigger than you thought and it's wide awake now. It scolds. *See flashing lights, go down another block. No lookie-loos.* It aches. *Not my time. Not today. I ain't going down like this.* It speaks to your feet. It's your brain—it can do that. *Run. Run.*

You fight it. With another part of your brain, the common sense part. You hold fast there, knowing you might be shot down where you stand.

The sirens grow louder.

"Be cool, man," you say. "Be cool."

He's breathing hard. And you are.

More cops roll up. More guns. All on you. Just like that, a walk home becomes a mouthful of sidewalk. Becomes handcuffs. Becomes the back of a cop car and a call to some legal aid lawyer. On the phone you tell her, "I ain't done nothing. I ain't seen nothing. I was just walking home."

ZEKE

In my nightmares I see flashing lights. I see them in the glint of sun off the other cars' hoods in the rearview. I see them in the glare off the road signs and in bouncing headlights. I see a white car with a ski rack and I ease off the gas on instinct. Just in case.

I wanna fly, you know? I wanna put the pedal to the metal, knowing I can afford the cost of a ticket. It's gonna be what, fifty bucks? A hundred? I don't know. Never been pulled over. Never wanna be.

Watch the needle like a hawk instead.

Every time.

Tonight, the lights behind me are real.

My pulse pounds under every part of my skin. Blinker on. Glide to the shoulder. Lower the window, then freeze, with my hands at ten and two. I already can't breathe.

Not one, but two police cars. I expect them to flank me. They don't even slow.

My car rocks in their wake. They are flying.

A prayer slides out of me, unbidden.

Relief, for myself.

Hope and despair, for the poor souls at the other end of their call.

Find a gap, ease back into traffic. Other cars rocket by me. I'm that annoying driver everybody can't wait to pass. Their slipstream is my security blanket. They'll get pulled over before me, for sure.

I'm only a few minutes' drive from the Underhill Community Center. I'll make it there before full dark.

My old car chugs its way down the exit ramp, weaves through the neighborhood. It's hard, coming down from expressway speed. Feels like I'm crawling.

Peach Street is all lit up like Christmas. Some kind of big mess.

I crawl. Watch the needle like a hawk. Use my signals.

Fifty bucks. A hundred. That's good money and all, but what's the cost of freedom?

All I know is what it's not worth: my life.

KIMBERLY

The clock on the office wall reads 5:27. It's two minutes behind my cell phone. My shift technically ended at five.

Zeke's late.

I've been pretend-packing-up my purse for almost half an hour. Put the lip gloss in, take the lip gloss out. Gloss. Put the lip gloss back in. Stand up. Loop the purse straps over my arm and take a last look at the desk. I'm like a background character in a cartoon. Can you get a repetitive stress injury from being ridiculous?

I should go. Instead, I unloop the straps and sit down again.

There's a file folder open on the desk. Doesn't matter which. It's only there so I can close it with a flourish, stuff it in the drawer, and breezily declare, "I was just on my way out."

I scroll to see what everyone's posting. Another couple of minutes won't hurt anything.

There's a discussion going on between several well-known organizers from around the country. Kelvin X and Viana Brown love to go head-to-head about protest tactics. Kelvin thinks he's clever, and he always sounds good in a thread of one-liners, but most of his ideas are unrealistically militant. I toss hearts onto a couple of Viana's best zingers. *Violence is not the answer; violence is the question.* She is always spot on.

The big viral item of the afternoon appears to be an article featuring Senator Alabaster Sloan.

I scroll past that one. I don't want to think about Senator Sloan. The Reverend. Al. Whatever.

"Hey." Zeke's voice comes out of nowhere.

I leap about a mile. Zeke's right there, on the other side of the desk. Even not reading the article had pulled my attention all the way into my phone, apparently.

"Oh, hey." My smile feels dramatically extra-glossed. Did I overdo it? Are my lips shining like a mirror right now? God. I fumble for the edge of the file folder. "I was just about to take off."

"You might want to wait a few minutes," he says. "There are cops all over Peach Street. Looks like a big raid or something."

When I leave, I won't be going toward Peach. The hair salon where I work is down that way, but my apartment is a few blocks in the other direction. I guess Zeke doesn't know that. Or . . . did he just invite me to stay? Does he want me to?

My tongue darts out over my lip. Comes back coated in gloss. Ugh. Sticky. "Um—" I scrape my teeth against the gunk. "Sure, that's a good idea."

Zeke isn't really paying attention to me.

I plop my purse back on the desk for the dozenth time. If it was animate, it would be pissed at me for jerking it around. "They've been out in force lately, haven't they?"

"Our community actions are making them nervous." Zeke smiles. He has a great smile. Not too glossy or anything. "Everything we do in the neighborhood to empower people, to create awareness, is frightening them. They want to keep us in check."

I lean on the edge of my desk. No, that probably makes my hips look too wide. "They're succeeding, aren't they?" It's an honest question.

Zeke looks at the desk. "Yeah."

There's not much to say after that. Except something about how we're going to change things, right from here. Together.

But that would sound too corny.

Our room is in the heart of the community center. It doesn't have any windows. "I guess I should get home," I tell him. It's pizza night with my roommate. "How long until it passes, do you think?"

The phone starts ringing off the hook.

MELODY

Police lights and caution tape? That's straight-up black-person repellent. People avoid that certain block on Peach Street while the cops close in. Ain't nobody want a piece of that mess. At first.

Then word gets out. What's really going down.

A child, dead. A girl.

Then the truth gets floated: *officer-involved shooting.*

Reporters pop up at the corners.

Then her name gets out: *Shae Tatum.*

What? They wrong. They gotta be. I would have kept walking, if I didn't hear someone say it. 'Cause that can't be right. Can't be.

Shae wouldn't be out alone at night. Ever. This couldn't happen.

Hold up, though. . . . It's Thursday. I dropped her off at tutoring at 3:30. Sometimes she walks home alone. It's only five blocks. But she'd have been home hours ago.

Already got my cell in my hand, like always. Dial Shae's momma.

It rings on into nothing.

Gotta get closer. I can't see past the people. Too short. *Think thin.* It's not so hard to slide to the front when you're small. Crane my neck, but there are too many police cars. The block is lit. Uniforms wandering this way and that. Milling.

The body on the sidewalk. Black coat. Pink shoes—

No. No. God, no.

The wail comes out loud. My green gloves tug at the yellow tape.

POLICE LINE—DO NOT CROSS.

I will cross anyway. But strangers put their hands on me.

Shae.

No way to go forward, no way to go back. There's a crowd, thick behind me, everyone crying and cursing and fussing. Rows and layers of people. More witnesses than anyone would know what to do with. They hopping. They shivering. How many of us got a really good winter coat? Naw, you mostly bundle and scurry. Like Shae was.

I can picture it. I can picture her going and going. Headphones in, like she always had.

Shae.

TINA

Shae wore headphones
for courage.
The sound of voices
in her ear made her feel
less alone in a big scary world.

JENNICA

The bell above the door jangles. *Customer!* It rings out the news way too cheerfully. I'm tired of smiling today.

I'm pouring coffee for the old guy already at the counter. He's a regular. Not a chatty one, just likes to watch the news. We have a rhythm.

When I turn around, my stomach shifts.

Oh. It's only Brick. I'm relieved and stirred all at once.

"Hey, Jen."

He calls me Jen here, because that's what's on my name tag. He's respectful like that.

Brick perches on one of the counter seats. "How you doing?"

"I'm good." I slip him a menu. Sometimes he orders. Either way he always leaves money on the counter. Hard to argue with that.

"Just good? But I'm here now." He smiles and winks.

I don't know what he's playing at. He likes me, but not like that. At least, he's never tried to grab me or nothing. If he's after me for sex, he's going about it different than any King I've known. Sometimes I get a glimmer off him, but it always tucks back away.

I'm mainly glad he comes alone. He's not trying to run game to get me back with Noodle. And Noodle's his main man, so maybe that's why he doesn't try to get fresh with me himself. Respect. Not that Noodle deserves it.

Brick scrolls through his texts. "Gotta iron out some wrinkles between my boys."

"Don't forget to starch them," I joke.

Brick grins. "I heard of that," he says. "Is that a real thing?"

"Sure." My mom used to starch my dad's work shirts. It was old school. The memory floats, like a cloud of starch dust. Standing under the ironing board, around my mom's knees. Puffs of steam, watching the powder float down. Thinking it magical, like snow.

Like snow.

Long before snow ruined them.

Brick grimaces. "Who wants their fabric all stiff, like cardboard? Hard to work it out in my head."

I let myself smile, but it's tight. Can't forget what his boys do. Can't ever forget. "Not stiff, more like . . . crisp. If you dig neatly pressed uniform shirts, or whatever."

Brick wears a black denim shirt with red trim. Red cap on backwards. Variations on a theme. He looks good.

He turns his phone over so he can't see the screen. "Lemme get some pie."

I serve him, and he chats at me about whatever. He likes talking to me, I think. He always did. We get along.

"You wanna come up to my place tonight? I've got people coming over."

He already knows what I'm going to say. "That doesn't make it different from any other night, does it?"

He shrugs. "What can I say? I'm the host with the most. Can't keep the ladies away."

Most of the ladies. It goes unsaid. "Thanks, anyway," I say.

He sighs. "I miss having you come by. We had some good times, didn't we?"

I slide Brick's pie plate away, try to clear my mind. No good comes from thinking in reverse. Instead, I focus on how it's pizza-night Thursday. What will go on my half, what will go on Kimberly's. She's more predictable. I like to shake it up. Because I can. Tonight I have to work later than usual, but the food will still be waiting for me when I get home.

Brick's phone is buzzing off the hook, but he stays right with me.

"Are you gonna check that?" I ask. He's barely glanced at it in ages.

"I should," he says. "Don't want to. Somebody's got beef and they wanna drag me into it."

"Where's the beef?"

Brick offers me half a grin. Hmm. He usually laughs too hard at my bad jokes. He's trying to look out for me.

He glances at his phone. Double takes. Picks it up and scrolls.

"Hey, do me a favor," he says. "Pop on the local news."

"Sure." The remote is right there below the counter, by the silverware bin. A couple of clicks and I'm seeing what he meant.

The six o'clock news leads with it. "Officer-involved shooting . . ."

"They always try to sugarcoat it." The old guy down the counter shakes his head. Time to refresh his coffee.

The clatter of the glass pot, the smell, the steam rushing up—all familiar. Familiar as the sterile-sad voice overhead.

"Police say a full investigation will be conducted. They decline to release the name of the suspect pending notification of the family."

"Suspect," the old guy grunts. "Dollars to donuts it's just a kid."

Brick pays closer attention to his phone. "Maybe one of my guys. My phone is blowing up."

My hand moves, almost of its own accord. Across the counter to cover his free hand.

BRICK

As I stroll out the diner, Noodle's texting me up down and backwards. *Where u at?*

Taking care of some business, I answer.

Can't exactly tell him I'm doing what I do most evenings. Eating mediocre diner pie and slow playing his ex.

Srsly, Noodle types. *Get down here. It's lit.*

It might never happen, me and Jennica. Maybe it shouldn't, either.

Ten cruisers on Peach. Paddy wagon rolling in.

Get clear of it, I instruct him. What is he thinking messing around with this? He's reckless. Dives headfirst into a mess and expects to come up clean.

Can't, he says. *We're throwing down.*

Sigh. Sometimes I wonder what Jennica ever saw in Noodle in the first place. He has only two settings: pissed off about everything or high enough not to care about anything. She deserves better. He's my boy, but come on. She's too smart for him. She deserves some nuance. Some sweet. I have more to offer her than Noodle ever could.

I'm biding my time. I could close this deal anytime I want, though. I know what to say to make it happen. She moves like a frightened rabbit. She would fall into my arms, like she keeps falling back into Noodle's. I could save her.

If it was any other girl, I might go on and get it done. See how it all shook out. We'd run fast and hot like a struck match, then flame out just as easily. But Jennica's not just any girl.

She's gotta know, she's safe with me. However long that takes. Slow burn. Something Noodle could never comprehend.

I tell him again, *We don't need trouble. Get out.*

Can't, bro. Everyone's here.

Goddammit. All right. Tuck my collar, glide toward the scene. My ride's parked between Peach and the diner anyway. Easy enough to swing past and see what's up. At least long enough to smack Noodle upside the head and bring him home.

Moments like this, I miss Tariq Johnson more than ever. I need a second with a better head on his shoulders. Noodle's loyal, and tough. He takes his marching orders without pushback—usually—and he knows how to keep the rank and file in line. But I need someone to bounce ideas off of. I used to have these conversations with T, before he got shot. And Jennica, too, when she was on the inside. Now I'm on my own. Juggling the big decisions without a sounding board ain't easy. Can't take Noodle's word for what's going down. Gotta see it for myself.

The shouting reaches me two blocks out. What the actual . . .

OFFICER YOUNG

Crowd control is usually a bullshit assignment. Boring as hell. We stand on a street corner during a march for breast cancer awareness, or whatever, and watch the chattering ladies stroll by, carrying their signs and balloons. We stare at pink shirts, hats so long the color loses meaning. We try not to think about breasts, even though they are all around us and the word is everywhere, too.

There is something musical about the shouting and chanting; we are lulled by it. There is energy pouring out of the comparatively small bodies in front of us. There is something powerful about the passion and anger directed at this disease, something moving about the idea of people coming together to make change.

We stand there, vigilance level set to automatic. Our eyes flick here and there occasionally. We admonish people for sneaking through the barricades. Sometimes they cross them anyway. We're part of the fabric backdrop. Everyone moves through us.

We get our toes run over by strollers a couple of times. Sometimes we get an apology. We give directions to the porta-potties. We stand with our thumbs hooked over our belts because we think it looks cooler than letting our arms dangle, plus the department discourages crossed arms because some captain took a course in nonverbal communication and determined that the messaging is unfriendly.

That's what it's supposed to be. Tonight it's not that.

Tonight, the only splash of pink has great meaning.

Tonight we stand with our arms crossed.

We put on our most menacing stares. If anyone steps on our feet, we can respond with appropriate force. If anyone has to pee, it's their own damn problem to solve.

There is something menacing about the shouting and chanting; we are disturbed by it. There is energy pouring out of the comparatively dark bodies in front of us. There is something unsettling about the passion and anger directed at us, something terrifying about the idea of people coming together to tear our blue line down.

We stand there, vigilance level set to the max. Our eyes flick here and there constantly. We threaten people for leaning over the barricades. Our batons are at the ready, and so are our guns. No one moves through us.

We're each handed a Plexiglas shield to carry in front of us. It makes us feel better and worse at the same time. We have fleeting thoughts about nonverbal messaging, but we do what we're told. We stand in a line, ready to serve and protect.

WILL/eMZee

The best time to tag is the middle of the night, but after school is when I'm free. I've made my peace with it.

The best time to mural is at dusk. Early enough that you still got some light, late enough that you can hide your face if you need to.

It's not unusual for me to see a big police hoopla. SWAT teams enjoy moving around dusk as well. No rhyme or reason. You'd think they'd prefer full daylight. *All the better to shoot you by, my dear.* I picture them cackling like cartoon villains, dressed in their strange new urban camo.

I guess we should have known they were coming for us when someone went out and made fabric. Urban insurgency.

It is unusual to see such a big gathering of onlookers. That's what really holds me up.

I'm supposed to be heading home. Long before now, actually.

It should be dark, but it doesn't look it, with all the floodlights. It should be cold, but it doesn't feel it.

The crowd is getting heated.

The body, people keep saying. *Move the body.* The ambulance is down the end of the block. Only vehicle on the street with its lights off.

But they don't move the body. They don't move her for hours. The sun goes down. They roll in lights. Walk around her like some set dressing. She is out of sight of the crowd, but the cops circle like vultures.

People gather, watching. Shouting. Cops come stand at the edge of us, with bullhorns. They order us to disperse.

We are not to wonder. We are not to feel. We are not to question the things we see before us.

We surge against the police line tape. It is not a wall. We are held in place because we let ourselves be . . . for how much longer? How much longer?

I slip from the crowd. Pull my spray cans from my satchel. Black. Gray. Red. White. Pause a second . . . Blue.

Shake. Listen to the telltale ball-bearing rattle.

Speak. My arms arc over my head.

I write the words in big letters on the side of a brick building. This space, I've been saving. It deserves something huge and beautiful. Something that would take more than a night to complete.

I don't know why, but I do it. Tell myself I can paint over it later.

Write the words: BLACK POWER.

Host: *We're here with special guest Professor Xavier Charles of Columbia University, monitoring the escalating tensions in Underhill tonight. Professor, what's your take on the situation?*

Prof. Charles: *Tragedy all around. The authorities are going to need to proceed with greater caution than they've displayed so far tonight.*

Host: *Are we looking at a possible riot?*

Prof. Charles: *We're looking at a community being actively disenfranchised, and targeted by law enforcement. You want to talk about tensions running high, don't look at the people on the street. They have reasons to be angry.*

Host: *So, in your view, rioting in Underhill is a real possibility tonight?*

Prof. Charles: *The police are not treating the citizens with respect. Bad policing results in unnecessary violence. Case in point, a thirteen-year-old girl was murdered tonight.*

Host: *Allegedly . . . The investigation hasn't returned any results yet.*

Prof. Charles: *An unarmed child was shot to death by a police officer. The police department already publicly confirmed the basic facts of the case. Let's be clear—we're talking about a murder.*

Host: *We're talking about the actions of a police officer on duty. It's irresponsible journalism to throw around criminal accusations—*

Prof. Charles: *I'm not a journalist. I'm a political science and African American history professor.*

Host: *To say murdered suggests—*

Prof. Charles: *I'm aware of what it suggests. The historical legacy of police violence against black citizens bears it up.*

Host: *History isn't at issue here.*

Prof. Charles: *Look at Watts in '65, look at LA after Rodney King, Ferguson after Michael Brown, Baltimore after Freddie Gray.*

Host: *Riots.*

Prof. Charles: *You want to call it "riots" because you want the focus to be on so-called black violence and so-called black criminality. You want to do anything possible to justify the reality of police officers acting with lethal force on a community.*

Host: *That's not—*

Prof. Charles: *You want to say it's okay for a police officer to respond with knee-jerk lethal anger at the mere idea of a threat against his person, and at the same time you want to say it's wrong for a community to rise up in peaceful anger in response to repeated, systematic abuses at the hands of the power structure. That logic doesn't hold.*

Host: *Peaceful anger? A riot?*

Prof. Charles: *Look at the live feed. I see a group of people exercising their First Amendment rights to free speech and to assemble peaceably. You've had the camera focused on the crowd this whole time. Who there is breaking the law? Yet you're already calling it a riot.*

Host: *A potential riot.*

Prof. Charles: *You see a public gathering of the black community as a potential riot—*

Host: *Look at them!*

Prof. Charles: *—and they see every police officer as a potential murderer.*

Host: *That's unfair.*

Prof. Charles: *Yes. But it's a parallel, and a racist double standard that news media and law enforcement perpetually ignore.*

Host: *You're saying there's bias on both sides?*

Prof. Charles: *I'm saying you have the cameras turned the wrong way. The whole time we're talking here, the live feed playing on the split screen is focused on the crowd of angry blacks. The scroll bar says "escalating tensions threaten to spill over." If you want to talk about responsible journalism, you should also show what they're protesting. How many hours later, and that child's body is still in the street?*

Host: *The police are surely following an investigative protocol. We can get more information—*

Prof. Charles: *They're making choices about what to prioritize.*

Host: *The crowd is growing and they don't have a permit to demonstrate.*

Prof. Charles: *Did they have a permit at the Boston Tea Party?*

Host: *You can't compare—*

Prof. Charles: *No matter what they tell you about the First Amendment, this country will never grant us a permit to tear down the establishment.*

Host: *That sounds dangerously close to treason, Professor.*

Prof. Charles: *On the contrary. It's a deeply American idea. The fundamental right to oppose tyranny is the entire basis for the Declaration of Independence, which we widely regard as a foundational document of the United States. But it wasn't at the time. It was, in fact, a document of resistance against the Crown, after which the newly independent states created their unified government under a new flag. The US Constitution, the actual foundational American document, establishes law for this new nation, in which black Americans, then enslaved, were counted as three-fifths of a person and denied basic human rights and citizenship. You can call it treason, but it is a deeply American idea for the disenfranchised to rise up against the power structure, in an effort to secure actual equality and the benefits of liberty on their own terms.*

Host: *You're calling for a revolution.*

Prof. Charles: *I'm calling for systemic social change. There are myriad ways that change could happen peacefully. We might still be British subjects if the Crown had responded to the colonists' desire for self-government with compassion and forethought. In this nation today, we still have leaders who stubbornly pursue their own self-interest. Instead of investing in social services, we have militarized policing.*

Host: *We need to take a break. Last thoughts, Professor Charles?*

Prof. Charles: *You have the cameras turned the wrong way. Even through this discussion, the feed hasn't shifted. You want to blame* *poor black communities, but violence begets violence. The problem begins with the police and the politicians who deploy them. I'll remind your viewing audience that there are students in the streets of Underhill right now, filming the police from within the crowd and posting the footage online. We should all be looking in all directions. The revolution—*

Host: *Thank you, Professor. We'll be—*

Prof. Charles: *—may not be televised, but it will be YouTubed.*

Host: *—right back with an update regarding Underhill Police Department procedures.*

@KelvinX_: Light it up, ya'll. #underhill #riseup

@Viana_Brown: We wait no longer. We stand still no longer.
#standupspeakout

> **@Momof6:** Kids today. SMH.

> **@BrownMamaBear:** My thoughts and prayers are with
> Underhill!

@WesSteeleStudio: The mainstream media will tell you LIES about
what happened tonight in Underhill. Wes Steele makes the real story
known: click for video. #HeroCop #MakeItKnown

> **@WhitePowerCord:** Self-defense is a human right.
> #BlueLivesMatter

> **@WhitePowerCord:** One less criminal on the streets. Hoo-rah.
> #HeroCop

@BrownMamaBear: Will there be peace in our time? Praying for all the
little brown babies tonite. #blessings

> **@Usual_Suspect_911:** Why r u up here talkin bout blessings?
> Aint no GOD in this mess.

> **@BrownMamaBear:** My prayers are with you, young brother.
> #blessings

> **@Usual_Suspect_911:** You trippin. Prayers aint enough.
> #WalkingWhileBlack

NIGHT ONE: THE FALLOUT

PEACH STREET

The opposite of calm is a frenzied feeling. It is the scratch of wool mittens, necessary to stay warm. It is the foam that spills out from the hole of a beer can, the pop-rush-damp, a first careful sip, then a chug.

The opposite of calm is concentric circles, the ripple effects of a stone in a pool. One smooth black stone—plop, rush, shimmer, and the stillness is broken.

The opposite of calm is the skitter of pebbles. When the people are distressed, so is the surface of the street. Every crack in the sidewalk echoes their scream.

WITNESS

"Man, nothing." How many ways can you say it? "I was walking home. Turned the corner, came upon the cop and the dead kid. That's it."

"What did you see?" the officer asks again. The room is small and growing smaller by the minute. You wonder if people are watching you through the dark window in the wall. You assume you're being recorded. "Describe exactly what you saw."

"Cop and the dead kid."

"The officer and the suspect. Did you witness the shooting?"

"Naw, man. It was over already. Kid was on the ground, cop was kneeling over her."

"The suspect was on the ground?"

"Yes. Lying there dead."

Cop nods. "The suspect was on the ground. Was the suspect lying face-up or face-down?"

"Face-up. He turned her over to check for a pulse."

Cop's voice sharpens. "Did you see him do that?"

"Naw, you could tell by the way the body was turned."

"I'll ask you not to speculate, then. Was the suspect lying face-up?"

"Yes."

"So, the suspect was facing the officer at the time of the shooting?"

Steam fills you up. You let it slide out your nose, like a bull. Let it slide out your ears, like a cartoon. "How you gonna call a thirteen-year-old girl a suspect?"

"Answer the question. The suspect was facing the officer at the time of the shooting?"

"I told you, I ain't see it."

Cop sighs. "I expect your cooperation in this matter."

Cooperation? As in, lying to support the cops? Screw that. "Now you want me to speculate?"

"Boy—" Cop looks like he's about to blow a gasket. Whatever that is.

The legal aid lawyer clears her throat. "What do you expect to gain from this line of questioning?"

Cop breathes in and out a couple times. Almost makes you laugh. Someone's been to anger management. You know a little something about that yourself. You're sitting here hoping they don't look up those records and use it against you.

"Ma'am, we're trying to determine an order of events."

"My client has been clear about his experience of the incident. If there's nothing further, and there are no charges to level, then he's free to go."

You stand up, following her lead.

"On TV they can tell that shit." Mistake. Too impulsive. You're baiting a hook, and you're the only fish in the room.

"Excuse me?" Tall cop wheels around.

Lawyer puts her hand on your arm.

"Forensics, right? You got some lab techs somewhere who can tell if she was shot from the front or from the back."

Tall cop flinches toward his cuffs, a reflex. "You wanna be charged with impeding an investigation?"

Lawyer sweeps you out the door using the full meat of her arm. "My client has been fully cooperative. If you have further questions, you may direct them to my office."

You are walking, suddenly and briskly through the precinct, the lawyer's small arm around you, propelling you.

"Not another word. To anyone, ever, about this. You hear?" Her strength comes from somewhere invisible. The bull inside you paws against her grip. You're spoiling for a fight. They've tipped you past the breaking point. You'd march straight back in there, tell them how it is. You have a daughter, almost thirteen.

The night air is surprisingly chill. It was hot in there. You walk, walk, walk. Stop next to a parked car. The lights come on and the doors click unlocked.

"Tell me you heard me," the lawyer says.

You stare at her blankly.

"Don't talk to anyone. No reporters. No one. No matter what."

"They wanna silence me?"

She sighs. "It's for your own good. You didn't actually witness the shooting. There's nothing good that can come from speaking out."

You do the sensible thing, nod.

She hands you a card. "I'm dead serious. Not a word."

Dead. The image has been floating there all along, but the word brings it into full focus. Smooth young cheeks, gone slack. Eyes unfluttering. Sleeping but not sleeping.

"Need a lift?" she offers.

"I'll walk."

You need time, and space. To clear your head. You have a daughter, almost thirteen.

TINA

I am the last to know
most things.
Mom crying means there has been
an occurrence
or maybe it is just one of those days.
I don't ask questions
put on my headphones
and wait.

DeVANTE

"My roommate is driving me nuts!" Robb storms into my dorm room. I turn down the music.

"Still?" It's the third week of January. Freshman year, second semester. You'd think they'd have pulled it together by now.

Robb throws himself down across my bed and starts fiddling with the throw pillow fringe. All the guys make fun of me for that damn fringe, but Ma said we needed to dress up the place a little. Whatever. Between the throw pillows and the homemade quilts and the cookies she sends, my half of the room is cozy as hell and everyone knows it. Where do they all come sit when they're feeling out of sorts? That's right.

So, I'm making friends left and right around here. Ma knows what she's doing. Can't deny her. Not that she'd let me.

"He never wants to do anything interesting," Robb gripes. "Studies around the clock."

"It's almost like he's in college or something."

"I know, right?" Robb sighs.

I half laugh. "You know you're gonna have to make your peace with it eventually. Half a year to go."

I don't want to hear about this from him. His roommate is black and the way Robb complains about him . . . I don't know, it's not racial in a serious way, but it feels like it might be underneath. Robb doesn't quite get that some of his aversions are coded.

"It's madness," Robb says. "We have scheduled music hours and quiet hours."

"Sounds fair."

It's hard being the one everyone comes to gripe to. I've already decided that I'm applying for RA as soon as possible. Might as well get paid if I'm doing the work, right? And it does feel like work. It doesn't really seem like my suitemates or any of the guys on the floor really like me that much.

Robb's my one good friend on campus so far. All semester he's been cool to me, when some of the other guys around here come across pretty standoffish. I wasn't expecting that. I thought there'd be more of a community feel, but for some reason that doesn't work when you're one of only two black guys on the whole floor.

It's weird. All my friends from high school were white. I feel perfectly comfortable here. But I also feel like I'm coming from some other place, or they think I am, and there's a distance there. If it wasn't for the damn throw pillow situation, I'd probably have no friends at all, and be stuck in my room all the time, like Robb's roommate.

Sometimes I feel guilty for not making more of an effort with him myself. Black guy to black guy, or something. But I also don't want that kind of obligation.

"Dude," Robb says. "Twitter's blowing up."

"Yeah?"

Robb's thumb flicks over the screen. "Another shooting. Cop versus kid. In the hood."

It's when phrases like "in the hood" slip out of his lily-white ass that I have to give him the side-eye. He doesn't notice. He's too into his phone.

"That sucks," I say.

"They gotta stop this crazy shit, man, seriously."

"Tell it to the history books," I say.

"It's the twenty-first century," Robb answers. "For crying out loud."

I bite my tongue. We've been crying out loud for quite some time now, haven't we?

"Whoa. Check it."

"What?"

"This is the same neighborhood as that other famous one, Tariq Johnson."

That other famous one? Come the fuck on. "Oh yeah?"

Robb scrolls. "Yeah, they're saying it's the same exact street." He doesn't even look up. "How messed up is that?"

"Pretty messed up." It's easier to agree with Robb than try to get into a conversation.

Robb rolls up off the bed. "I'll be back," he says.

No doubt, no doubt.

When he's gone, I pull up the news on my laptop. It's good to stay current. And it's happening not that far from here, really. Less than six hours away.

News of the shooting is popping up all over everything. It stabs me all the way through. My eyes get thick. I pull on a sweater and tuck myself among the cozy pillows.

My mind replays the scene with Robb from moments ago. How . . . excited he sounded. To him, it's all a story, all a theory. It's not everything he sees when he looks in the mirror.

I close my eyes. Things had been feeling okay with Robb, finally feeling okay with some of the other guys, too. My gut says this is going to shake us up.

TYRELL

Differential equations are a slice of heaven as far as I'm concerned. My pencil slides across the page, and I lose myself in the math. Solve for x. Solve for y. The more complicated the better. Mental gymnastics is better than meditation for making the whole world disappear around me.

"Yo, T," Robb says, bursting into our room. All semblance of calm slips away.

"Tyrell," I correct him for the thousandth time.

He barrels in like he didn't even hear me. "Yo, you hear the latest?"

"I've been studying."

"You gotta check your Twitter at least sometimes, dog."

"I do." I'm just not on it 24/7, *brah.*

"Check this. Some kind of shooting happened." Robb flips his phone toward me so fast that only the key words jump out at me: *Police shooting. Child. Underhill.*

"That's tragic," I mumble. My skin tingles in little ripples, like goose bumps.

"Cops shot a girl. Only thirteen, and retarded or something."

"Don't say 'retarded,'" I correct him automatically.

"Yeah, whatever you call it." He waves his hand.

Breathe. Robb gets under my skin without even trying, and at the moment, it seems like he's trying. *Ignore him.* Focus on the next problem set in the textbook in front of me.

"That's all you got to say?" Robb looks annoyed. "That's your hometown, dog."

I'm well aware of where I come from, thanks.

He pushes the phone closer, like it's going to make me see something I didn't already.

I turn away. "So?" The cold feeling starts to rush in.

I don't want to think about home. Definitely don't want to think about people dying there.

My head is full and pounding, out of nowhere. My fingers curl around the lip of the desk.

Shootings are way too common. Anytime one happens anywhere, it reminds me of Tariq. Not that I forget about him the rest of the time. T's always with me. I carry him, like a satchel, everywhere I go. I don't mind. He's still my best friend. I carry him, and he helps me carry everything else. Sometimes it's like I can even hear his voice.

This is different. It's not in my mind—it's physical. A head-throbbing, throat-clogging, stomach-aching feeling sets in when the news hits too close to home.

Breathe in and out. Hold the edge of the desk. It'll pass. It'll pass.

"So, did you know her?" Robb says.

It'll pass. "You think I know every black person in Underhill?"

Robb rolls his eyes. "I'm not racist like that, yo. It's just, if there were riots where I come from, I'd be all over it."

"Lots of dissatisfaction down there at the country club?"

Robb laughs. "I know, right?" He doesn't even feel the dig.

"News at eleven," I say. He thinks we're buddy-buddy. A couple of guys, just joking around. It will never make sense to me. I've stopped trying to understand.

Robb scrolls through his phone. "Peach Street," he says.

A shiver goes through me. "What?"

"Dunno. They're making a big deal about where it happened."

The story writes itself in my head. I can see the street, the convenience store. The block I'd avoid like the plague, except I can't because I have to walk down it to get just about everywhere.

"Dunno," Robb says again. Scrolling. "Oh, wait, it's the same block where—"

He's going to say it, and I don't want him to. He doesn't know.

"I don't want to talk about it!" I push the words at him. I'm rarely this direct with Robb, but he can't take a hint. I need to sit with it all in my own mind. Calculate the odds of a second shooting happening in the same exact place. Like a vortex. A Bermuda Triangle, right down the street from my so-called home.

He smirks at me. "I don't get you."

That's right. You don't. You don't get me. And you don't get to get me just because you want to. You can't have me.

"Leave me alone." I reach for my headphones. I need better ones, the kind that really block out all the noise.

Robb huffs over to his bunk. I breathe in and out slowly until I can see straight again. Until my fingers uncurl from the edge of the desk and it becomes bearable again. The truth, that my best friend was shot for no reason, by a man who will never be prosecuted.

"This is wack," Robb mutters, still fixated on his phone.

When you've lost someone, the way I lost Tariq, nothing makes sense anymore. "Mmmhmm," I mumble. Robb doesn't know from wack.

BRICK

Noodle was right. The block is lit. Quite literally. Floodlights and flashing lights, and Noodle in the middle of it talking about trying to move some product.

"Unwise," I tell him. "Just let it shake out. Come on."

I don't like the look of things here. The crowd is on edge and it feels like things could all boil over. We gotta bounce. 'Fore it's our faces on the news.

"Come on." I grab his arm. Nothing's moving tonight. And even if it was, Noodle's not going to be the one to do it. We got kids for the nickel-and-dime shit.

We start pushing back, back, away from the center of this mess. We're almost out when the scream comes.

"Shae!"

The deep cry pierces, like something being torn to shreds. A sound both full and empty at the same time. And close. "Shae?" Bill Tatum tears through the crowd, a wild man. "Shae! Shae!"

The murmurs begin. *Oh, God. That's the father. Her father.*

Cops move toward the place where he will emerge.

The next five minutes play out in my mind in sped-up slo-mo fashion: *He'll run at them. Try to bring them down with his own hands. Then he'll be laid out beside her and they will feel justified.*

No time to think. I'm moving.

I use my size, my power to part the crowd. People jostle around me. No complaints. The urgency wins.

We meet at the edge of the caution tape barricade. My hands go up, blocking his path. "Tatum."

He bursts forth into my arms. He's tall and wiry, but I am a wall.

"Let me through! Shae!"

I am a wall. A shield. A punching bag.

"Shae!" he screams. "Answer me, baby!"

He pummels me. I've taken worse, but just barely.

"Back it down, bro," Noodle shouts. He's trying to get an arm in.

Tatum pushes hard, slips past me. A man possessed.

I catch him again, this time from behind. My arms X across his narrow chest, locking him to me.

Holy fuck.

We're facing a crescent of cops, guns drawn. "Hands in the air! Freeze!"

Tatum strains against my grip. "That's my baby. Let me go! That's my baby!"

"Back it down," Noodle shouts, as if reasoning with a madman is possible.

Keeping hold takes all my willpower. "I got this," I tell Noodle. "Get us a doctor."

"Doctor?" Noodle echoes.

"You killed my Shae! Get up baby, Daddy's here."

"One of them ambulance guys." I can hold Tatum for now but he ain't gonna stop. We are two big black men under the gun, and still, I can feel it. He ain't gonna stop.

The cops call out in a cacophony.

"Hands in the air!"

"Stop right there!"

"Freeze, asshole!"

"Put your hands up!"

"Show your hands!"

"You can fucking well see our hands!" I answer. "It's her father. You get that?"

Noodle edges away, one step. But he can't, really. He's in the crescent with us. We are three big black men under the gun.

Noodle looks to me, uncertain. If I order him to go anyway, he will go. My bones hum with the power of it. Even as my muscles ache with powerlessness. Under the gun.

"Stay cool," I order.

"We need a doctor!" Noodle shouts.

A Mexican-looking dude in an ambulance suit runs toward us. He pauses, becomes a part of the crescent.

"It's her father," I tell him. "You got something to knock him out?"

He glances sideways at the cops, takes one step forward. Pauses.

Tatum bucks and screams. We'd be on the ground already but for the crowd behind us, and the television cameras.

"He ain't deserve to get shot," I scream. "Fucking sedate him!"

The paramedic takes another step. "You got him?"

"I got him."

"Going in," he announces to the police. They shout at him, but he comes toward us with a syringe. He has a ring on his finger. Probably some little rug rats at home. He meets my eye, brown man to black man. All I gotta do is hold on.

"Give him more," I tell him. "It wasn't enough."

"That's the standard dose," the paramedic answers. "It'll just take a moment to kick in all the way."

"You sure?" Even as I'm asking, Tatum begins to slacken in my arms.

The paramedic's dark eyes are clouded with worry. "You good to get him home?"

"I got this." But over his shoulder, the crescent is firm. "They gonna let us walk away?"

He looks at me, looks at Noodle, looks at the crowd. "Walk him straight backward. Right now. No hesitation."

Our eyes are locked. Brown man to black man. He pulls in all his breath filling his chest and broadening his shoulders. He takes one step back, takes my place as the wall.

I move, on faith. Straight back into the crowd, dragging Tatum with me. The cops are shouting, but the crowd enfolds us.

The stone-cold ache of the crescent is with us, all the way to my car. Out of sight, out of mind, my ass. We shuffle Tatum into the backseat. His listlessness is no comfort. "Shae, baby. Daddy's here. You're okay, baby."

Noodle starts to hop in the front seat.

"No, sit with him."

"Man," he complains. "He's all spread out. What you want me to do back there?"

"Fuckin' Christ," I shout. "Just sit with him."

"Shae, baby," Tatum moans.

The paramedic didn't give him enough. Black pain is deeper than Western medicine.

In the car on the way home, even through the sedative, he keeps repeating, "My baby. My baby."

EVA

Daddy comes home late, and he's not alone. When the garage door starts creaking, I run to hug him like usual. Our routine is for me to hang up his coat while he takes off his uniform shoes.

I wait by the door. Mommy said Daddy had a problem at work today, and I am to be well behaved and not cause any trouble.

"We've already had dinner," I tell him. "We covered your plate."

The other men with Daddy are also in uniform, and looking Very Serious. The cold air comes in on their clothes.

"Come in," Mommy says. "I'll take your coats."

I get a bad feeling in my tummy. Everything is wrong.

Daddy kneels in front of me, which is not from our routine. His cheeks are bright red with cold. I lay my hands on his stubble. "What's wrong, Daddy?"

His whole face folds up. "Eva, baby."

Daddy never cries.

OFFICER YOUNG

We holster our weapons. Crisis averted. Still, nothing is calm. The dark sea of worried, angry faces still looms behind the barricade. They shout. They hiss. They hold up their phones, filming us.

"You blocked our shot, idiot," snaps the officer to my left. O'Donnell.

Chip Mendez caps his syringe. "Gonna shoot a grieving father on national TV? Really?"

O'Donnell sniffs.

"If that was the plan, then I saved your ass, O'Donnell."

"Shut up, Mendez." O'Donnell sneers. "Get back in your rig."

My eyes comb the crowd. That's the job, after all. The father is gone. We've just come face-to-face with the leader of the 8-5 Kings. And his lieutenant. They're easy to recognize. We got their faces up on a wall in our precinct.

O'Donnell might've been set to shoot, but I doubt it was at the father.

Every glint of silver is a double take. Weapon? Phone. Weapon? Phone. No one wants to screw up tonight. But here we stand, in the open. A thousand eyes on us. A thousand unseen hands out there. All angry.

"No respect for authority." O'Donnell curses. "We need to shut this down."

He's right. The gathered faces didn't flinch when we drew our weapons. Not a good sign.

O'Donnell's radio hums with static. "Sit rep, O'Donnell. Stable?"

O'Donnell squeezes the button at his shoulder. "That's a negative," he reports. "This side is hostile."

"Status?"

"We've had to draw weapons."

Brief silence. Then, "How many are you looking at?"

O'Donnell looks at me. I shrug. Glance at crowd. I'm no expert. I shrug back, hold up two fingers. Best guess.

"Can't tell for sure. A couple hundred, easy," O'Donnell says.

"All hostile?"

O'Donnell speaks into his radio. "They refuse to disperse," he reports. "They're behind the line but only for now."

"Pull back," comes the order over the radio. "Tactical unit coming in."

We don't turn our backs to the crowd. We amble, toe to heel, in reverse.

"We need masks," O'Donnell says. "Asap."

"Masks?" I echo.

The canisters whistle overhead, each trailing an arc of smoke. The white-gray cloud that billows up sets people choking.

The line we held firm for hours is shattered. So long, tenuous peace. The string of yellow tape bursts and drifts to the ground as people run and scream.

KIMBERLY

"Her body is still in the street?" Zeke says. "What's it been?"

The clock reads 11:27. Six hours exactly since I looked last. Dang, I really need to get home. I have to be up to work morning hours at the salon, and then back here for a couple of hours in the late afternoon.

Even though this organizing work feels more important than cutting hair, SCORE isn't what pays the bills.

"I really have to get home," I say. "I'm sorry."

"You've gone above and beyond tonight," Zeke says. "Thank you for all your hard work."

I gather my purse, for real this time. "I can come back tomorrow as soon as I'm done at my job."

He nods. "We're going to need all hands on deck."

The rest of the UCC is usually bustling, compared to the SCORE office. Tonight it's past closing. Everything is quiet. The community room with all its colorful chairs, unoccupied, feels strange and ghostly. In the dim light, the carpet looks worn, the chairs well used and wonky. Amazing, how people and voices and chaos can make a space come alive.

The building is silent and yet there's noise. Faraway noise pressing toward me from someplace beyond.

The front doors of the place are two tall wooden arches. This part of the building is historic. They're locked. I'm never here this late. I forgot that the staff entrance is around the side.

A heavy knock comes at the wooden door. Again. It shakes in the frame.

"Hey," says a voice. "Hey, anyone home? Help!"

My feet take me back a step, even as my arms stretch forward to open the door. Pause. "Who's there?"

"This Rico. Yvonne? Open up!"

There is a big brass key sticking out of the right-hand door. My fingers start to grasp it when there's a sound like glass shattering.

"Shit. Help! Open up!" The voice grows more urgent.

My fingers are on the key ready to turn, but I'm scared now. "Come to the side door," I say. "I can open that one." The staff entrance is a glass door. I want to know exactly what is on the other side before I make a mistake.

On the other side of the glass, people are running, shouting, frantic. The strobe of police lights echo against the bricks.

A light-skinned man with a scraggly beard lurches around the corner, his eyes wide and fearful.

"Rico?"

"Where's Yvonne?" He's holding his hand to his head. Blood seeps between his fingers.

"Come in," I say. Maybe I'm not supposed to, but there's an instinct when someone is bleeding in front of you. Rico staggers forward. I settle him at the social services intake desk, which is the closest thing. "Wait here."

The clinic is on the back side of the building. We share a wall and a door, but it's locked.

Zeke startles when I burst back into the office. "Oh, you scared me. I thought you left."

"It's—go look. It's loud out there."

"Whoa." Zeke moves up beside me. His hands wrap warm and firm around my arms, just above the elbow. He's touching me. "Everything okay?"

"Yes—" That's the automatic answer. His thoughtful frown pulls the truth out of me. His hands on my arms make me safe to say it. "Actually, no. I don't think everything is okay."

TINA

It is hard to sleep
the world sounds like broken bottles
smells like gasoline and fire
looks like police in boots and helmets
it is bad enough to hear all the sounds
without the crying smoke
Mommy comes into my room
into my bed and holds me
she teaches me the names for things
which helps
riot gear tear gas Molotov cocktail
we have plenty of reasons to cry tonight
other than tear gas
which really doesn't help anything at all

ROBB

After midnight, and it's still totally lit in Underhill. A bunch of guys from my floor are clustered into the lounge watching the coverage. Basically everyone, except Tyrell, the math-headed recluse. How's this for math? If everyone else is doing something maybe you should be doing it too.

The footage right now is a split screen, between a distinguished-looking news anchorman, and Peach Street in Underhill. The street is crowded with people chanting, surging toward a growing wall of police with riot gear. The camera angle juggles and adjusts from time to time. It must be a handheld, and they're walking around trying to cover what's happening.

The live footage turns cloudy with smoke.

"Oh, shit," says someone behind me. "No way."

"Way," says DeVante. "Remember Baltimore? Ferguson?"

Urgent, pounding music echoes from the television. A looming voiceover announces *This is a National News Network Special Update. Breaking News.*

A familiar reporter's face comes on. The hot chick with the big lips. "Tensions are escalating tonight in Underhill, at the scene of the police-involved shooting of thirteen-year-old Shae Tatum earlier tonight. We're receiving reports that police have deployed tear gas canisters in their efforts to maintain control of the crowd."

The live image is blurring and jouncing at the same time. Smoke and silence come from that side of the screen. Then the live feed cuts away, and we see the scene from an angle, from a different camera, with plumes of tear gas rising up in the near distance. The slim blond man on screen has a cloth pressed to his face with one hand, and a microphone in the other. Screaming, crying, furious people run in all directions around him.

Hot chick continues, "Reporters on the ground estimate that several hundred people have gathered to protest in Underhill tonight. We're live with the ongoing coverage. National correspondent Sean Toffee is on the scene in Underhill. Sean?"

She sorts the papers on her desk and the lapels of her tailored suit jacket widen, giving a better shot of her chest.

"Daaaaamn," I groan. "Can we get a scroll bar with her number?"

A few guys laugh. Tom, a senior, smacks me on the back of my head. "Get a grip, dude. There's rioting."

I roll my eyes. Come on, can't I think a girl is hot and still care about, like, race relations?

Wick, my next-door neighbor, says, "Leave it to Robb to try to get laid in the middle of a national crisis."

DeVante says, "Rioting? That's a white man's word."

We all look at him. Everyone in the room is white, except DeVante and two Asians. I mean, a Filipino and a . . . I forget. Chinese, maybe. Whatever—he grew up in Portland.

"Dude, there are people throwing shit through windows," says Wick. "How is that not a riot?"

"Sounds like a reasoned response to militaristic policing," DeVante answers.

I squint at him. "What the fuck are you talking about, bro?"

He throws a couch pillow at me. "I'm not your bro."

The pillow comes hard, like a brick. I block with my forearms. Weird. He's not the type to get worked up. DeVante's usually pretty chill.

"Sorry," I say. And I mean it. Maybe it feels particularly shitty to see rioting when you're black. I don't know.

"Wait," Wick says. "So, you're cool with rioting?"

DeVante sighs. "The point is, it's more complicated."

"Of course it is," says one of the Asians. The Filipino.

DeVante says, "Everyone wants to say violence isn't the answer. You have to remember that violence is also the question. That's what we don't talk about."

ZEKE

The Underhill Community Center's front doors are open. I stand beneath the wooden archway, trying to look fierce. I'm no kind of security guard, but I'm all we've got.

Yvonne bursts in the side door and immediately draws up short. Kimberly freezes amid her collection of wounded neighbors and shivering homeless people. It's not that I thought she was wrong to bring people in, but it was definitely a bold move. Without permission. And now we face the music.

Yvonne sighs. "I wondered why all the lights were on."

"What are you doing back?" I'm relieved to see Yvonne but she took a big risk venturing out to get here.

"It's my job, honey," she says.

"So, you're not mad?" Kimberly asks.

"This is what a community center is for," Yvonne says. "If we don't open our doors now, what good are we?" She pulls out her big ring of keys. "Who wants to bust into the clinic with me?"

Kimberly follows Yvonne down the hall. I pull more paper cups and paper towels out of the supply closet.

Our little crowd has grown to about twenty-five. People seeking shelter, seeking warmth, seeking first aid.

We distribute blankets from the clinic, stragglers continue to dribble in. We stick on bandages, bust out crackers and peanut butter, read news updates out loud to the room. By the middle of the night—middle of the morning, really—things seem to have calmed down.

"How are you all getting home?" Yvonne asks. "Anyone need a ride?"

"I've got my car," I say. "I can bring Kimberly home."

Loud and renewed sirens pick up out front.

"On second thought," Yvonne says. "Better to wait for first light."

Kimberly and I retreat to the SCORE office with a couple of blankets. The chairs are not that comfortable in here, and we're both too exhausted anyway.

"I have to lie down," Kimberly says. She goes behind the other desk and pushes the chair away. She curls up in the space under the desk. I completely get the impulse, to pack yourself away in a small space, safe, with walls on all sides.

"Here." I spread the blanket over her and sort of tuck her in. Maybe it's weird to do that. I pull my hands back just in case.

"Thanks." She smiles up at me. So pretty. Sleepy eyes are kinda sexy, I guess. Meanwhile she's probably like, *Why are you still sitting here touching my blanket?*

"Well, I hope you can get some rest."

"We did a good thing," she says.

"You did this." I would have stayed back here in the office all night, not helping anybody.

"Different kinds of helping." She yawns.

"I guess . . ."

Her face slackens in sleep before I can come up with the rest of what I want to say. I scoot a few feet farther away and lie down with my back against the wall. Far enough to be proper, but where I can still see her.

Different kinds of helping. Kimberly's good on her feet, quick thinking. I like to plan. Days, weeks, months in advance. But tonight we took care of things, together. We're a good team, I think.

STEVE CONNERS

"I'm worried," my wife says. "Will should really be home by now."

She seems small all of a sudden, curled against my side. I know she's worried. I've known it for hours, and yet the calm quiet truth is somehow more startling than anything that came before. We've crossed over, out of the yelling and weeping and the pacing and the "When I get my hands on him . . ."

The clock reads close to midnight, and he's not answering his phone.

"We should call the police," I say.

She freezes in my arms. "No. I don't want them looking for him."

"What?"

"The news," she murmurs. "They'll be trigger-happy tonight."

Sometimes I forget, the difference between walking down the street looking clean-cut and grown, in a suit, and being a teenage boy you can't wrestle out of a hoodie. Those damn low-slung jeans.

I shouldn't forget.

"You think he's in Underhill." I mean for it to be a question, but it comes out flat.

"That boy should know better," she snaps.

"Maybe he has a girlfriend," I say. "Maybe they lost track of time."

"Hmmph." She shoots me sharp side-eye. If Will walks in fine, and it turns out he was with a girl, she'll grill him sideways . . . and not about being late.

"I'll take a look in his room, okay?"

She says nothing. Wants it done, but doesn't want to grant permission.

It is a trespass. And yet in the moment it feels right. Needed.

A slight laundry-hamper odor hits as soon as I open the door. Random piles of dirty socks are to be expected from teenagers, I'm told. It's not terrible. His room is not as neat as the rest of the house, is all. It would be hard to be; I keep things crisp. But he's a good kid.

His walls are covered with drawings. He's really quite talented. I feel somewhat objective in saying that, since I'm only his stepfather. We've grown closer in the last couple of years. But it was hard at first. To adjust to a small person's energy and whims whipping through my condo. Now the space is all of ours, more fully than I could have imagined.

Most of his schoolbooks are piled on the bed. The guilt surges up through my chest. He's a good kid. It's not my place to do what I'm about to do.

I lift his pillow. Nothing. Kneel by the bed, lift the tails of the comforter, which is already in disarray. Covering my tracks will not be a problem.

How many socks does this child own? And how can they all be dirty? They are knotted like fists and they multiply when I touch them.

The never-ending laundry is concealing a stack of thin gray binders. They are so chock full of page protectors that they are widened like shark jaws. It looks scholarly and illicit. The one on top is full of Polaroids of graffiti art and murals, neatly organized in photo-protector slots. The older ones have regular photos, index card sketches, and random slips of paper poking out.

I gave him the Polaroid camera for Christmas. I thought he'd find it fun, and he seemed to really love it. Now I can see that he really does. He's taken dozens of photos. The album is almost full.

The art is striking.

I know Will admires street art. He comments on it all the time, if we pass some. He's got an eye for it, too. He can talk about what works and doesn't in even a small patch of color on some bricks.

He's much more into it than I realized, I guess. And he has a favorite artist, apparently. All of these pieces are signed with the same little squiggle: eMZee.

JENNICA

The customer bell over the door jangles at 11:58. I hope it's not a regular. I'm not inclined to give anyone a break right now, when we're about to close.

"Not a chance," mutters Troy, the line cook. He's already shut down the fryers and he's scraping grime off the griddle. "Send them packing."

"Yeah, got it." The half door to the kitchen is still swinging as I push back through it.

Oh. It's a regular, all right.

"Hey, Brick."

"Hi, Jen." There's no one else left in the diner except Troy, but Brick still shortens my name. Easier that way.

"You know we close at midnight, yeah?"

Brick nods. "I came to take you home."

Oh. He's done this before. It's awkward. I don't mind that much when he comes at night, to sit at the counter and keep me company if business is slow, like earlier. It's sweet.

Ever since Noodle and I split up, I stopped hanging with his boys. No one seems to care except for Brick, who keeps coming around. I don't mind, it's just awkward, because sometimes it seems like maybe he wants more from me. But he's never so much as leaned in.

I close down the diner. Grab the to-go container of salad and chicken strips Troy prepared for me after Kimberly texted to say she was not going to be home in time to pick up our usual pizza.

The chaos in the neighborhood is worse than it looks on TV. One small lens can only hold so much. The diner is ten blocks from home. A comfortable walk on a normal night. Tonight the sidewalks are full of people running and shouting.

It's not a bad idea to be with Brick. I'm safe, riding with him. The leader of the 8-5 Kings. Nobody will touch us. His low red car is a bubble floating on the surface of things. Out the windshield, it's as if I'm still viewing it all on a screen. I don't want it to come any closer.

At the stoop, I unlock the door and turn to him. If he comes in, it will get extra awkward. There's a line we cannot cross, and it's unclear whether he knows it. He's looking at me with those eyes that seem to see something in me. But I can't have it. The best choice is to lean in and kiss him on the cheek. Quick and gently. "Thanks."

He squeezes my shoulders. "You know I got you."

Once he's moved back down the stairs, I go inside. I let myself into the apartment. Kimberly's still not home. I text her:

I'm home. Where are you? You safe?

She answers:

Safe. At UCC, helping out. Don't leave home!

I curl up on the couch to wait.

@WhitePowerCord: #Underhill What a mess. Barricade them in! Let them destroy themselves. It wont take long.

@Viana_Brown: Protest is our right. Our voices matter. Our lives matter! #Underhill

> **@Momof6:** Doesn't anyone trust cops' judgment anymore? 😢

> **@BrownMamaBear:** What will it take for black children to walk safe in their own neighborhoods? #BlackChildrenMatter

@WesSteeleStudio: White officer on duty, black suspect dead. Guess who's under the microscope? THE WAR ON POLICE IS REAL. Click here for Wes Steele's latest hot take. #SteeleStudio

> **@KelvinX_:** Will someone please take this asshole's microphone? I'm busy. #UnderhillRiot

> **@WhitePowerCord:** TRUTH WILL OUT. #HeroCop

> **@KelvinX_:** There isn't a shovel big enough for @WesSteeleStudio's bullshit. Anti-white racism is not a thing. Cops are the aggressors. Just look at #Underhill tonight.

> **@WhitePowerCord:** Can't handle the truth? We will hand you your ass. #WhiteMightWhiteRights

> **@KelvinX_:** All those who feed on the racist White-Power structure will eventually starve. Our day of liberation is coming. #UnderhillRiot

> **@WhitePowerCord:** Fuck these niggers. We're gonna take it to them where they live. #MakeItKnown

> **@KelvinX_:** Give us equality or face the consequences. #YouHaveBeenWarned #UnderhillRiot

DAY TWO: THE AFTERMATH

PEACH STREET

In the light of day, the street appears unchanged. The feeling in the air, the one that can't be shaken, is intangible.

The people step gingerly as they go about their business. So as not to break the silence. They scurry heavily. The cold is bone deep.

They avert their eyes from the caution tape. Caution is in their blood.

WITNESS

You wake, and it's already in your bones. The memory of what you've seen. You can't shake it.

You pour coffee, and it looks like pavement. You crisp some toast and it looks like skin. You make the bed and it looks like that moment when they pull a sheet over the body.

You can't shake it. The house is full of things that speak of girlhood.

Your daughters' pink socks.

Their dolls.

The glitter explosion of art magnetted to the fridge.

A robot dressed like a princess sits in the middle of the dining room table, its neck cocked like it's ready to listen.

These things make you inexplicably angry.

Well, not inexplicably. You understand where it comes from and that understanding only amplifies the anger.

Things of innocence should not spark rage. Things of innocence should not spark fear. Things of innocence should go on and on and on, until they end in something poignant, beautiful. Should go on and on, until they grow.

JENNICA

"Hey," Kimberly is saying. "Do you want to sleep some more here, or move to your bed?"

Groan. Stretch. The couch blanket feels thin and the chill of the night has already reached my bones. "What time is it?"

Her warm weight settles beside me. Her hip fills the arc between my chest, stomach, and thighs. My knees curl up, as if I can tuck her into me. A reflex. She runs her hand softly over my back. When I shiver, she strengthens her touch.

"You okay?"

My brain is fuzzy. Half-sleepy. "I guess."

"You're cold. Come on into your bed." She tugs. I moan. This is familiar. Sometimes we fall asleep on the couch, trying to watch one more episode of whatever we're into. Then one of us wakes up in the middle of the night and has to drag the other one up. My sleep brain would rather stay in this semi-warm spot that is really not warm enough.

My bedsheets will be cold at first. Kimberly pulls me down the hall anyway. She folds back the bedding and I crawl in.

Pale light streams in through the blinds.

"It's almost morning."

"Yeah," she says. "It just got clear enough to come home."

I've slept through some crazy, is what it sounds like.

"What's going on out there?" I split the blinds' slats. The street looks like the street usually does. "You only just got home?"

"Yeah. It was . . . bad. For a while." Her voice is strained.

I'm awake now. "Did you get any sleep?" I grasp her hand, and she slides into the bed beside me. She's warm.

"A few hours at the center. Wait," she says. She leaves the room.

Comes back a minute later, in soft pants and oversized T-shirt. Pecking at her phone in her hand. She plugs it in to charge. "I have to get up for work in like two hours."

"Ugh."

She climbs back in with me. "Zeke was there," she says. "I was kind of waiting for him. If I'd left on time, I would have missed the whole thing."

I'm sleepy again. I tuck my hand under my cheek and yawn to signal it. "So you got to hang out?"

"Yeah, and it was crazy and busy and everything, but . . ."

"What?"

"It's probably nothing."

"What?"

"There was this moment, I don't know, where it seemed like maybe he wanted to kiss me?"

I used to think it was easy to tell when a guy was interested. If they're into you, they try to get with you. Period. They're not subtle. But thinking about Brick lately . . . it's not so clear anymore.

"He should want to kiss you," I say. "If he knows what's good for him."

Kimberly scoots closer and I roll to meet her. Wrap my arm around her stomach, rest my head on her shoulder. Sometimes it is best not to be all alone.

TINA

I like to run, I love to skip
I own many, many hats
When it is dark I go fast
too
When it is cold, I go faster
still
Momma holds my hand
Not too fast.
Slow down, baby girl.
Not everyone has a Momma
you're
Not always with your Momma
outside

WILLIEMZEE

The shower steam follows me into the hallway. Soapy heat collides with the scent of frying bacon.

Great. The last thing I need today is a man-to-man breakfast with Steve.

Sure enough, Steve's the one at the stove and Mom is nowhere to be seen. We have Pop-Tarts, right? I slink toward the pantry. Steve's back is turned but my growling stomach gives me away.

"Really?" he says. "It's so bad you're gonna skip out on eggs and bacon?"

Caught.

"Whatever." I throw myself into a kitchen chair. Who am I to turn down first-class service?

"Order's up!" Steve smiles.

"Eggs and bacon, hold the lecture."

"Eggs, bacon, toast, and fruit." He sets the plate in front of me. And a mug. "Hot chocolate."

With whipped cream? Hell. I'm really in for it.

Steve sits down across from me with his own plate. "Your mom was worried sick."

"I caught enough of that last night. Don't drag it all back up."

He sips coffee. "It's not that simple. When she worries, it affects everything."

"I know."

"You're a good kid."

I avert my eyes.

"Shae Tatum—"

I see her body in the street. Feel the heat.

"—it has her shaken up, okay?"

"Yeah." It's safest to nod and eat. How fast can I empty a plate of eggs?

"This kind of tragedy reminds us all of how black bodies are treated in this country. How easy it is to make a mistake when you look like us."

The white-hot center of me ignites. "Why you wanna put it on her? She's the one who died."

"I didn't mean—" He shakes his head. "It's so easy for what we do to be misinterpreted."

"She didn't do anything. Media is reporting the cop's version of the story. That's not how it went down."

"How do you know?"

Steve doesn't know I tag, but he knows I go back to Underhill.

"Cone of silence?" I say. That's what Steve calls it when we keep a secret from Mom. It's from this old TV spy show, *Get Smart*. He says it is important for men to have discussions between themselves.

He nods. "Usual protocol."

I hesitate. That means he will not tell Mom what I say unless someone is going to get hurt, or if he thinks it is in my best interest. But he's gotta cover his bases. I get that.

"Never mind."

"Will . . ."

"Never mind." I toss two Pop-Tarts into my backpack and bounce.

STEVE CONNERS

The email comes before I'm even at the office. New shared calendar appointment, with John at 9:15. My office.

The strange part is the location. Usually John has me come to him. Maybe it's disciplinary. It shouldn't be. Everything about my performance is on point. I'm sure of it. I make sure of it. Daily.

Something big is happening, to compel John out of his office. To be sitting on the wrong side of the desk is a position of weakness. He knows this. He's making a strategic choice. It won't be disciplinary. It'll be the opposite.

Like asking for a favor.

I make sure to arrive in the office by 8:45. If you're on time, you're late. It's easy to straighten up, clear the desk except for one fat file, which I'll leave open until they arrive. I dust the tops of the Nigerian carved-wood statues on my bookcase, smooth out the Zambian fabric swath hanging on one wall. My wife picked out these decor elements, on the theory that it gives people a sense of my heritage. It's not meant to be political.

I water my plant, arrange its leaves so the fullest part is forward. Adjust the blinds, such that there is a slight glare on the spot where John will be sitting. Then I pose behind my desk.

John enters my office, alongside a man in uniform. I don't know how to read the bars and badges, but he appears high-ranking. Underhill PD. Another officer comes in behind them.

I stand to greet them.

It rolls out in front of me, a blood-red carpet.

The officers glance around, taking in my decor. I figure anyone walking into a PR exec's office and finding a black man sitting there is going to get a sense of my heritage. So it is political.

What isn't?

"Have a seat." My arm sweeps forward to invite them.

They perch in my wing chairs. They squint into the sun. For a moment, I allow them to squirm. The leather of my desk chair settles underneath me.

They nod. Blink.

"Oh, John, would you adjust the blinds?" I tip my hand negligently toward the window. Not meeting his eye, which is more than enough to let him know. I've sat at the knee of a master. I've learned to play the game.

The officers relax, grateful. I appear both thoughtful and in charge.

EVA

Everyone at school knows it was my dad. His name was on the morning news and so was the name of the girl. Shae Tatum. A girl only a few years older than me. She was in sixth grade.

Other kids look at me and point. They whisper behind my back.

Teachers speak in voices extra bright. They whisper over my head.

He was only doing his job! I want to shout.

But I'm supposed to say nothing.

BRICK

Sheila cries when I tell her about Shae. When her face falls, I learn what that saying means in real life.

Maybe it was a mistake to come in person. I wanted to. Thought it was right. I don't know. I don't know anymore.

I've dropped her off a cliff. She loves it when I visit. Her eyes light up, she bounces. "Hi," she exclaims, when I walk into the breakfast room. "Look!" Sheila shows off her sparkling blue backpack. Her smile is a hundred watts and brightening.

But when her favorite person comes bearing terrible news . . . Extreme high to extreme low. I ask the cook to leave us alone for a minute. Pull up a chair next to Sheila and take her small hands in mine.

I was younger than this the first time I tasted grief. I remember, and I don't want to remember. If I could use my power to spare Sheila of this loss, I would do it. If I could give all my money to make it untrue, I wouldn't hesitate.

Her cries echo off the wood-paneled walls. She will wake the whole house. Any minute now, other residents or staff from the home will come running. Sheila knows that dead means gone, not just out of sight but gone forever. We go over it anyway.

When I reach over to hug her, she fixes me with a look worse than death. I am the bad-news man. I can offer no comfort.

It breaks me. I hold myself as still as I can, but in every other way I am falling apart.

One of the nursing aides rushes in. "Melody!" Sheila screams. "Shae is DEAD. Goodbye forever. We will never see her again."

"I know, sweetie." Melody gathers Sheila against her. They are practically the same height.

Hovering beside them, it hits me. At thirteen, Sheila is the size of a small adult. Shae was taller. A head taller, maybe. I can picture them, bobbing along the street side by side. What I picture next is Shae bobbing along by herself. In the dark, on the run . . . nope. In my mind's eye, she's still clearly a child.

Is it only because I knew her?

MELODY

We stand at the corner of Peach and VanBuren, fighting about the route we will take to school. Tina holds my right hand, Sheila holds my left. They are crying.

Sheila wants to take the same route because it's our route, and patterns are important.

Tina doesn't want to go by Shae's building. It's too sad.

"We can't skip Shae," Sheila cries.

I squeeze her hand. "You know she's not there. We can go to her house, but she's not going to come out." The routine has changed. It will be an adjustment.

They sniffle. It's too cold for this, and we're gonna be late.

"Switch hands." I shuffle their tiny selves around me. "Now, we'll take our usual route but you can stand on the street side." I shake Tina's little hand. "And you can stand on the house side," I tell Sheila.

"You can even close your eyes," I tell Tina. She clusters against my side, and we make our way. But she does not close her eyes. She looks straight at the sidewalk. Sheila walks with her head up.

The steps of the building are decorated with all manner of tributes. Flowers wilting in the winter air, small stuffed animals, signs and cards and even balloons. My eyes sting.

"If we knock on the door, what will happen?" Sheila asks.

"We'd probably make her mommy sad," I answer. "It's already a really sad day."

"When Tariq died, lots of people knocked on our door," Tina says. "Sometimes it made Mommy stop crying."

A weird little stab of old grief cuts through me. Tariq Johnson's murder two years ago feels fresh again this morning. Probably to Tina most of all.

"We'd be late for school. Let's say bye to Shae's house and keep going."

"Bye."

"Bye."

"On the way home, we can knock," I tell them.

TINA

Saying goodbye usually means
you will get to say hello again
soon.
We shout it from the doorway
from the street
back and forth
until we can't hear each other
anymore.

ROBB

The footage out of Underhill from last night is unreal. Everyone is posting it. I see it over and over in my feed. Most of the clips are the same after a while, but I check them all anyway.

My favorite, the one I find most striking, is of a young kid throwing a bottle through a storefront window. It was shot on someone's phone, it's all vertical and weird, but you can see his face in a semi-close-up. He's crying and furious all at the same time. First there's this pause where he looks down at the bottle in his hand, then his face goes monstrous for a second while he puts his whole arm into the throw. He watches it land, then you just see him run away, crying. It's awesome. At the tail end of the frame, as the little boy leaves, the phone gets juggled and red and blue lights flash somewhere in the shot and then it's cut. I keep trying to find out what happened next. Did they catch the kid? The cameraman? Social media is asking, but no one has it yet. I keep checking.

On my way into poli-sci, I bump into Kwame, this guy who's in two of my classes. We roll on the same wavelength, I guess.

"'Sup?" We slap hands. He passes me a flyer from a stack in his arms.

"We're planning a vigil," he says. "In memory of Shae Tatum."

"That doesn't sound like much. What does it do?"

"Raises awareness on campus."

"Yeah, but what about some kind of action? You know, to send a message?"

Kwame nods. "It's a marathon, not a sprint," he says. "Student organizing got it done in the '60s and it'll get it done in our generation, too. It's gonna look different, though."

I wave my phone. "More technological."

"Well," Kwame says. "You should come by the Black House later, if you're interested in the work we're doing."

"Sure thing, sure thing." I grin. DeVante's always going down to the African American Student Center. I could tag along. The more I watch of these videos, the more I know something has to be done.

KIMBERLY

"It's a relief," says the woman in my stylist's chair. "Don't you think?"

"What? Sorry." My hands can weave perfect plaits without my mind checking in. I'm elsewhere, but the customer doesn't need to know that.

She flips through a copy of *O*. "A break from the coverage. At least you're showing regular TV in here."

On the monitor over our heads, *The View* is playing.

"Yes, it's tragic," I murmur.

"You're so distracted," she says. "Heh. Must be thinking about a man."

"What, no, I, no—" I sputter.

She laughs like an auntie. "Must be a hot man."

"He doesn't know I'm alive," I tell her. It's the easiest thing.

Auntie eyes me in the mirror. "Mm-hmm. Looking like that, he knows."

My face flushes. "Stop."

"Girl, you got it going on. Don't let no one tell you different." She flips the magazine page. "Mm-hmm. He knows."

ZEKE

"SCORE, how can I help you?"

A pleasant woman's voice says, "Ezekiel Jacobs, please."

"This is Zeke. Who's calling?"

"I have Senator Alabaster Sloan for you, Mr. Jacobs."

"You're kidding."

Her laugh is warm. "Hold, please."

Reverend Alabaster Sloan? Now Senator. My palms tingle. I dry them on my thighs. This man marched in Birmingham as a child. Up against dogs and fire hoses.

I stand up at my desk. It feels right, to take a call like this standing up.

"Ezekiel?" I'd know his voice anywhere, even if he hadn't been announced.

"Zeke. You can call me Zeke, sir. Hello."

"Talk to me about the situation on the ground."

I shift my grip on the receiver. "We're basically on lockdown, sir. Last night's protests brought significant backlash from law enforcement. Tear gas. Rumor is, they'll be enforcing a curfew tonight."

"I've heard that, too."

That confirms it, I guess, if the news has reached DC. "People are pretty upset."

"Rightly so," the senator agrees.

"The situation was mishandled, and the cops are escalating. But we'll get blamed for it."

"I agree. The coverage is . . . problematic."

That's an understatement. "They have tanks, sir. Just parked around the neighborhood. They're putting up barricades."

"It doesn't help that Wes Steele is all over the internet with his videos."

"The 'war on cops' guy? I can't even stand to watch him."

"His following is growing," Senator Sloan says. "Shae's story has gone national, in a bad way."

"What are you saying, sir?" It settles into me, the reality that this is not a pure condolence call, not merely a show of support. It's a warning.

"Steele's been ranting nonstop on his shows. You don't have to watch, but you need to know about it."

"I know about it. They're all over our social media feeds spewing their racist rhetoric."

"Henderson is Steele's latest cause célèbre. He's rallying the troops."

"That's so messed up." I should have better, smarter things to say. "Why does anybody even listen to him?"

"He plays their deepest fears like a banjo. It's all too easy for white America to believe we're out to get them. Much easier than examining their own biases and complicity."

That's how I want to sound. Formal and intellectual. "Yeah, I get that."

"Steele runs toward the spotlight, wherever it is. This story started out with increased attention, because . . ."

"Because of Tariq Johnson. No one has forgotten his murder, or the media firestorm that followed."

"Every news outlet wants another piece of that pie."

"That's sick."

"That's America." The senator sighs. "I've considered attending the child's funeral."

Wow! "I'm sure your presence and support would be appreciated." I hope I sound chill, but not too chill.

"I'm just as interested in supporting community efforts," Senator Sloan adds. "My presence draws attention, but I want it drawn to the right things. What are your plans?"

"Yes, sir. Thank you." I flex my shoulders, consider where to begin. This conversation is a dream come true.

●●●

Kimberly walks in just as I'm hanging up the phone. She glances at me. Double takes. Smiles. A question on the corners of her lips. She's looking at my face. My overjoyed, can't-believe-what-just-happened face.

I leap out from behind the desk, extend my hands to her. She takes them. Our fingers connect and I'm reminded of lying down close with her last night.

"You'll never guess who that was." I draw her hands in and out from my chest, one by one, a little boogie.

She tips her shoulder. "Who?"

I let go of one hand and spin her around under my arm. She's smiling. "Al Sloan! The senator."

She pulls back. Her eyes widen. "Oh?"

"He's coming here. Isn't that great?"

Kimberly shrugs, ending our little dance. "He's been here before."

"I know, but that was two years ago. Tariq Johnson, right? I saw him speak then."

Kimberly averts her eyes.

"SCORE was brand new then. We grew. People got involved. You know. You've been with us almost since then. Except you stuck with it, when a lot of people didn't."

"Yeah."

"Sloan was organizing around the hoodie march back then. Didn't it inspire you?"

"You could say so."

"What's wrong?"

She shakes her head. The hesitation is strong. "I—I also knew Tariq Johnson," she says finally. "I used to babysit for his sister."

"Oh, wow."

"Yeah."

"So it brings up bad memories? Everything that's happening, and Sloan coming to town?"

She shakes her head swiftly, then beams. "No. It'll be great. Of course. It's great news, Zeke."

I love to hear her say my name.

DeVANTE

Everyone's talking about what went down in Underhill last night. They all seem to know everything about what happened. We shuffle into the Black House common room for the vigil planning meeting and people all around us are bantering about this tweet and that image, things I haven't seen. I've been watching the coverage, too, constantly, and yet somehow I feel like I'm behind the curve. So what else is new?

I never feel quite at home in the Black House. It's supposed to be this sanctuary from the whiteness of everything else, and it is, kind of, but in other ways it puts me on edge.

I'm not used to being with a room full of black people. It's super exciting and different, but it's never been something I craved. It doesn't make me feel at home. Sometimes I get scared that I'm secretly racist, because it's so much easier to hang out with white people. Not that that doesn't have its problems, too.

I glance at Robb. He wanted to come with me tonight, which is cool I guess. He knows Kwame, who invited him. But he's my friend, and we arrived together, so I feel like people are looking at us like, *Who's the white guy and who's that oreo who brung him?*

TYRELL

I like living in the dorm. It's simple. Food is right downstairs in the dining hall. You don't even have to go outside. Swipe the meal card, and it's like manna from heaven. I'm gonna get fat. And I'm gonna like it.

I take full advantage of every swipe. I bring my books. Eat, then study, then eat again.

Some kids come down and use a whole swipe for a bowl of cereal. One of many things I don't understand about this world.

They be trippin', bro. That's what Tariq would say about it. Even now, two years later, it's hard to stop his voice from sliding into my head.

Harder today than usual. I don't want to watch the news, but I can't help seeing it. Her name, her face, is everywhere. Around the cafeteria, soft mutterings:

"Can you imagine?"

"God, her parents. I feel so bad for them."

"What kind of cop can't tell the difference between a little girl and a gangbanger?"

"Never walk wearing headphones. That's the moral of the story."

"I can't imagine."

I bend over my tray, keep full attention on this bowl of oatmeal. Bite my tongue. You can't imagine? Really? It's happening in front of you. Some of us don't have to imagine.

Cinnamon, raisins, brown sugar, sliced almonds. What I can't imagine is a world in which someone pre-slices your almonds for you.

My spoon keeps stirring. The truth is, I'm full. For now.

I make myself walk an hour every day, for a bit of exercise. Put in my headphones and let the music carry me. In the last few weeks, I've even started jogging.

I go at dusk, right before I head down for my dinners. The sunset sky settles over the trees. I loop through the wooded walks of campus, across the quad, weave among the dorms. I become a dark shape moving against the gathering night, and somehow it is okay. People move out of my way when they see me coming, but otherwise I am barely noticed.

It's amazing.

Girls scurry around in clusters after dark, all but holding hands. Occasionally they seem a bit wary of me. They might hug the outside of the sidewalk, keep their eyes on me. I don't begrudge them. I know what it is like to walk afraid.

Every few weeks we have to sit through yet another talk about campus safety. I see their worried faces, hear them fuss. I feel for them, I do, and yet a part of me is content with this arrangement. I've never been in a world where the least safe person on the street is a white girl. Some kind of twisted logic applies in this place.

I've never felt safer.

The security guards scoot around in tight little golf carts. Most of them are black. They think they are very menacing, and it makes me want to laugh. They are battery-powered, they are siren-less, and they are all that it takes to keep the peace. This is paradise.

MELODY

Picking up the girls after school is the no-brainer part of the day. I mean, usually. Today's gonna be different. I know it the second I step out of the building.

It's a twenty-minute walk from here, one way. I lose count of the cops I see in the first five minutes. There's a few on our block. Many more when I turn on Peach. A couple dozen cops, easy, and all their cars and trucks taking over the street.

A construction-looking truck turtles along the center line, dropping those kinda metal fence barricades like you see at a parade. Dudes in neon vests scurry behind it, grabbing them up and lining the street. It's usually parked cars all along the block, so the street seems wide open, to one way of thinking, and totally packed at the same time.

Peach is the most direct route, but I don't care. I'm taking the side streets. Gotta hurry, though. Can't be late.

I meet Sheila and Tina at the side door of the school, right near their special education classroom.

Usually they bounce along the sidewalk, begging for time on the playground. Today they stand quiet by the pillar, holding hands.

Usually it's the three of them. As two alone, they look lonely and small. Sheila and Tina are about my height. It was Shae who was built taller and thicker. She made them all seem bigger, I guess.

We walk quietly together. The usual route. Can't help but to worry what they'll think of the barricades. They must've heard all the people out last night. Must've been scared.

"Shae's house," Sheila says.

Tina adds, "We're going to knock."

"I am going to knock," Sheila says. "We decided."

"Okay," I agree. I did promise.

Brick pops up along the way. Can't be a coincidence. Sheila runs to him.

"Hey," I say over her head.

"Hey." Brick puts up his hand for a high five. That's . . . odd.

I raise my palm to clap his, and it's lucky I'm slow. It wasn't meant for me. Tina steps forward and slaps his gloved palm with her mittened one.

"How's Miss Tina today?"

"Shae is gone," Tina reports. "Shae is dead."

"Yeah, I'm sad about it, too," Brick says. He strokes Sheila's back, keeping his arm around her.

"We're stopping by her house on our way," I tell him. "If you're here to pick up Sheila, maybe you can wait until after?" She'd be disappointed otherwise.

Brick nods and falls in step. "You seen Peach Street?" he says, probably rhetorical. "It's a gauntlet. Pork central."

I smile. "So, you're here to walk us home?" That's sweet. Unexpected. But to be real, I can't decide if he makes us safer or not. Three small women alone, versus three small women with the beefy leader of the 8-5 Kings? Brick is something of a target in and of himself. But I can't deny it *feels* safer having him along.

We walk hand in hand in hand in hand, with the girls between us. Maybe this is what it's like to be married with children. Feeling needed, safe, loved, worried, scared for what the world will do to them. Feeling strong and weak all at once.

Sheila and Tina let go of our hands when we reach the Tatums' stoop. They bound up the steps and Sheila knocks, as planned. They rush inside when Shae's dad opens the door. Brick and I follow. We pile the coats inside the doorway.

Mr. Tatum shakes Brick's hand. "I owe you."

Brick shrugs. "Nah. It's good."

It's awkward when men who don't really know each other try to hug. They get all stiff and where-do-my-arms-go. Like robots.

Shae's mom hugs the girls and cries. They sit on the sofa together, all snuggly and tearful.

Mr. Tatum comes outta the kitchen with two mugs. "We got mulled wine. My sister-in-law's been making it like there's no tomorrow." He smiles in a broken way. A way that means he ain't sure about there being no so-called tomorrow.

I'm technically working, but I don't know how to say no. I grip the handle. I can just hold it without sipping. A sniff or two won't hurt.

He goes away again and comes back with hot chocolate for the girls. Shae's favorite. Then he disappears toward the bedrooms.

Brick and I hover in the doorway, holding our mugs.

"You okay?" he says. He kneads the muscles along my shoulders with his big strong fingers. It feels nice. A little strange, 'cause we don't really know each other 'cept to say hello to. But nice.

"Me?"

"Yeah. How you doing with all of it?"

"I guess I don't really know yet." That's the truth. "It's too fresh." It feels realer, here in the Tatums' living room. The air is thick with grief, turned humid by tears.

"You on duty?" Brick says, clinking his mug against mine. Guess he noticed I'm not drinking.

"Yeah."

"When you're not, you should come by my place sometime."

Wow. Brick's place is legendary. He gets DJs up in his own house to lay a beat. I bet it's awesome. Or would be, if I was a club-scene kinda girl. "Oh, sure."

"I get the music going around nine."

"Every night?"

He shrugs. "Couple times a week. When I feel like it. I usually take Sunday and Monday off."

"That's when you cross-stitch?"

He smirks against the rim of his mug. "Don't knock my hobbies." He drains his mug, then hands it to me. "Switch."

We swap mugs, my full for his empty. He's thoughtful. Not gonna let me turn a full cup back over to Mr. Tatum when we leave.

Brick's hand moves up and down my back, massaging gently. It feels damn good. I ache over Shae, but some other kind of pain, some other thing dissolves away beneath his touch. I find myself gazing up at him. Who is this guy?

NATIONAL NEWS NETWORK SPECIAL REPORT

Host: *The police department has instituted a curfew for the Underhill neighborhood, effective from midnight to six a.m., beginning tonight. We're here with prominent activist and community organizer Sam Childs to discuss the effects of such crowd control measures. Mr. Childs?*

Childs: *Policing against nothing. It will only inflame tensions that might otherwise dissipate. This could've been all over by now, if the police weren't trying to escalate.*

Host: *It's their duty to keep the peace.*

Childs: *They broke the peace to begin with! They were the instigators at every level in this.*

Host: *The officer-involved shooting of thirteen-year-old Shae Tatum brought citizens into the streets last night.*

Childs: *Police are the aggressors. This is racism and police brutality 101. It's a cycle.*

Host: *Isn't it possible that increased policing and curfews could prevent such shootings?*

Childs: *Only if you believe in taking away people's freedom for their own protection. Those restrictions would never fly in a white community.*

Host: *Riots aren't happening in white communities.*

Childs: *Unarmed white children aren't being shot by police, either.*

Host: *So, it all comes down to race?*

Childs: *Racism leads to bias. Bias leads a so-called "good" cop to see a criminal in a black child. Fear causes him to pull the trigger too soon, without a moment of pause for the benefit of the doubt. He sees a black face and he has no doubt.*

Host: *You weren't there. You can't assume that moment of pause didn't happen, or what went through the officer's mind.*

Childs: *An unarmed child died! You really want to stand by the claim that Henderson displayed good judgment?*

Host: *I didn't—*

Childs: *He made a deadly mistake, due to bias. And here come all his defenders to say it wasn't a mistake?*

Host: *Police officers make split-second decisions—*

Childs: *To say a thirteen-year-old girl should have known better than to be running down the street wearing headphones? That she deserved to lose her life because she was tall for her age?*

Host: *No one's saying—*

Childs: *Absolutely, you are. Every argument about trusting a cop's best judgment, or an officer's need and right to protect himself, is built on the premise that something about what happened last night was not wrong. A thirteen-year-old girl. Unarmed.*

Host: *And the curfew . . . ?*

Childs: *(Shrugs) Let's not forget that Shae Tatum was shot around five p.m. If the police want to protect the citizens of Underhill, maybe they should think about decreasing their presence, not militarizing it. If they want to prevent wrongful shootings, maybe they should think twice about making it harder for people to legally walk the streets.*

JENNICA

When Noodle comes around, sometimes it's like the sun is shining for the first time in forever. I turn my face into him and everything is warm. When he comes around other times, it's like the sun will never shine again.

How many times do I have to say no before he hears me?

How many times can I stand to?

"Hey, gurrrrrl." He drags the word out so long it sounds dirty. There are times when I know I will never be clean of him.

"Go away, Noodle. I don't wanna keep doing this."

"I wanna keep doing you." He leers.

My eyes roll of their own accord. I'm out of energy. What I miss about him has nothing to do with sex. It doesn't make sense, how you can look at someone and love them and hate them and want them to hold you and never want to see them again, all at once. The head trip is some kind of roller coaster.

I whisper to myself over and over, in my mind. *He's not a good person. He's not a good person. You can't. You don't want to. Don't do it.*

But when his arms go out, it's too hard. Way too hard to say no.

KIMBERLY

It's a little bit about his hands. The way he moves paper across the desk so efficiently. Long slender fingers. I love to watch him dial the desk phone—quick and smooth, like he's strumming.

It's a little bit about the way he tilts his head while people talk to him. He really listens.

It's a little bit about that one time, when he touched my shoulder, and the shiver went all the way through me. The funny little dance we did . . . I would have let it go on forever, if—

He caught me off guard earlier, bringing up Al, that's all. Zeke can't ever know what happened between me and Al. Reverend Sloan. The senator.

I can pretend better, so he never finds out.

Just look at him. He's so adorable. So dedicated.

It's a little bit about his mind. He has ideas. More than that, he knows what to do with them. You never see him confused. He's got everyone's respect.

It's a little bit about his smile. White teeth, pretty close to perfect, like maybe he wore braces once. The quirky, jaunty question mark at the corner of his lips; would you call that a dimple, or merely something in that vein? A tiny dart of his dark tongue over those lips, and I have to check myself from staring.

He's fine.

ZEKE

She's fine. Can't tear my eyes from that big, sexy behind of hers. Why is she wearing cute pants like that to the office? Nobody needs to look that good while filing correspondence.

She glances over her shoulder. Catches me staring. The receiver feels wrong in my hands all of a sudden. I fumble it down to the cradle. It's been a minute since I finished the last call. My fingers work to make up time. Dialing the next call. Over and over until I reach the bottom of the sheet.

Then she's there. Right in front of the desk. "Oh, hey, Kimberly." My voice sounds like shredded wheat. She thinks I'm an idiot.

"Zeke, I was wondering—" She pauses. "Is this an okay time to ask a question?"

She's so thoughtful. She pays attention to everything going on around the room, and what everybody needs.

"Sure, of course." When I turn my face up to her, to show I'm listening, she smiles. Wow, that smile. A shower of feelings crashes over me.

"Do you maybe need a new notepad?" She has a fresh yellow legal pad in her hand, like the one I'm already using. Which, I now notice, is full. I've covered all the pages, and my notes from the last call are scrawled straight on the cardboard backing.

I laugh out loud. "Uh, yeah. Looks like I do."

Kimberly laughs along with me. Those sparkling eyes.

I'd better be careful. I can't go falling for anyone right now. This movement is bigger than me. I feel the call with it. Can't walk away. Don't have time to get dizzy.

ROBB

DeVante comes to my room. "I got your text about the vigil," he says. "I'm going down to the Black House now. You wanna come?"

"Yeah, yeah." I glance at my phone. It's six-thirty already. The vigil starts at seven.

I tug a few scraggy strips from the spiral rings of my notebook. They crumple easily into a tiny paper nugget. I toss it across at Tyrell. It lands in the gutter of his math textbook. He looks up and pops out an earbud. Just the one. Always.

"Yo, T, you coming to the vigil?"

"Tyrell," Tyrell says. "No, I have too much work." He sticks the earbud back in.

I expected as much. I turn to DeVante. "Let's bounce."

A large group of students gathers at the fountain. We're early. We get near the front. This is where most of the campus demonstrations take place, on the cobblestone plaza surrounding this fountain.

Behind me, the crowd is growing and growing. The glow of the candles starts at the front, one flame passed from wick to wick. It spreads back and back. It looks like Christmas Eve. At the far edges, the people who don't have candles switch on their phone lights and hold them to the night sky. We are surrounded by bluish-white light, like an aura.

Kwame gets up on the edge of the fountain's rock wall. "We're gathered tonight in memory of Shae Tatum. Let us begin with a ceremony of libation."

He holds up a palm-sized pitcher of oil, pours a few drops onto the stones and a few drops into the rippling pool of the fountain. "Tonight we call forth the ancestors as we gather in their memory, particularly in the memory of those who have died due to police brutality and those who have died in the struggle for liberation and peace. Let them be remembered not only for their deaths but for their lives. In their name, we carry forward the struggle."

"Shae Tatum," someone begins.

"Emmett Till," says someone else.

Then other names rise up, spoken in many voices. The soft calls burst overhead like fireworks, each carrying a whole story, a whole life.

"Martin Luther King, Jr."

"Sandra Bland."

"Tariq Johnson."

"Medgar Evers."

"Eric Garner."

"Philando Castile."

"Viola Liuzzo."

"Trayvon Martin."

"Malcolm X."

"Bobby Hutton."

Shivers run up my spine. There are so many names. I don't know one to say out loud that hasn't already been said, but other people do and the names just keep coming. I'm embarrassed that I don't know who they all are. I promise myself I'll remember. I promise myself I'll look them all up.

"Michael Brown."

"Freddie Gray."

"Shae Tatum," Kwame repeats, to close out the naming. We stand in silence together as the candles flicker and burn.

TYRELL

Across the quad, through the trees, the glow of the candlelight is strong. When the vigil breaks up, not everyone blows out their candles. They walk the paths, flickering like fireflies. It is hard to ignore, so I close the blinds.

I'm not the person Robb and DeVante think I am. If the other shoe drops, it's gonna mess things up for me.

They think I'm not interested, or that I don't care. Whatever. They can think what they want. I can take the heat.

Not everyone has to march. The fight is bigger than they know. I'm part of it, just by being here.

I win if I graduate.

STEVE CONNERS

The police aren't making our job so easy right now. I'm supposed to weigh in on messaging, figure out how to position the police actions as positive. Difficult when everything is such "a hot mess," as my stepson would say. I've never been fond of that phrase, but it makes perfect sense in this context.

"We need to streamline and clarify the official communications around the incident," John tells the officers clustered in the conference room. Union reps and a handful of brass. "In this climate we can't underestimate the value of perception."

"You mean a climate in which unchecked police violence is unacceptable?" I can't help myself.

"What Steve means is—"

"Steve can speak for himself, thank you." Pause. Breathe. Be politic. "You have me on this case to provide a black perspective. Believe me, that's the black perspective."

"I don't follow," says one of the brass.

"Police violence is unchecked in black communities, and the powers that be are comfortable keeping it that way. That's the existing perspective of most black Americans."

"But—"

"Look, no one has made it clear what Henderson thought he was doing." I lean forward. "There's no narrative from the police side. The child was running away and got shot in the back. That's the best they have to say?"

The brass stir uncomfortably. "Obviously he thought there was a weapon in play."

"I've been over the public statements. That hasn't been made clear. At all."

The union rep folds his hands. "I think it's clear enough."

"Are we really expecting the public to make that assumption? He shot an unarmed child in the back."

"So, we need to say there was a weapon?"

"There wasn't one. That much, we know."

"Henderson thought there was a weapon."

"Did he?" I ask. "If he did, why wasn't that part of the initial statement?"

"He ordered the suspect to stop running. She didn't."

"Is that a capital crime now? Running while black?"

"Resisting arrest. Failing to respond to a police officer."

I wave my hand. "Those are misdemeanors, aren't they? Anyway, which is it? Was she shot because he thought he saw a weapon, or because she was resisting arrest?"

"A number of factors contributed to his decision to discharge his weapon."

"How many of those factors were simply bad judgment?"

John interrupts my flow. "This is what I meant about clarifying and streamlining the narrative."

It's not complicated, people. "You need to fire Henderson."

The union rep shakes his head. "Before there's been any hint of due process? We'd take so much flak for that."

"The public respects due process," the brass agrees.

"For police officers, but not for thirteen-year-old black girls?"

The room falls silent, then fills. With a slow cold certainty that nothing has changed. We are back at the beginning. The impasse is a roadblock guarded by tanks and AR-15s. A Grand Canyon–wide gap in logic and practice.

EVA

Ham and peas and potatoes. It is one of our favorite dinners, but tonight everything tastes like chalk.

"I have the right to defend myself," Daddy says.

"We're not supposed to talk about it, Darren," Mom says again. She glances at me. "Not at the dinner table, okay?"

They want to protect me from what is happening, but they can't. They get to stay at home and keep the TV off. They don't have to go to school and hear about it from everyone.

"I have the right to defend myself," Daddy says again. When a bad thing happens, sometimes you get stuck in one place.

"No one's arguing that you don't."

"Damn right they are. I'm supposed to stand there and let myself get shot when someone draws on me?"

An elephant is in the room. And it's packing. The air is double charged.

"There was no gun," Mom says gently. "They confirmed it."

"I thought there was."

"Just keep telling them your version," Mom says. "It's your right."

"A girl," Daddy says. "Thirteen."

"Don't think about it," Mom says, which is the strangest thing to say. How can we not think about it?

"I thought there was."

Silence.

"I thought there was," Daddy repeats.

OFFICER YOUNG

Boots. Batons. Shields. Service weapons.

We will patrol tonight.

Our goal is to protect the people.

But the world has changed. The city is out to get us.

We will patrol tonight.

Our goal is to keep the peace.

TINA

From high up in my window
they look like toy soldiers.
Little dolls with plastic legs
you can bend only so far.
They are not toys and yet
they are not willing to bend.
I close one eye and squeeze
them between my fingers like ants.
Tariq taught me that trick,
and also how to hold up a fork
and send someone to jail.
We laughed about it.
No one is laughing now.

BRICK

Curfew is a fucking joke. Who do they think they are, to pen us in like that? The streets are strange and calm and empty. We can't stand for it.

Caution tape be damned. This is our neighborhood. Sheila, Shae, Tina—they should be able to walk in peace.

Anger defines us. The shape it takes in each of us is who we are. How we move. Sinewy like a snake, stealthy like a cat, the swirl of a tornado or the steadiness of a rock.

They would take it from us, our anger. Render us motionless and mute. We can't stand for it.

Nothing is simple. Nothing has ever been simple. This neighborhood, our hearts, our homes. Our jobs, our shame. The way we kowtow and cower. Shuck and jive to keep going one more day.

They would shove us into small boxes. Smaller and smaller until our bones are dust. Build cities out of our shells, our shards.

We can't stand for it.

@UnderhillSCORE: We have questions. Who has answers? #UnderhillPD #StartTalking

@Momof6: This could happen to any cop. #StopWhenTheySayStop #NoBrainer

> **@KelvinX_:** Resisting arrest IS NOT a crime unto itself. #KillerCop needs to answer for HIS crimes. #NoKidDeservesToDie

> **@Momof6:** Resisting arrest is a crime!!! When everyone obeys the police, there's no problem.

> **@KelvinX_:** A 13yo child is dead. The onus should be on cops to protect our children.

> **@BrownMamaBear:** Heartbreak after heartbreak. Pray for all the brown babies out there.

> **@WhitePowerCord:** Sure, play the black card. She was BLACK, she couldn't have done anything wrong. He's a WHITE COP, he's obviously evil. STFU. #BacktheBlue

@UnderhillSCORE: Where are the politicians? Where are our leaders? It must stop. It must change. Who will take us where we need to go? #YouthRiseUp

@WesSteeleStudio: When Police come under attack, none of us are safe. The cop-baiting traps the mainstream media won't show you out of Underhill. Unbelievable video footage!! #HeroCop #MakeItKnown

> **@Momof6:** Blessed are the peacemakers, for they shall be called children of God. #BlueLivesMatter

@UnderhillSCORE: We don't retreat. We don't back down. We demand answers. We demand our rights. #TodayForShae #TomorrowForAll

DAY FOUR: THE FUNERAL

PEACH STREET

We have been here before. Black bodies have lain in the street, with white men standing over them, in uniform. We have been here a thousand times before.

This stretch of land has known tragedy and grief. It has known deep and fleeting joy. This stretch of land has known sun and snow and rain, cleats and Jordans and clicking Mary Janes. The joyful slap of double-dutch rope, the colorful chalk squares of hopscotch, the blood of skinned knees and shards of afternoon Coke bottles.

This stretch of land remembers when it was earth, longs for something out of reach.

WITNESS

You shave carefully in front of the mirror. No nicks. There is no such thing as smooth enough today.

You lotion up while your wife fusses with the iron. She clatters the thing more than necessary. She does not approve. But she can do in two minutes what would take you an hour, and she is gracious.

She holds out the shirt on one finger.

"Are you sure?" she says, not for the first time.

You roll your shoulders. The white fabric is still warm.

You are sure of nothing.

Her kiss offers either judgment or permission. Hard to tell. You only smell shaving cream.

You button your good black suit. You promise yourself closure.

TINA

No.
I don't want to go.
Mommy says *WE ARE GOING.*
When she speaks in capital letters she means business
I mean business too
NO.
NO!
No
more
funerals.

ZEKE

Alone in the office, I practice my move. "Kimberly, would you like to have dinner with me?"

It's all hypothetical, of course. I wish I could turn this particular setting off in my brain. I don't want her to feel weird, or like I'm putting pressure on her. I'm not her boss, not exactly. But sort of. And that makes it weird. And possibly inappropriate. I'm not sure. I think I get a vibe off her that says she won't hold it against me. But I don't want to be one of those guys who thinks he's the exception and end up making her uncomfortable.

When the door opens—and I jump out of my skin—it's not even Kimberly. Of course it's not. She's not due in for an hour.

It's Yvonne. Looking dead serious.

"Hey." I greet her with a smile anyway. "What's going on?"

"It's the funeral this morning," she says.

Right. That's enough to bring anyone down. "Yeah, I heard that on the news."

Yvonne shakes her head. "There's a problem. Unexpected." She looks downright shaky all over.

"How can I help?"

Yvonne sinks into the chair on the other side of my desk. She bursts into tears. Whispers. "She was a child."

My hands fumble toward a tissue box that I know is somewhere. . . . There it is.

I pull one. Two. Three. Fork them over. "I know. It's a tragedy."

She lets it go for a minute. I don't really know what to do. My impulse is to go over and hug her or something. We're friends, I guess. But she's sort of my boss, and again, there's an underlying no-touching rule about the workplace that's hard to get over. I settle for pulling more tissues. Maybe there is no comfort, anyway, in the face of human cruelty.

Yvonne takes a deep breath. "I'm sorry," she says. "I'm supposed to be smooth and in charge."

"Hey, don't worry about it," I assure her. "This is a rough one for all of us."

Her tearful smile contains a thousand years of suffering.

"There are protestors," she says finally. "At the funeral. They showed up with signs."

"Not my SCORE crew. We didn't arrange for that."

"No." Yvonne clears her throat. "Not us. Not on behalf of Shae."

That doesn't compute. "They're protesting the funeral?"

Yvonne nods. "Someone organized a group. I don't know from where."

She turns her phone to face me. The image on the screen strikes hard. All the breath rushes out of me. The background is filled with the chests, knees, and arms of several adults carrying posters and banner sticks. The focus is on a small girl, not more than ten, standing at the front of the group. Her long blond pigtails fall over her shoulders, framing the hand-lettered sign at her chest:

SHE HAD IT COMING.

KIMBERLY

Zeke's call makes no sense, and neither does this vision of the small clump of white women outside the funeral. From the corner of the church steps, they sprawl out in front of me, a sea of hateful signs, hateful faces. It is impossible to comprehend and yet it's taking place in real time. The edges of two different worlds collide and the aftershocks would bring me to my knees. But I have a job to do.

It's easy enough to count the women. Twelve. They have children with them. Four small, pale beings bundled in colorful coats and hats. They are one small, silent island, but they loom large, even amid the hundreds of people coming up the steps for the funeral.

I don't know who they are. A women's group? Church ladies? Cops' wives? A book club? I don't know who they are, but I know who they follow. A woman in the front has a Wes Steele Studio logo on her jacket. One of their signs reads END THE WAR ON COPS. Another reads EXPOSE THE BLACK CONSPIRACY #MAKEITKNOWN.

I post from the SCORE account, tagging every news outlet on our list. The news media will show up sooner or later. The ones who are already on-site are actively filming.

My still shots of the group lack the power of video, but to film too long means I have to stop posting. I take a 15-second short every now and again. Try not to focus on how I'm eating through data.

This is history. This is worth it. This is the twenty-first century's Birmingham. This is radical segregationist stay-in-your-inferior-place bullshit and we can't stand for it.

It's bizarre to see my pics—mine—going viral.

Zeke texts. *You OK?*

I'm good. I'm on it.

I'm on my way. Hang in there.

Hang in there. That's what they want, too. This is a twenty-first century lynching and they've come with their picnic baskets to witness the spectacle.

As if she's read my mind, one of the women whips a square of cloth from her bag, spreads it over the pavement. She settles the smallest of the children onto it, pouring out Tupperware. String cheese and grape halves and Goldfish crackers. The toddlers loll against the handle of her sign, which reads:

HENDERSON DESERVES A MEDAL, NOT A PUBLIC LYNCHING.

Click. Post. A picture is worth a thousand words.

TINA

Shae was my friend
She's gone now

Tariq was my friend
not only my brother
He's gone now

I am supposed to say *Tariq died*
but gone sounds nicer
I am supposed to come to terms
which means to accept it.
This is confusing
because it is not up to me whether it is true

Tariq is dead
but gone sounds nicer.
It does not mean I don't know what is real.

Words can mean different things
Why doesn't everybody know this?
Now I say it the other way out loud
Tariq is dead.
Shae is dead.

Grown-ups are goofy sometimes
In my head, gone sounds nicer.

BRICK

Sheila likes riding with the windows down, even though it's too cold. Today, I let her. We're going to her best friend's funeral, so she deserves a pass on the stupid stuff.

She buzzes the window up and down, eyeing me. Her smile is huge.

She leans out and giggles, straining against her seat belt. Her cheeks redden, her eyes sparkle, and she glances at me out the corner of her eyes waiting for me to crack down, like I usually do.

Maybe she doesn't care about the window. She just wants to get a rise out of me.

"It's too cold," I chide her. "Stop that."

Buzz, buzz. Side-eye. Grin.

It's not about the window. It's the fun of breaking the rule. Huh. That's my kid sister all right.

"Come on, goofball. Are you trying to freeze us out?"

I wonder if she finds healing in her own reckless laughter, or if the game just takes her to another place.

The spire of the church pokes up at the end of the block. Cars everywhere. There's going to be nowhere to park. Should've realized that earlier.

The 8-5 Kings better show up in force. My word is law.

And yet I've been hearing about it for two days. *Why we gotta show at some kid's funeral?*

What goes unsaid: there's a funeral every day in Underhill. For someone too young.

The implication slams me like a hit. Why do we care about this one, and not all the rest? Because of Sheila. Like losing T, like losing a member of our ranks, this one hits home.

"Respect." I'm in charge. We care when I say we care.

"Breeeeeeeeeeze," Sheila drawls, pulling for my attention. The window goes all the way down.

"We're almost there, goofball. Roll it up."

I reach across and poke her tummy. Hysterics. Kids are so simple sometimes. When I pull my hand back, she stops suddenly.

"Is it bad to laugh on a sad day?" Sheila asks.

Not so simple.

MELODY

They roll in the tiny coffin. Music plays. Organ swelling, choir moaning, that kind of thing. Can't help but get thick in the throat. Tina's small hand slips into mine. Her mother sits at her other side, stroking her back. It's interesting. Often she slides away into her own separate world, not wanting to be touched or bothered. But when she wants comfort, it's here for her in spades.

In the middle of the service, Sheila comes to me, crying. She slips down the aisle from somewhere behind. I wrap my arms around her and pull her into the pew with us. There is room. We can make room. She tucks herself onto my lap.

A second later, a long shadow crosses us. Brick looms over me.

He takes Sheila's hand. "Come on back. Sorry," he says to me.

Sheila presses herself against me tighter. She doesn't need to worry. I won't let go. "It's okay, she can sit with us."

"She needs to sit with family."

I shake my head. This is what he gets for sending her away.

"There are all kinds of family."

His body tightens up.

Maybe it's a slap in the face. Maybe that's a risk worth taking. Turn my head, send a glance toward all Brick's boys in their row.

"You made your choice a long time ago."

JENNICA

They come into the diner together, two men in nice clothes, well layered, with signs folded in their bags. I bring them menus and water and they ask for tape to repair a thing.

They order bacon, egg, and cheese sandwiches and fries. When they ask to borrow the tape, I think absolutely nothing of it. I bring it, and they say thanks. They smile politely.

I could've said *Sorry, we're out* and sent them across the street to the corner store to buy some. They don't look like they're from around here. I did notice that. We don't get a lot of clean-cut white boys out to eat in Underhill.

Their signs are horrible, confusing, upsetting. I stay behind the counter as they do up their tape job, looking satisfied with themselves. I hope they finish before their order comes up. I have to bring them their sandwiches, but it would be easier if I could pretend I didn't see.

They leave me a decent tip. I'm surprised they're willing to eat in a diner in this neighborhood. They must've been really hungry, to accept food prepared by black hands. Except, by the look of them, I doubt they even know what it means to be hungry.

OFFICER YOUNG

I don't agree with their signs. I'm not racist. People should live and let live.

Certainly, they should live and let Rest in Peace. It was a kid, after all. It's distasteful to show up with hate signs at someone's funeral, regardless of how you feel about things. There's such a thing as basic decency, after all.

I hook my thumbs over my belt, put on my sternest expression. No one gets through me. Not today.

I'm not worried about it, though. They're all just standing there with their signs. Exercising their First Amendment rights. They're not even yelling.

They're not here to start a fight.

DeVANTE

"Can you fucking believe this?" Robb marches into the lounge, where I'm trying to study. Econ is kicking my butt already and we're only a couple weeks into the semester.

"Which part?"

Robb holds up his phone. It's open to the Twitter feed of Underhill SCORE. Picture after picture of the white protestors and their rabid, home-made signs.

Tiny flames erupt beneath my skin. My voice, though, barely sim-mers. "They misspelled the N-word. Kinda undercuts the argument, don't you think?" My fingers fan the pages of my textbook. I really need to focus. I don't have time for this.

"She was a little girl! Why are they picketing her funeral?"

I rub my temples. "Uh. 'Cause they're messed in the head?"

"It makes no sense."

"It's racism. It never made any sense."

Robb paces. "For a child."

"Remember that school shooting? All the elementary schoolers? People planned to picket at the funeral."

"That's batshit."

I shrug. It infuriates me to my marrow, and yet the world keeps turn-ing. I still have an Econ quiz at two. "It happens all the time after hate crimes. The shooting in that nightclub in Florida."

"The gay club?"

"Yeah. They're cool with domestic terrorism as long as it's ultra-wack white Christians doing the terrorizing."

"Ultra-wack," Robb echoes. He tosses himself down on one of the couches. Great. Now I'll have to endure his popcorn thoughts.

"Look, I gotta study."

"Sure, sure." Robb scrolls through his phone, occasionally clucking in disgust. He never seems to study. I don't know if he gets good grades like magic, or if he just doesn't care if he does well. A job in his dad's company is already waiting for him.

There are earbuds in my backpack, somewhere. Here they are. Whew. I pop them in, even though I was enjoying studying in silence. I really don't feel like music right now.

My thumb stops on an album of thunderstorm sounds. Yup. That feels fitting.

WILL/EMZEE

When the bell rings at 11:40, I don't go to the cafeteria. I pack up my books, take my coat from my locker, and bounce. No one stops me or asks questions. Easy as that. Skipping is a no-brainer, it turns out.

All I know is, I can't sit still anymore.

I've been prepping for college. Steve's big on academic achievement, and I've got the goods, you know? I can put pencil to paper and come up with some solid thesis statements or whatever.

Today, I don't know. Four more years feels like a long time to be cooped up in a classroom, waiting for real life to kick in. Real life's alive and kicking all over Underhill, right this very minute.

Or else it's got a bullet in it. And it'll all be over before it begins.

The apartment is quiet in the middle of the day. Too quiet.

The pile of textbooks stares silently back at me from the middle of the dining room table. This homework feels like nothing now. No meaning to it.

On the other hand, my backpack, my hoodie, a half-dozen cans of paint—they scream to me.

What went down with Tariq Johnson, well, you could chalk that up to bad luck. A freak thing. Call it gang banging, put it in a box with things that don't make sense, and padlock it away.

But this girl now? Shae?

You can't call that nothing but racist. Tragic. The cops are gunning for our annihilation, one innocent at a time. They say they ain't, but they keep on shooting. What's that?

I should do my calculus worksheet now . . . but why? Because, screw it, I could spend ten years getting a PhD or whatever and still get shot on the street like a dog. LIKE A DOG. Worse than a dog, actually. With a dog, they stun you or Tase you and throw you in a net. They don't shoot to kill dogs. Say it's inhumane. I'll paint a dog, being killed. Watch the news cover it as a blight on the community. I'll paint a black man being killed. No news. Cruelty to animals = sickness. We are less than animals now.

TINA

We Don't Call It a Picnic

Ladies, ladies
loud ladies
big ladies
chewing ladies
sipping ladies
humming, Lord Jesus
humming, my baby
humming all the way to the cathedral sky
crying ladies
hugging ladies
stories and stories and stories
all sad
laughing anyway

checkered tablecloth
fried chicken and greens
biscuits and mac and cheese
vocabulary word: cliché
means
always delicious

princess tablecloth, like someone's birthday
pies and cakes and cookies
yum

red tablecloth
iced tea and lemonade
and someone's uncle, Arnold Palmer
vocabulary word: family
means
blood and beyond

plain black tablecloth, plastic
photos and notebooks and tears
because
they don't make deathday tablecloth

TYRELL

"Hi, Tyrell." The background hums with sounds of chatter.

"Tina? Where are you?" My brain zings upright. Is she lost? Is she in trouble?

"I memorized your number. I can call you from any phone."

"That's very smart. Whose phone are you using?"

"The one on the wall."

"Which wall?"

"The church. It's a funeral," she says.

Oof. "You're at Shae's funeral right now?"

"There are too many people."

"I bet. Does your mom know where you are?"

"She's busy."

"What is she doing?"

"Holding Shae's mom's hand. She's crying a lot."

"I bet." I rub my forehead. I'm really not sure how to help Tina from here. "Don't go outside, okay?" I've seen the news. The mess over there is hard to fathom.

"There are too many people outside, too."

"Yeah, exactly."

"Did you know there are six different ways to make macaroni and cheese?"

"I bet there's more than that," I say. "Why do you think there are only six?"

"There are six macaroni pans on the table downstairs. They all look different."

"Which one did you like best?"

"The ones without any crunchy stuff on top."

"Oh, but the crunchy stuff is my favorite."

"You can have it."

I laugh. "You're all about the cheese, huh?"

"Tariq says cheese and noodles are the perfect food."

"Yeah, he liked his mac and cheese, didn't he?" My eyes close of their own accord. Let the memories scroll across the screen of my mind. With Tina on the end of the line, it doesn't hurt as much. My heart doesn't try to stop.

"Everyone likes mac and cheese, silly."

"Who you calling silly, silly?"

Tina giggles. There is a small pause. "I won't go outside," she says. "There are lots of police out there. I don't want them to get me."

Oh, my heart. "You stay with your mom, and you'll be okay." I want to add, *I promise*, but it doesn't seem very wise, all things considered.

EVA

We light candles in the living room. "In honor of a young life lost," Daddy says.

"We could go to the funeral," I say.

"No, we can't," Mommy says. "No one wants to see Daddy there."

"Because he did a bad thing?" It doesn't make sense, because when you do a bad thing, you're supposed to apologize.

"He did his job." Mommy is what Daddy calls a broken record, saying the same thing over and over.

"But what happened is a tragedy," I say. This is the word everyone keeps using. The worst of the worst possible thing. The most terrible kind of sadness.

Daddy puts his head in his hands.

"It's complicated," Mommy says. "Let's pray."

Host: *Shae Tatum's funeral in Underhill.*

NNN Commentator: *This is the wildest thing I've ever seen. Protesting at a child's funeral?*

Guest Activist: *There's a history of counterprotest. Remember, the "God Hates Fags" contingent showed up at Matthew Shepard's funeral.*

Commentator: *What is the point? It's insult to injury. What do they hope to accomplish?*

Guest: *It's a stunt.*

Commentator: *It's twisted.*

Host: *And yet, legal. First Amendment protections.*

Commentator: *Hate speech is not protected. This is hate speech.*

Guest: *We have freedom of beliefs in this country. That doesn't mean we have to tolerate cruelty.*

Commentator: *We tolerate a lot in the name of religious faith.*

Guest: *When a serial killer says God made him do it, we don't let him off the hook for his crimes. Are we supposed to accept murder as a protected aspect of faith?*

Host: *That's a false parallel.*

Guest: *Actually it's not.*

Commentator: *But the white supremacists will turn around and say the same. That the mere presence of diversity impinges on their beliefs.*

Guest: *It doesn't. It's not the same.*

Host: *Why not?*

Guest: *Because exclusion and liberty can't co-exist. Exclusion means you don't have liberty and justice for all. Full inclusion is, or should be, an American value.*

Commentator: *The minute you accept the premise that intolerance is a valid point of view, you lose freedom.*

Guest: *Exactly.*

Host: *Isn't that intolerant?*

Guest: *No. Empirically. My existence makes no threat to the personhood and liberty of a white supremacist. His existence does make a threat to mine.*

Commentator: *He perceives a threat, though.*

Guest: *He also thinks white people are better and more deserving than non-white people. His perception is not reality. More importantly, his perception does not get to define MY reality.*

Host: *Freedom of speech—*

Commentator: *I get it. It's the difference between beliefs and actions.*

Guest: *You can believe you're better than me all you want—*

Commentator: *But look at their signs. "She had it coming"? And* what was trending on social media this morning from the same people? "The only good n—— is a dead n——." I won't say that word on air . . .

Guest: *Thank you.*

Commentator: *That message is about more than a belief. It's a call to action. That's troubling.*

Guest: *My liberty does not stop a white supremacist from enjoying his own liberty. His existence and beliefs are specifically about limiting what someone who looks like me can do in society. How is that freedom?*

Commentator: *White supremacy enforces liberty for whites only, at the expense of all others. Which is the system we're already living under.*

Host: *The system—*

Guest: *If a police officer is justified in shooting any citizen who appears to possibly have something in their hand, then we'd see similar proportions of dead "suspects" across races. If this justification only holds when the citizen is black, then black people are not safe anywhere. Not while holding a cell phone, not while driving lawfully, not while listening to headphones. As long as bias is our reality, black Americans are not truly free.*

KIMBERLY

We sit side by side on the steps of the church. Zeke rubs his forehead, looking tired. "I'm starving. You wanna get some food?"

"Oh, sure."

He jolts upright, dropping his hand. "I mean, uh, no. I mean, Kimberly, would you like to . . . or maybe not . . . I didn't mean to suggest . . . I just said it." His cheeks are all flushed. He's adorable when he's flustered.

"I'm hungry, too," I said. "There's a diner where my roommate works. If her manager's not in, she can hook us up with some free dessert or something."

"Sounds good," he says, relieved.

He's bending over backward to make clear that he wasn't asking me out. Got it. I let him off the hook with a smile. "You act like you've never eaten out with a friend before."

"Friend? Right. Yeah." He shakes his head. "That's totally normal."

Now my cheeks are flushing. We're side by side now. Maybe he won't notice.

We walk in silence for a block or so. Should I be trying to make conversation? My head is kind of swirling with everything that happened this morning and I don't know how to shake loose of it. I can't get the image of those kids and that hateful sign out of my head.

"You're really good at the media stuff," Zeke says. "What did you major in?"

"Oh, I didn't go to college."

He blinks long and slow at me. "Really? Why not?"

"I got my cosmetology license," I say.

He nods. "That's great. And do you like what you're doing now?"

"Yeah, sure," I say. "I make decent tips at the salon. And I still have some time to volunteer." I wave my cell phone at him. The battery is down to one red sliver of life.

He grins. "Sure. Well, we're glad you're on board."

We. Okay. I get it. Still, it's no effort at all to smile back. He has that kind of draw. "Right."

"I mean, uh—" His long fingers dance in the air between us. "I mean, I'm glad you're here."

My face is hot, hot. "Thanks. I'm glad you're here, too. Although, I mean, I guess none of us would be here if not for you, so . . ." *Gah. Awkward much?* My brain screams at me. *SHUT UP.*

"I'm proud of the work we're doing," he says. "SCORE is going to make a difference around here. I really think so."

"Me too." My hand twitches with the impulse to reach out and hold his. But I can't. That would be weird. I don't know where he is with all of this. It's okay. We're friends. Colleagues. He wants to share a meal with me. It's enough.

We arrive at the diner. Jennica is working, which I expected. The place is not too crowded. She greets us and seats us near a window. Prime table placement. She lays down the menus for us, but I stay standing.

"Excuse me for a minute. I'm going to wash my hands."

I make huge eyes at Jennica and tip my head toward the bathroom. It's a one-seater, which I know, but she follows me in there anyway.

"Is this him? Zeke?"

"Yeah."

She smiles and smacks my arm lightly with the backs of her fingers. "Oh, he's cute."

"Right?" I can't hold it. I slip into the stall.

"Totally. And he's into you."

"You were there for like two seconds. How can you tell?"

"I know what guys are like. He was looking at you."

It feels like I'm going to pee forever. I speak over the sound of it. "So, wait, is this a date?"

"Why wouldn't it be?" Jennica says.

"We were both hungry after working the funeral. Not exactly romantic."

"If he didn't want to spend extra time with you, he'd be eating by himself." Jennica starts washing her hands. "I have to go back. I have other tables."

I squeeze my way around the stall door. My reflection in the mirror is frazzled and all my makeup is worn. "Gah. I'm so not dressed for this. Maybe it's not a date."

"If he pays, it's a date. Go get him." She grins and slips out the door.

●●●

Forty minutes later, Jennica lays the check on the table. She glances at me out the corner of her eye, as she positions it delicately in the middle of the table. Exactly between us. It is all I can do not to laugh.

Moment of truth. Zeke reaches for the check. When he does, I put my hand forward also.

"I got it," he says.

"Oh, you don't have to do that," I blurt, fumbling toward my purse.

"You worked hard today. The least SCORE can do is buy you dinner."

Ah. So, he's treating but as a SCORE work meal. What does this mean?

"Well, thanks," I say. "That's really nice of you."

He smiles. "This was fun."

"Yeah, it was. Thanks." How many times do I need to thank him? Sheesh.

Zeke stands up. He plucks my coat off my chair and holds it while I slide my arms in. I make an excited face at Jennica while my back is to him. She gives me a double thumbs-up.

We step out to the sidewalk.

Zeke says, "I'd, uh . . . Kimberly, I'd like to buy you dinner another time, if you might be interested."

JENNICA

They're cute together. Kimberly claims not to know if he's interested in her, but it's so obvious. I mean, come on.

I'm happy for her, but there's more to it. Something under the skin that doesn't sit right. Maybe I'm jealous, which is awful and unfair. Kimberly deserves everything.

I'm butterfingers all afternoon. Feel it all slipping from my fingers.

When the door bell jangles, I know without turning who it's gonna be.

Noodle. He had to choose tonight to drop by. It's like he's got some kind of radar for when I'm lonely, when I'm sad, when I'm vulnerable. How does he do that? How does he read my mood from all the way across the neighborhood? When we were together, he couldn't read my mood from across the room.

"What are you doing here, Noodle?"

"I came to see you, baby. I missed you."

Maybe. It sucks how much I want it to be true. "Then why don't you ever text me back?" He's hurt me too many times. I'm supposed to be strong. I *am* strong.

"I've been busy," he says. "This girl who died, all the chaos. Haven't you been busy, too?"

"Sure, of course." I wave at the rest of the diner. "In fact, I'm busy right now." If I walk away, maybe he'll go. Not so much.

"Table for one," he says, following me.

"Why don't you just sit at the counter?" I suggest. Noodle doesn't pay his check, let alone tip the way Brick does. I don't want him taking up a whole table when it's about to be the dinner rush.

"Nah." He tosses himself into a prime booth that could seat four. "This is cozy."

I pull in one big breath, gather my courage. "If you're gonna sit there, you gotta spend at least fifty bucks," I inform him. "It'll come out of my tips, otherwise."

Noodle grins. "Sure, sure. You know I'm good for it."

"Up front," I insist.

He reaches into his wallet and pulls out a fifty. "Most expensive cheeseburger I ever ate," he says, grinning.

"Well done with fries and a shake?"

He grins. "I haven't changed."

Lord knows that.

As I return to the kitchen, my cell vibrates in my apron pocket.

This is me, texting you.

And then, while I check on my other tables.

You look hella sexy in that apron.

And then, while I'm refreshing the coffee.

Do that hair flippy thing that I like.

And then I stop looking. The phone vibrates six more times.

"Order up," Troy calls.

I march back to Noodle's table with the burger. He's all smiles, all surface chill.

"What, you don't write me back?" He pouts. "After giving me all that grief?"

I push the plate over to him and smack down a bottle of ketchup. "Stop it. I'm working."

"Aren't you gonna ask me if there's anything else I need?"

The words almost rush out of me, by habit. But . . . "No." I walk away.

He texts twice more. I don't look. The diner gets more crowded, and Noodle's taking his time with the fries and shake. I want his table to turn over.

When I finally circle back to clear his dishes, he says, "No, seriously. I hate to think you've been waiting by the phone." His hand teases my hip.

"Of course not," I lie. "I have a life. It's just . . . if you're gonna drop by like this, it'd be nice to hear from you in between."

"We're not together anymore," he says. As if I need reminding. "You got no claim on me. We're chill. We're casual. I thought that's what you wanted. Just friends, and shit."

"We're not getting back together," I assure him. "I'm not expecting anything."

"Then why you giving me grief about a few texts, baby? We cool?"

"Sure. Yeah." I want him to go. I want him to leave me alone before it all becomes too much and the inevitable happens. I'm not strong. Not nearly strong enough to fight all the things he reminds me of. Being held. Being part of a pair. Having someone who would always, always bring me home.

As if I have willed it, Noodle grabs his coat and slides out of the booth. He seems not to notice that I'm holding his dirty plates in my hand. He wraps his arms around me and pulls me close. "Love you," he says. "Miss you." He holds me just long enough that my body wants to relax into him and let him carry me away.

He leaves, and about ten minutes later, my phone vibrates again. This time, I check, just in case it's not him.

I really miss you, Noodle texts. *Come home with me tonight?*

It may or may not be true. The truth is that I've missed him and he knows it.

STEVE CONNERS

"What are you doing in my room?" Will demands. He marches in through the open door and tosses his backpack onto his bed.

I drew the short straw on who gets to talk with Will. Actually, I lobbied for the gig, although at the moment it doesn't exactly feel like a win.

My wife is hopping mad, too mad to have this conversation in a reasonable tone. "I will tear him limb from limb," she announced, the moment she hung up from the school attendance office. They called to report that Will missed his afternoon classes.

I offered to talk to him first, since she was threatening to take a metal spatula to his backside, as if he was still young enough to be cowed by the fear of a spanking. It seemed like a good plan at the time, but it failed. The second he walked through the door, she lit into him like there would be no tomorrow. So I came in here to wait.

"Mom already read me the riot act," Will says.

"I heard."

"So, leave me alone."

"Let's go get some ice cream," I suggest.

He blinks, then scoffs. "What am I, seven?"

We used to go for ice cream when he was small. When my wife and I started seeing each other, he was so young, and already jaded by the world. By the men of the world, in particular. It took a long time to worm my way in, and looking at him now, I'm not sure if I ever fully got there.

"Rocky road," I say. "Cookie dough. Are you really gonna make me go down there alone?" Ice cream outings used to be good for us. We got to talk a little, even if it was only about the merits of various toppings.

"I want to be alone," Will says.

"She might not be finished," I tell him. "If I go out there and have to say we didn't talk, you better believe you're gonna hear more from your mother."

It's a cheap shot, I know, but desperate times.

Will considers me. "I'm getting an entire banana split," he says. "With extra everything."

"You can order whatever you want." I clap him on the shoulder. He flinches.

BRICK

We stand at the window, looking down at the night. My condo overlooks the park, and the neighborhood beyond. They've placed floodlights at each corner. They've linked up rows of metal barred fences to keep people from gathering on the grass. So instead, people fill the streets, pressing and surging and chanting.

"You seen these barricades," I tell Noodle. "We can't stand for it. This is our turf."

"You wanna walk up and tell the popo that? They will carve you up. Pigs." He spits into an empty glass on the windowsill.

"Maybe we carve them up first. Let them know whose space they're stepping into."

Noodle huffs. "Sure, right. We'll get right on that." He sips his drink with a grin.

He thinks I'm not serious. Thinks I wouldn't rather be down there screaming with everyone else. It's not a planned protest. It's organic, spontaneous. A pouring out. We may be disorganized, but we are unified. And we are loud.

Behind us, the never-ending music thumps on. I could lose myself in it, find some honey to wriggle against me, soft and warm. There's someone for me. Always. Any woman I want. The one in the hot-pink mini skirt. Damn. The one with the shaved head and earrings like Olympic rings. Hmhmmm.

It's ten-fifteen. In an hour or so, I ought to shut this party down. Make sure everyone gets home safe, before the midnight curfew.

Or.

Or, I could shut it down now, and take the party to the streets. Bust into my arsenal and take it to the cops. Show them a taste of what Underhill really has to offer. There's enough of us. We could do some damage.

I wish—goddammit. I wish I could have this conversation with someone else besides Noodle. Anyone.

No, not anyone.

Jennica isn't the most bookish person I ever met, but she asks the right kinds of questions. The stuff she doesn't know shows me what I know and don't know. The shit she knows is on a whole other level. She knows how to stay calm when everything is flying off the handle.

"No joke," I insist. "We gotta go down there."

Noodle takes down his drink in a gulp. "Why, so they can throw us in jail? You want a replay of the other night?"

"Throw us in jail for what?" My throat is tight and my fists are like rocks.

"Aw man, you know they'll find something. The whole point is they come after us for nothing now. We can get high and forget about it." He reaches for the bottle. Offers it to me. Even though he knows I don't drink anymore. Gotta keep a clear head.

Clear head.

Clear head.

"You think it'll blow over?" I try to breathe. I shouldn't give a whit about Shae Tatum. I don't. I mean, I wouldn't, if not for Sheila. I know good and well that I walk a line. I'm no innocent bystander. If I go down with a pig bullet in me, it'll be my choice. My fight. I do what I gotta do.

"Naw," Noodle says. "They're gunning for us. Don't make today no different than yesterday. Tomorrow, either."

I look at him hard. *Gunning for us.* Sure. We live under the gun, Noodle and me. By choice. Cops roll up on us, it's 'cause of who we are, 'cause of what we do, not how we look.

This is different.

There's such a thing as innocence. When they start coming for our littlest ones, we can't stand for it.

WILL/eMZee

Usually I do homework on the bus. Tonight, I'm boycotting homework. It's bullshit.

Without a book or a math problem, the ride is long. Interminable.

The news says the curfew's coming down at midnight, preventing people from being out late. So what's different about that? They're always patrolling. Always ready to roll up on guys like me. I know how to duck and cover. Screw 'em. I have things to say.

I paint the dog thing:

RULES FOR DOGCATCHERS: STUN GUNS ONLY, GENTLE TOUCH

RULES FOR POLICING BLACK COMMUNITIES: SHOOT FIRST, ASK QUESTIONS LATER

After the fact, my fingers are ink-stained. A hole in my glove I didn't notice. Steve will blow a fit if he catches the stain on me. He doesn't know it's written all over me already. Indelible.

Anyway, I'm not going home. Not yet.

I want to see what goes down. I want to paint it.

Put my mark on the world.

OFFICER YOUNG

They're coming for us. Dressed in red and black, the colors of the 8-5 Kings. A handful of Kings lead the protest, and they'll stay out walking and chanting past curfew. There is heavy media coverage and citizen journalism. We are instructed to discharge a weapon only in the event of very last possible resort. The reminder echoes in the back of my mind. Because, isn't that always true? Isn't that what we're taught in the first place?

I know how to do my job. Shooting is always the very last possible resort. This is how we live. They remind us anyway. Firing into a crowd is dangerous. We are being filmed.

The street teems with angry people carrying signs. First Amendment. Chanting:

"Unarmed! Not a threat! Unarmed! Not a target!"

Unarmed . . . so they say.

I'm scrolling, I'm scanning. Faces and bodies and hands. Looking for weapons. The glint of screens in the darkness comes from everywhere. Glint after glint.

My fingers itch toward my gun. No, toward my baton, which I will reach for first. I'm committed to that. No mistakes.

My heart races. It is hard to remember to swallow.

I have a shield. A vest. A helmet. A baton. A gun. They have to go through a lot to get to me. They won't get there.

I'm scrolling, I'm scanning. Glint after glint.

Twenty minutes to go. The crowd will thin. It will. When the curfew hits, anyone who remains gets arrested.

@UnderhillSCORE: We don't retreat. We don't back down. We demand answers. We demand our rights. #TodayForShae #TomorrowForAll

@TroubleInRiverCty: Shae Tatum's crime: running while black. #convicted

@Momof6: I feel sad for police officers working today. This is the treatment they get for trying to serve and protect?

> **@Momof6:** Do what you've gotta do down there in #Underhill, fellas. We've got your back.

> **@Momof6:** Respecting cops is the law. Right to protest be damned. #BlueLivesMatter

@Viana_Brown: The world is on fire. Stay safe out there, friends. #TodayForShae #TomorrowForAll

@WhitePowerCord: Like monkeys in the zoo. Making sounds and throwing feces. Ooh Ooh. Fenced in! Tear gas! Tase their asses! #PassThePopcorn

@KelvinX_: Underhill, take your stand. #TodayForShae #TomorrowForAll

DAY FIVE: AND THE DAYS THAT FOLLOW

PEACH STREET

Come the light, the street goes quiet. Business as usual, despite a lingering feeling of aftermath.

Curfew is a promise of one thing, and a threat of something else. The tension in the neighborhood makes it hard to move around.

The neighborhood is at war, day and night. The ice-cold pavement seethes with fury. The weather may be the only thing keeping them from lighting it up.

WITNESS

The squad car rolls past your house a few times nightly. *Blip-blip.*

The small sound speaks much louder to you. *We are watching. We know who you are. Where you live. Remember that, when you speak about what you saw.*

You draw the curtains tighter after the third time, turn the lights down as low as you can stand. Think about the girl. About the cop. About what is required of you.

You heat a pot of water. Stand by the stove, remembering the war in your wife's eyes. Try to reconcile the dueling pleas for safety and justice. You prepare a mug. Chamomile is supposed to be soothing. But you're out, so you settle for Lemon Ginger. You can cut the spice with honey.

The water roils and hums. The head of steam gathering in the kettle is emblematic of something. You watch the first curls escape through the tiny hole. Snap off the heat at the first hint of a whistle.

Blip-blip.

You can take the hint. Enough already.

You sip your tea. Think about your children, asleep in their beds, already so inured to the *blip-blip* that they do not even stir.

EVA

There is always a cruiser stationed outside our house. Daddy says it is to keep us safe.

There are a lot of people who are out to get cops. Especially cops turned famous by circumstance.

When your name is on the national news, Daddy says, it tends to bring out the crazies. "There's a target on my back," he says.

So there is always someone watching. I'm not to answer the door.

They don't flash their lights or anything, but the warmth of the red and blue covers us like a blanket anyway. We are protected. We are part of something bigger than any one of us.

I can snuggle under the covers and know that no one is going to hurt me.

Still, it is hard to sleep.

I don't like knowing that someone might want to hurt me.

TINA

Momma says
the world will never take care of me.
Helpful people are there to help little white girls.
I am on my own.

I read and read
the book about Helpful People:
police officers
firefighters
teachers
doctors
lawyers.

I want to believe
anyway

But I don't.

I tear and tear
the pages out, one by one.
I am tired
of being disappointed.

DeVANTE

"I get it, man," Robb says. He lounges on his bed, while I slouch in the beanbag chair. I'm currently trouncing his ass at Mario Kart.

The more he says that, the more it reinforces that he doesn't get it. I shake my head. "I don't want to keep having this discussion. You aren't afraid when you walk down the street. You have no idea what that's like."

I glance toward Tyrell, as if he's going to back me up. He has his head buried in a calculus textbook. Headphones on and bobbing his head to the music.

"Damn." Robb curses as his kart flies off a mushroom into the abyss. "I'm on your side. I'm not saying it's right."

I zip around the cartoon curves. I'm comfortably in first place. This is my arena. "You think the issue is police officers making mistakes."

"A huge pattern of mistakes."

I shake my head. "Black people doing nothing wrong, getting shot by police. That's the issue."

"Right, that's the mistake."

"My point is, the issue isn't mistakes, it's bias. The underlying reason the so-called mistakes are happening."

"So-called mistakes?"

"The cops always stand by their actions, because the person was acting suspicious."

Robb rolls his eyes. "They must've done something."

"There it is!" I snap at him, grasping the truth like a steel trap. *Whee-hee!* My kart soars across the finish line, creating the victory sound. "You don't believe they're innocent."

"Sure, I do. Not that they actually did something wrong, but the cops thought they did."

"You don't get it. Being black is enough to make you suspicious to police."

"Shae Tatum, running from him. That's just dumb."

"She was a child. And had headphones in. She might not even have heard him. That deserves a death sentence?"

"Of course not. I've been watching all the coverage," Robb says. "That's why he shot. Obviously it's messed up."

The conversation goes in a circle. I'm ready to be done. I set my controller aside, as Yoshi dances in victory on top of the winner's podium. "Look, we've got an organizing meeting at the Black House tomorrow. Come if you want to."

"They're thinking of going down to join the protests in Underhill, aren't they?"

"Some people are talking about it, yeah."

"Hell, yeah. Someone's got to stand up."

Yeah, I'm done. I drag myself up off the beanbag. "Lots of people are standing up. It's on TV every night."

"I know. Look at what's going on with the Kings. We're looking at gang members turned resistance fighters."

"And getting arrested left and right."

"Hey, Tyrell," Robb calls. "Tyrell!"

Tyrell pulls off his headphones. "What?" He's annoyed, and at the moment I don't blame him.

"Kings versus cops. Who comes out on top?"

"That's a stupid question," he says. He shoots me a look that's half sympathetic, half baffled. Headphones back in place.

Robb waves his hand. "Say what you want about me being white. At least I care about what's happening. I'll be at the march, with bells on."

"With bells on? You're going to bring superfluous metal objects to a public demonstration?" I force a grin. "Don't stand next to me, white boy."

Robb laughs. I slap the doorframe on my way out of the room.

TYRELL

They don't know. They can't know. They dip into this movement like they are going for a swim. Put on the right suit, slick your hair back, and glide. Tip your head at just the right moment for a breath above the surface, cry out "Justice!" Keep your arms and legs moving, feel the burn in your muscles like you're doing some good. . . .

My arms flail. My legs flail. They don't know. They can't know. The full burn. The feeling. Of drowning.

ZEKE

I swing by Carl's barbershop for a shape up. Kimberly's bound to like the clean-cut type, based on the way she dresses. I can do clean-cut.

I own jeans, T-shirts, polos, a couple button downs, one blazer.

"Why you suddenly so big on the outfits?" my sister asks. I've got her in my room looking at the combinations with me.

"Just help me out, would you? Do me a solid for once. No commentary."

Monae's eyes narrow. "Who is she?"

"Shut up."

The items on the bed look like a bunch of fabric to me. I can tell which ones go on which half of my body, but that's where my fashion talents end.

"Do I know her?"

"Monae."

"Do you want my help or not? I need to know who it is so I can dress you right."

Sigh. That makes a certain amount of sense. I'm reluctant to admit it, though. Monae has a sly look about her. "You're just being nosy."

"Price of admission."

"I never said there was anyone."

Her brow arches. "Deductive reasoning. You suddenly care about clothes, there's a woman in the picture." She eyes me up and down. "Would I like her?"

"You don't like anybody," I chide.

She laughs. "Nothing wrong with having high standards."

I pick up a polo and settle it inside the blazer.

Monae howls. "Boy, you are hard up."

"What's wrong with it?" I'm honestly mystified. "The blazer makes it nice, right?"

Monae wipes tears of mirth from her eyes. "Here." She plucks a button down. "If you want to wear the jacket, pair it with this."

"Over jeans?"

"Yeah, unless you're taking her somewhere really fancy. Wait, let me guess, this is the girl from SCORE?"

"What girl from SCORE?"

"The one whose tweets you're always gushing over."

The grin steals over my face against my will. Caught. "She invented #TodayForShae, #TomorrowForAll. Now everyone's using it. That's her hashtag."

Monae swoons and makes kissy faces at me. "In other words, she's used to seeing you in that dank little office in a ratty T-shirt? You don't need me. You can't go wrong by comparison."

I toss the rejected polo into her face. "Shut up. She basically jump-started the movement that's happening. You can't tell me that's not impressive." I slip my arms into the chosen shirt. Button it up and start tucking the tails into my waistband.

"Hmm, I think don't tuck it in for now," Monae says.

"Really?"

"And leave the top two buttons open. You don't wanna look too buttoned-up. Casual. With the potential to be tidy."

That sounds good. I grab the blazer by the collar, toss it over my shoulder. "How do I look?"

Monae laughs. "You look hard up. But you'll do."

KIMBERLY

Zeke's apartment is small, and surprisingly girly. Lavender walls and paintings of flowers and dancers. Throw pillows with silver sequins. Everything matches and looks really nice. He makes us tea and serves home-baked cookies from a tin. The intrigue continues. Who is this guy?

We had a nice dinner out, and he paid with his own money this time. He puts my leftover lasagna in the refrigerator, all responsible and careful. That's the detail I enjoy the most. He thinks I'm going to be here long enough that my leftovers ought to be chilled.

"We also have some beer," he says. "It looks like we're out of wine."

"The tea is good," I answer, sniffing the lemon steam. Tea and cookies. It's sweet and wholesome, and somehow both fitting and opposite to what we are doing.

When Zeke sits on the couch beside me, I set aside the tea. I offer him the sexy grin I've practiced.

He smiles. Leans toward me. "I want to kiss you now," he says. His face is close to my face. He pauses, and I'm nervous. Maybe we are both nervous.

"Then what are you waiting for?" I whisper. This time, I feel his smile.

His lips are soft. It's not unpleasant. But I don't know what to do. It's supposed to be instinctive, or something, but what if it's not? What if I'm not good at kissing? What if he tastes me and knows right away that I don't know what I'm doing?

My hands find his shoulders. His tongue plunges in and out and I try to move mine in response. Like dancing, except not the way I usually step on everyone else's toes. I hope.

My hands squeeze his shoulders and part of me wants to wrap my fingers around his neck and pull him closer, but how can he get any closer, and there is another part of me, in the back of my brain, that won't let me lean into it at all.

My palms pump against his shoulder bones, pushing him away.

"What's wrong?" Zeke is alarmed. "What happened? Did I hurt you?"

It takes a moment to catch my breath. Zeke's hands slide down my back, soothing and comforting but also sending shivers through me. All my muscles are awake and intrigued by him.

"I'm sorry," I blurt out.

He rubs my back. "Don't be sorry," he says. "You don't have to be sorry."

"I'm sorry."

"No," he says. "Do you want to stop?"

"No. I mean . . . no. I don't want to stop."

Zeke waits anyway.

"It's . . . there's something you should know."

"Okay." He listens to me, all sweet and open. He's paying such close attention, but how do I really tell him?

"I don't, I mean, I haven't . . . before. I've never . . ." Why is it hard to admit it out loud?

"You've never had sex?"

"No."

"Oh." He lets go of me altogether. I've ruined it. Now he knows and he can't see me the same way.

"Is it, like, a religious thing?"

"No, I just haven't had the opportunity."

"That's probably not true," he says. "Lots of people have been into you. You just didn't know it."

It's nice that he thinks that. "Maybe," I say. "Except it's me."

Zeke frowns, making a the-whole-world-should-see-what-I-see face. "Don't you know how amazing you are?"

My I-hope-it's-sexy grin. "Sometimes."

He leans forward. "Good."

"It's not that I doubt myself. It's more like . . . I don't think most people really see me."

"I see you," he says.

"Maybe." I lower my gaze. It's baiting and coy and I don't like myself much for doing it.

"You are beautiful," Zeke says. "And not just because you're so freaking hot."

I laugh out loud.

His hands cup my face. "If you even give me the time of day, I'm the luckiest guy." His thumbs stroke my cheeks. "And if no one has ever recognized all the amazing things about you, they didn't deserve you anyway."

"There was one man, once," I whisper. "Nothing happened, but I thought for a minute that maybe . . ." Even now, I can lose myself in remembering. The shivers that used to come over me when Al—Senator Sloan—would look my way. I can't believe he's coming back here. I'll have to see him. It's a weight on my shoulders already.

He'll whirl in, shake things up, and whirl away.

It's different with Zeke. He's present in a way I can touch. He's real.

I cover his hands with my hands. My body is warm and eager and my mind is screaming at me to stop being so stupid. "Which way to the bedroom?" I ask.

He kisses me lightly on the lips. "We could wait, if you want."

"No, I'm ready."

"Are you sure?"

"I'm sure."

Zeke is beautiful and sweet. He will never let me down.

●●●

Beyond Zeke's bedroom, a door bangs open and closed again, shaking us out of our slumberous bubble.

"Roommate?" I ask.

"Not exactly." His voice is suddenly wary and distant.

I raise my head to look at him. "I have a roommate. Jennica. You met her at the diner."

Zeke's squinting at the door, as if willing it not to swing open. Or, probably, checking to see if it is actually locked. "I live with my sister. It's not weird," he rushes to add. "Better than staying at home, is all."

"Did you grow up around here?"

"My parents live about an hour away. I don't like making the drive every day."

"How do you like college?"

"It's better than high school, that's for sure. I'm about out of patience with school, though. This is my last semester. I'll be looking for a real community organizing job when I graduate."

"What will happen to SCORE?"

"If I can find a job here in Underhill, then I'll stay on as an advisor."

A jolt, like a current, courses through me. "You would leave Underhill?"

Zeke strokes my shoulder. "God, are you kidding? As soon as possible."

"Oh."

He rolls away, and the side of me that was touching him grows cool in the sudden open breeze of the sheets. All of me shivers. I pull up the blankets.

"Look," he says, coming back to me. He has a book. It's full of beautiful images from places around the country. "Don't you want to see the whole world?"

"My world is big enough," I lie. I remember dreaming that. I remember how quickly the dream died. The sharpness of reality, a thousand shards piercing my skin my muscles my bones. I am Underhill. Underhill is me. It's all there is and all that ever will be. To imagine a different life . . . I can't. That glass is too fragile to look through, let alone handle.

I pull the book from his hands and set it aside. I tuck my arm over his chest and he wraps his arm around my back. We shift and snuggle until we are comfortable and close.

"Can I stay?" I ask. "Can I stay here with you?"

"Of course," he answers, holding me tight. "Right now, you are the whole world."

JENNICA

I wake in the morning and the apartment is quiet. I can feel that Kimberly's not here. Even under the warmth of the blankets, a shiver runs over me. I slide toward the bathroom, start the shower. Tremble and wait, with my arms tucked close, for the steam to rise around me. Brush my teeth quick to get it out of the way. Get the bad taste out of my mouth.

When the world was not ending, we ate breakfast together. Cereal out of quick bowls, or pancakes if we had time to shake out the powder and stir water into it. Kimberly knows how to cook and I like watching. You'd think I'd know some things after working at the diner, but it's different here. Curled in my pajamas on the kitchen stool, studying how her hands go. Caring how it turns out. Waiting for her to look over her shoulder and smile.

It's hard to forget that she saved me. It's hard to forget all those good mornings, the sound of our dishes clattering into the sink beside each other's. She leaves for work a few minutes earlier than I do.

I would sit there, cupping the cooling dregs of my coffee and worrying about the day to come. She'd slide her feet into her shoes, slinging her purse strap across her chest. Then she'd walk toward me. Predictable as clockwork and soothing as a salve. She'd kiss my bare shoulder. "Be strong."

STEVE CONNERS

"Babe—" I stretch my legs out under the desk, switch the phone to the other ear. Rock back and study the ceiling.

My wife's voice is pulled taut. "You think he's still going down there? Don't you?"

"Can't blame him. Like it or not, he feels attached to Underhill."

"It's been eight years since we lived there," she says. "Why can't he accept the way things are now?"

"Look, he's just having a hard time. It's, I mean, everything that's gone on over there is enough to get anyone upset."

"We've bent over backward to give him chances he didn't have in Underhill. Now he's gonna go throw it all away?"

"Maybe he feels guilty. He's got a better situation now. A lot of his friends don't. That's, well, it's something to carry. You know what I mean?"

I swivel my chair toward the window. At first glance, it's all white sky and insulated glass. From my 23rd floor office, it's easy to stare at the grid of streets below and forget what it's like down there for a lot of people. And it's not as if I don't care. I handle several pro-bono portfolios for nonprofits. I write generous checks.

Will is more compassionate than I am. Or he's closer to it. I don't know. "Your son—our son—has a very big heart," I remind her.

She sighs. "The whole point of me moving us out of there was to get him in a better school."

"Right. Not because you love me and wanted to live with me or anything."

"Stop," she snaps.

I should know better than to needle her when she's already upset. "It was a joke," I say gently. "I mean, I think . . ."

Silence on the other end of the phone. Damn. I done stepped in it good, as my wife would say.

"You wanna make this about us right now? Really?"

"Babe, I'm just trying to lighten the mood."

"I can't—"

"I know. I'm sorry. Look, I'm worried about him, too. You want me to talk to him again?"

"Whatever you said last time has him all but dropping out of school, so . . ."

That's not fair and she knows it. But it's easier to let that one slide for the moment. Deep breath. "How can I help, then?"

EVA

Mom watches the news when Daddy's not home. "We need to know what they are saying about us."

They are saying Daddy is a bad cop.

"Shoot first, ask questions later. That can't be how we police our cities."

"People need to show respect for officers of the law. Period. You're out there doing your job, with people out to get you. In that kind of neighborhood . . ."

"This was a child."

"In that kind of neighborhood, age doesn't necessarily equate with level of threat."

"This was an unarmed child."

"Officer was under threat . . ."

"From an unarmed child?"

"The officer perceived a threat . . ."

"Perceived being the operative word."

". . . and took the appropriate action."

"People make mistakes," I say. "Why is everyone being so hard on Daddy?"

Mom takes me by the shoulders. "It was not a mistake." Her voice is hard. "Never say that again."

On TV they show her face again. Shae Tatum. Thirteen years old.

TINA

I am old enough
to walk
to the store on my own
my new favorite candy is Reese's.
I am old enough
to understand
Hands Up Don't Shoot
and all the people marching and shouting.
I am old enough
to listen
and to stop when they say stop
but everybody makes mistakes sometimes.
I am old enough
to know that
things are not always very simple
even when they should be.
I am old enough
to remember
people who are gone now
Tariq and Nana and Shae.
I am old enough
to die.

BRICK

So many arrests. I've spent enough of my time, my capital getting my guys out of lockup. We need a better plan. I pace behind my chair, near the windows, glancing out at the dusk. *Shooting time,* says the voice in the back of my head. *Cops and niggas in a game of chicken—who's more afraid of the dark?*

If that's not the lyrics to something, it should be. I'll write it in my notebook. Later, when no one's looking. Too busy now. Got some of my lieutenants gathered up on the couches, working it through.

"They ain't messing around with the curfew," Sammy says. "People gonna die."

"Aw, hell no. They're not doing this on my block again." I mutter it, but not enough to myself.

Sammy agrees. "This Kings' territory. How you gonna let it go down like that?"

"We can't walk out there with guns blazing." Noodle. Ever the voice of reason. "It's not like going up against the Stingers, right?"

My ass.

"They rollin' up in motherfucking tanks, yo," Sammy declares. He holds up his phone to the live footage. It's nowhere near curfew, but they're ready.

"You really wanna walk against that?" Noodle says.

I nod. "The right of the people to keep and bear arms shall not be infringed."

"They straight up infringing our rights, yo. They down there doin' it right now. What we gonna say back to that? What? We just gonna roll over like dogs?"

"Sammy, shut up, man," Noodle says, real easy. "Let's not get all riled up."

I laugh, straight up. Noodle is the king of flying off the handle. Some days he would pop you one for looking at him funny. Now he wants a reasoned and measured response?

Sammy's on a roll. "They wanna shoot us like dogs, yo. I seen this mural about it."

"I saw it." Rules for dogcatchers, rules for cops. That's good art. My man eMZee tells it like it is.

MELODY

"You should come by some night," Brick said. I dunno why I did. Not really my scene. Just curious, I guess.

The place is alive. I can feel it already, even walking down the hall. He must own the building, to get by with this kind of racket. Or at least all the neighbors know better than to speak up.

I seen kids in the elevator. Can't help picturing all their moms trying to get them down at bedtime. With bass thumping through the floorboards, rattling the bones of the place. I'm not down for that.

Brick's apartment is jamming. I didn't know any buildings in Underhill had a penthouse. Maybe he took out some walls, to get a place this size. It's like a nightclub.

Is a nightclub, I guess. Must be something like fifty people up in here. Dancing and drinking and being all loud. He's got a DJ turning the music live. He's got a girl tending bar who looks like a low-rent Beyoncé. Which is still pretty hot.

They drug test at my job. I'm not looking for a contact high to mess up my whole situation. But the music is pumping and it makes me wanna move. Throw my hands up and shimmy.

I admit, it's crossed my mind to wonder what Brick's world is like. To see it up close. To peel back a few of those layers that close him in. That's why I came, I guess. I didn't expect it to feel this easy. Throb with the beat and forget the world. Forget myself.

After a while, I realize I'm no longer dancing alone. Brick has moved through the mass of people to stand in front of me. Not dancing, exactly, but he still fits here. Presence, they call it. He's the kind of person who takes over whatever space he enters.

Brick glances me up and down. Appreciating my outfit, I guess. I didn't plan it out like that or nothing. But it feels good, him checking me out.

"Mel," he says. "You came."

"Melody," I answer.

He nods, lip curling like he wants to laugh.

"What?" I can guess what he's thinking: most girls let him call them whatever he wants.

"Come kick it with us a minute." He gestures toward the top of the room. No better thing to call it. Top of the room. His chair is a throne, almost. The couches arced around it are reserved for his handpicked few. The inner sanctum.

"Me? Why?" *Just go. Don't look a gift horse in the mouth, or whatever.* Although that saying never made much sense to me.

"Lemme bend your ear a minute," he says. His arm goes around me. "What are you drinking?"

The Trojans brought a great big horse to their enemies as a gift. If they'd looked in the mouth, they'd have realized it was full of soldiers. They'd have left it outside the gate. So looking a gift horse in the mouth seems like a perfectly good idea, really.

We're already walking. "Okay, I guess."

I don't mind his arm being around me. There's no denying he's fine. He's different here, somewhere between the hard way I've always thought of him, the way he goes around the neighborhood, somewhere between that and how he is with Sheila. He has a soft side. I've seen it. That makes him . . . interesting.

"House special." He hands me a glass. Whatever is in it has the perfect flavor. Sweet but not too sweet. Nuanced. I could slurp it like nectar, but I sip slowly instead. Cautious.

The couch is burgundy, almost purple. I can see the spot where I'll sit. At the right hand of the . . . whatever Brick imagines himself to be.

"I need your opinion about something," he says.

"You barely know me," I remind him. "What do you care what I think?"

"You've stepped to me twice already this week."

My heart beats faster. "I tell it like I see it." My big old mouth can't help itself.

"That's valuable," he says.

"Valuable?"

"You'll call me on my bullshit."

Side-eye, all over his ass. Wave my hand around the room. "This is all bullshit. Where do you want me to start?"

Brick laughs. His hand, on the small of my back. Like they do. "See?"

It's intoxicating, his orbit. Calling me out to lean in, but I'm still wary. "What do you want from me?"

"Sit down," Brick says. "We can use a woman's opinion on this."

"I think we got it handled, yo," says one of the guys.

"Shut up, Sammy," says the other. I recognize him. He looks me up and down. Not flattering, like Brick's way. More lecherous. I give him cold eyes back. He says, "What do you think about policing the police?"

I shrug. "I know it worked for the Panthers."

"But that was fifty years ago." Brick's hand is still on my back. "We're talking about making a response. To the curfew, to the cops."

"Oh." This, I know something about. "I have a friend who works with SCORE. They're planning a protest. You wanna know about all that?"

"Naw, we wanna fry some bacon." Sammy laughs.

I glance at Brick. "Really? You wanna be some kinda Huey P. Newton now?"

Brick stays serious. "Give me my spear and my rifle."

"I don't think you've got the chops for it," I tell him honestly. That's what I'm here for, after all. "They'll kill you all. It's a different time."

The couch is comfortable. Brick introduces me around.

WILL/EMZEE

My parents don't want me going to any more protests. As if they can stop me. They think they know everything, but they don't.

"I'm going tomorrow," I tell Steve over breakfast. I say nothing about my plans for tonight.

Tomorrow is a big deal. White Out, the white supremacist group, is coming to town. Not to Underhill but to the white side. Griffith Park. That's where we live.

"You only said I can't go to Underhill," I remind Steve. "They're bringing this mess to us. I'm supposed to look the other way?"

"I don't know," he says. "It sounds like there's the potential for violence."

Bring it. "So?"

He studies me over the rim of his coffee. "It's different than before."

"So you're back to being skittish?" I slam a slice of bacon into my face.

Steve lowers his cup. "The march for Tariq Johnson was a peaceful protest. It was designed that way and it stayed that way."

Bacon. It's one of the miracle foods. It gets even more delicious when you're pissed about something. Around a mouthful, I say, "It's not the protestors getting violent. It's the cops."

"This is civil rights 2.0," I argue. "Those guys never backed down from a protest. They faced down dogs and fire hoses. They got hit and went to jail and everything."

"They were trained in passive resistance." Steve frowns. "They still don't teach you that in school?"

"I know about the dogs and the fire hoses," I tell him. "You think that's what we're up against?"

"To be honest, I think they've moved beyond that," Steve says. "I think they'll straight up shoot." He pauses. "What I meant was, you think those protests in the sixties were a bunch of angry people getting together one day? And singing 'We Shall Overcome'?"

I shrug. Something like that.

Steve sips his coffee. "You can't compare the sixties to now. That's all I'm saying."

"Whatever."

"Know the history and know it right. We're not trying to repeat it."

"Because things are so much better now? Because we're all equal and we just have to work hard?" I glare at him. "That's bullshit, and you know it."

"Look at this house," he says. "You and I have opportunities we never would have had in the sixties. Don't discount the progress."

"Tell that to my friends who live on Peach Street."

"You want this to be a simple conversation." Steve sighs. He pours a fresh cup of coffee. "It's a very complicated issue."

"I know that. Geez."

The carafe clatters back into place. Steve leans against the counter, weighing his words. I don't care what he thinks. He doesn't know what it's like in the old neighborhood.

"You think they'll shoot? At nonviolent protestors?"

"Everyone has a cell phone," he says. "And the police are trigger-happy."

"Exactly," I say. "We have to take a stand."

"I work with these people," Steve says. "They don't see anything wrong with what has happened."

"But it's wrong." That sounds stupid and whiny. But it's all I can think to say.

Steve looks out the window. Maybe he can't face me while he says it. "I think they've moved past a segregation mentality. They're back to a slavery mentality."

"What?" In spite of myself, I'm interested in what he's saying. This part of it anyway.

"You've seen other White Out events on the news, right? They're carrying torches and talking about taking 'their' country back. They're not talking separate but equal."

"Duh. They're white supremacists."

"They're speaking for a lot of prejudiced people who are afraid to come into the light."

"That's why we gotta take a stand!"

"Will—" Steve pauses. "Your mom and I don't want you participating in these protests."

"You don't want me standing up for what's right?"

"We want you to understand what all is at stake. For your future."

"I do."

"They hate us." Steve's voice chokes up. "It's not enough anymore to push us to the side and pretend we don't exist. We've proven we won't stand for that. So they want to eliminate us."

"I know. And I don't want to let them get away with that." My voice rises in response to his emotion. "I don't want to grow up in a world that hates me and not be able to do anything about it."

"I want you safe," Steve says. "I love you."

There are a few things that scare me more than anything else. Grown-up tears are one of them. I grab my backpack, ready to flee.

At the doorway, I turn around. Steve is at the counter. The coffee cup looks small in his hands and he looks small against the kitchen.

"I love you, too," I tell him. Because I don't know if I've ever said it before. And we don't know what will happen. "But I have things I have to do."

EVA

The plump envelope sits in the center of the table. It is the ugliest thing we have ever seen.

We eat dinner around its edges, because to move it means putting it somewhere. And it's not clear where it needs to go.

So it sits there, right where I left it.

I am the one who checks the mail. I always do, after school. I like to sort it into piles. Things for Mommy, things for Daddy. Things for "Current Resident," which is me.

I save all the catalogs and coupons to make my collages.

The white bubble package is thick and bulky and heavy. It would not fit in the mailbox, instead it was leaning against the post, all slumped against the grass like a mail-order T-shirt. It had no return label, but it was addressed to "The family of Darren Henderson," which is me.

There was a manila envelope inside, one so worn and overstuffed that it was tearing at the edges. Poking out the seams, there were rolls and wads of bills. Cash money.

I rushed inside, plopped it on the table. Tore it open. So much cash money, rubber banded in small bundles. I wanted to unwrap it, toss it in the air, roll around in it like a lottery winner.

The note fluttered from the envelope. The note was typed on a piece of off-white paper and signed with a blood cross stamp:

ONE DOWN, ONE MILLION TO GO.

I wonder if it is a million dollars, but Daddy says no.

"It's probably fifty thousand."

Still enough to make my eyes bug out. Still the most money we have ever seen in one place.

But Mommy says the blood cross logo is a symbol of white supremacists. We've been sent money by the Ku Klux Klan.

More money than Daddy even makes in a year.

KIMBERLY

When it's just the two of us in the office now, it's different. We stay longer than we mean to. It is easy to get lost in the work, to get lost in each other.

"Did you call the local affiliates?" Zeke says.

We're sitting side by side at his desk. Our knees might be touching, but we pretend they aren't. Sometimes, when he takes a call, his hand drifts to my knee. I like it there. It is interesting, how different the world becomes when there is someone you can touch.

"Yeah," I answer. "They'll be there in the morning."

We are sorting through the various flyers and materials for the White Out counterprotest tomorrow. In a minute I will get up and go make more photocopies on bright-colored paper.

Zeke's hand finds my knee again. I will get up. Really. In a minute.

I put my hand on top of his. He leans in and nuzzles my neck. "You smell so good," he says. "What is that?"

"Should I go back to my desk?" I grin. "I think I'm distracting you."

"You're not going anywhere." Zeke kisses me again. "Everything else in the world is a mere distraction from you."

It is hard to believe this is my life.

Minutes pass and we are mostly kissing. Maybe this is why the work is taking longer than usual. Maybe I don't care. We will be here for hours. We will be here forever, and it will be all I could ever hope for.

Someone knocks on the door. Luckily. Zeke pulls back, sits up all straight and official.

"Yeah, come in," he calls.

I grab the flyers and stand up, as if I was already headed to the copy machine.

The door opens. A girl a few years younger than me pokes her head around it. I know her, from ages ago, from school.

"Hi," she says. "Do you have a minute?"

Zeke nods. "How can we help you?"

"Melody?" Her name comes back to me in time. "Hey, what's up?"

She approaches me, looking a bit nervous. "I remembered that you work here. Something happened—" she pauses, glances at Zeke. "I think you should know . . ."

"Should I step out?" Zeke offers. "Do you want to talk to Kimberly alone?"

He's so considerate. It makes my skin flush, even as I'm focused on Melody and whatever she's brought to us. I don't really think of her as the organizing type, but honestly, who among us was before Tariq died?

Melody squares her shoulders. "No, I just need to say this, so that you know."

"What's going on?" With a hand on her arm and the other in the air, I invite her to sit in a chair across the desk from Zeke. I pull my own chair away from his side and closer to Melody. We lean in to listen.

"It's Brick," she says. "You know Brick, right?"

"Yeah," Zeke says. He glances at me. He doesn't know the history there, either. Not even a little bit. There are things we haven't discussed, but he knows I know pretty much everyone who's anyone around Underhill.

"We know Brick," I confirm. I've known him since grade school, when he used to pull my pigtails, so to speak. Except worse.

"I was up at his place last night," Melody says. "His boys are pissed about what's going down, and they want to fight back. They're talking about taking it to the streets."

"The Kings have been breaking curfew," I say. "They're out there every night." I've been surprised, but it's happening.

"And getting arrested," Melody says. "Now they're talking armed resistance."

"Not a great idea," I say.

"Unless they're looking to get gunned down," Zeke agrees.

Melody shrugs. "He's talking it. I'm only telling it. Panther-level action, taking guns against the cops."

"That's suicide."

"It's also not what the Panthers were about," Zeke adds.

Melody nods. "We're dying anyway. We take some of them out with us. That's how we get ourselves on the map, Brick was saying."

"Damn," Zeke says, drumming his fingers on the desk. "We can't have that kind of thinking in play. It'll undermine the whole movement."

"That's why I'm here," Melody says. "If you hit up Brick before he goes off, maybe you can get him in on what's already up."

Zeke laughs. "You think I'm a miracle worker?" He glances at me.

"Brick is not one-dimensional," I say. This much I know is true. "He's smart, and he's strategic."

"And pissed as hell." Melody holds up her hands. "I'm just telling it."

"Maybe there's a benefit to working with him," I add. "He has guns. And lots of manpower."

Zeke looks thoughtful. "The whole point of a movement like this is to underscore the fact that we're not all violent, not all drug dealers and gang members."

"We need people to come together," I say. "We don't need to start a fight."

"Brick's looking for a fight," Melody says.

"So are we." Zeke rubs the back of his neck. His mind is agitated, I can tell by his sudden restlessness. "I just don't know what that alliance would look like."

Melody stands up. "Me either. All I know is, if you don't get to him, it's going off."

JENNICA

Thursday is pizza night. Kimberly always picks it up on her way home from the salon. We pull the blankets up and watch old episodes of *Grey's Anatomy* or *Project Runway* on her laptop. The screen is small, so we have to sit close together. It's okay if I rest my head on her shoulder. Sometimes, the best times, she wraps her arms around me. It's the only time I feel okay. It's the only time I can get clear on what it really felt like to be with Noodle. When I have someone there to lean on who's better. Kimberly is solid, warm. Noodle is like smoke or vapor. Fleeting.

He hasn't called. Hasn't texted. Not since the other night. I stare at my phone. Nothing. And I hate myself for wanting it, when everything is wrong.

I'm already on the couch when Kimberly breezes in.

She plops her purse on the counter. Her purse . . . and nothing else.

"Hey, Jennica." She swoops on down the hallway.

I sit up. Where is the sweet-hot scent of crust and cooked tomatoes?

A few minutes later, she's back, dressed in boot-cut jeans and a flowy, belted top. Clothes to go out in.

"No pizza?"

She smooths down the belt, glances at her reflection in the microwave door. "Sorry. I can't tonight."

"No big deal." I think the words sound light enough, even though my throat is closing.

Kimberly pops some lip gloss out of her purse. "No, you're right. I should have called. It's our standing date." She smiles and it is warm. Still, the apology is not the blanket I was hoping for.

"No big deal," I say again. "You look great. Have fun with Zeke."

"It's not a date. It's sort of a work thing. We have to go to this party."

Sounds like a date. "Well, have fun."

Kimberly sighs. "I'd invite you, but it's not a party you want to be at, you know?"

So it's like that. "I'm fine," I tell her. "Don't worry about it."

"See you," she says. The door closes behind her.

I curl up under the blanket, alone.

OFFICER YOUNG

It doesn't make sense that they would keep coming like this. They know what's going to happen. We have no choice. Curfew hits, and we go in. Like clockwork. But they just keep coming. Haven't they made the point? Nothing is changing.

As the seconds tick toward midnight, I stare into my locker. Every piece of equipment in there is designed to make me strong. Strong is not how I feel tonight, suiting up.

It feels like going to war, which I have done once. Stateside, when you walk around in your army fatigues, people clap. It happened to me in an Applebee's once, right after my tour. I was with my wife and my brother. We walked in, and someone—his kid was still actively serving, I think he said later—started up this round of applause for me. We got seated and all through the meal people kept coming over to say "thank you for your service." Most of those people have no idea about long, quiet nights in the desert. Or how bad it gets when the nights are not so quiet.

I'm home now. I'm going to work, and more and more it feels like going to war. Police officers are supposed to be tough, like soldiers. I've been a soldier. That's how I know there's no such thing as tough. It's all an act. There's too much to fear out there.

"Come on, rook," O'Donnell says, clapping my shoulder. "Saddle up."

Host: *Tonight, we're in conversation with Senator Alabaster Sloan and law enforcement expert Garrison Hobart, here to discuss the legal case of Darren Henderson, and the shooting of thirteen-year-old Shae Tatum. Protests continue in Underhill.*

Sloan: *Qualified immunity shouldn't be a get-out-of-jail-free card. There has to be accountability for law enforcement.*

Hobart: *Of course, but police can't be in fear of being arrested for actions performed while on duty.*

Sloan: *Why not? If it makes them exercise force more responsibly . . .*

Hobart: *They're well trained to react with professionalism.*

Sloan: *Should their first priority be their own safety at all cost?*

Hobart: *Yes.*

Sloan: *At all cost? Really?*

Hobart: *The point is, no one would ever become a police officer if they didn't have this immunity.*

Sloan: *So, you're saying people join the force to use violence without consequence?*

Hobart: *Of course not. The point is, using violence is often a necessary part of policing effectively. They can't do their jobs if they're afraid of being charged with a crime every time they discharge their service weapon.*

Sloan: *Why not? Wouldn't it lead to more responsible policing?*

Hobart: *No. It would lead to chaos.*

Sloan: *It would save lives.*

Hobart: *For example, often during an arrest, if the suspect isn't cooperating, you have to get physical in order to restrain them. Police officers can't be counter-charged with assault every time they bring someone in. That's qualified immunity.*

Sloan: *There has to be a line—*

Hobart: *There's absolutely a line. It's called "excessive use of force" and . . .*

Sloan: *AKA, police brutality. And yet—*

Hobart: *. . . and officers can be brought up on charges.*

Sloan: *Shooting an unarmed child is a far cry from putting someone into a wall a little too hard.*

Hobart: *There are shades to resisting arrest.*

Sloan: *"Resisting arrest?" You're talking about Shae Tatum?*

Hobart: *Many cases—*

Sloan: *I don't agree that a police officer's first duty is to protect his own life. They want to be celebrated for nobly putting their lives on the line, but also to have carte blanche to engage in self-protective action? You can't have it both ways.*

Hobart: *That's far too simplistic.*

Sloan: *This was an unarmed child who, at worst, was attempting to flee.*

Hobart: *Resisting arrest.*

Sloan: *Is not a capital crime!*

Hobart: *First responders are trained to protect themselves first.*

Sloan: *Firefighters run into burning buildings. Risk is inherent in the job.*

Hobart: *They perform a risk assessment first. There are times they don't run in, if it isn't reasonable or safe.*

Sloan: *Henderson shot her in the back. Where was the threat?*

Hobart: *It's akin to putting on your own oxygen mask before assisting others, in the event of a loss of cabin pressure while flying. A police officer's first duty is to his own safety, because he can't help anybody if he's injured or compromised.*

Sloan: *Why become a police officer, then? The safest thing would be to stay home. We should be policed by a group of people willing to genuinely put themselves on the line for* public *safety. Not just* their own *safety.*

Hobart: *For any officer to discharge a weapon, they must perceive a credible threat. You think officers should be willing to die* on the off chance *that the suspect who appears armed actually isn't?*

Sloan: Credible *threat. Which brings us back to the question you tried to dodge a moment ago. Where was the credible threat Shae Tatum posed to Officer Henderson? Innocent until proven guilty is the backbone of the criminal justice system. Why should police get to circumvent due process when they fire their service weapon?*

Hobart: *If their life is at risk, there's no time to impanel a jury to determine guilt or innocence.*

Sloan: *Their decisions are based on snap judgments, and they routinely snap to the negative in black communities. If this was happening in race-blind ways across the country, you better believe we'd be looking closer at police procedures and practices.*

Hobart: *Probably true. Systemic bias is a reality, one that exists high above the actions of a single officer on the street.*

Host: *There are two sides to everything.*

Sloan: *At least. But let's not erase the concept of accountability. We can't throw up our hands and say bias exists, so black people are going to die.*

Host: *We'll be right back, with more from Senator Sloan and Dr. Hobart.*

BRICK

They come to talk me down. Kimberly and her buttoned-up little activist boyfriend. Zeke is woke, but too brainy for the real world. All ideas, no clout.

He's the type that thinks it was Martin Luther King's powerful speeches that changed the world in the 1960s. It wasn't. It was bodies in the street. It was a hundred cocked guns in Oakland. It was the promise of a revolution to follow.

They come talking to me about tweets and flyers and buttons. *Naw, man. Let me hook you up.*

They need me.

They need me to show them how to really make a stink.

JENNICA

Brick's party is always the place to be. Does Kimberly think I'm stupid? *"It's not a party you want to be at."* I knew what that meant as soon as she said it.

I came anyway. In time to see Kimberly and Zeke sitting right up where I used to sit. Holding court with Brick. So I'm holding court with my good friend Jose Cuervo.

Screw them. Dance.

I don't even know what she's doing here. Some meeting. It'll be a cold day in hell before Brick shows up to volunteer at a SCORE meeting. They're barking up the wrong tree. I could tell them. But no.

Dance. Dance! Screw the revolution!

I miss this, if nothing else. The freedom of turning my body loose against the music. The softness of liquor in my veins. It's been ages. Kimberly barely ever parties, says it doesn't agree with her. So I've kept off it all, too, because we have fun together. I haven't even missed it.

Doesn't agree with her. Ha. Right now, tonight, I remember how crazy that used to sound. How could this feeling not agree with anyone?

Anyway, here she is, trying to live the life she wants me to walk away from. Hypocrite.

"Jennica." Kimberly. She's here now, with me on the dance floor. She puts her hand on my arm. "Jennica?"

I shake her off. "Leave me alone."

"What are you doing?"

"Nothing. Dancing." I writhe toward her, then away. The beat is strong, good.

"Let's go home," Kimberly says. Her warm eyes are concerned, and I hate it.

"I want to stay." She's with Zeke anyway. "It's cool. You should finish your date."

"We're working," she says. "It's not a date. I care more about getting you home safe."

Bitch. Now she wants to be the perfect roommate?

"I'm fine. I'm blowing off steam. I haven't danced in ages. Just go. Have fun." See? I can be the perfect roommate, too.

Kimberly's reluctant.

I turn to Zeke. "Get her out of here. Show her a good time. I'm counting on you."

Zeke pulls Kimberly aside. "She wants to stay. She doesn't seem that drunk," he says.

I smile inside. I'm *trying* not to seem that drunk.

"I don't want to leave her here like this," Kimberly says. "It's a girl thing."

"You wanna stay?"

"No," Kimberly says. "But—" She looks over her shoulder at me.

Damn it. I come forward and hug her. "I love you," I tell her. "I promise it's okay. I'm okay." Nothing will happen. I'm perfect. I'm beautiful. The music will never end and I'm here for it.

"You have your phone?" she asks. "You'll call me if you need me?"

"Of course."

They fade into the crowd. Everything fades, except Jose and me. He knows how to tango, how to swirl me right. Perfect. Beautiful. Music and music and music.

KIMBERLY

"She didn't seem very drunk," Zeke says. "And she wanted to stay, what were you supposed to do?"

"I don't know. Friends shouldn't leave each other in that kind of situation, is all." It's wrong. All wrong. "I shouldn't have left her."

"She seemed okay."

"No, she didn't."

Zeke rubs my back lightly. "Text her, if you're worried."

"I did, but she's mad, so . . ."

"So, not responding doesn't mean anything bad."

"I don't even know what she was doing there. She hates those guys."

"They are a lot to take."

"They're kind of a joke to me. I mean, not exactly. I know they're dangerous and all. But I grew up with them." I guess I want Zeke to be impressed with my chill or something. The Kings used to scare me, big time, but Jennica helped me see them for the puffed-up little boys they are. I know they could still hurt us. But they're quick to flinch if you don't cower.

"It's crazy, the way they jump at Brick's every order."

"We don't have to work with them," I say.

"Yeah, we do." Organizing 101. Consolidate community leadership around a common goal.

"They want to fight the cops. SCORE can't get into that kind of thinking."

"If all you have is a hammer, every problem looks like a nail," Zeke says. "We can give them some alternatives to the hammer."

The image in my mind is Brick, holding a big-ass hammer that suddenly turns into a flock of butterflies, fluttering around his head. The expression on his face makes me giggle out loud.

"Maybe Sloan will have some ideas."

Ice water.

JENNICA

On the dance floor everything feels fine and good. In the bathroom, the whole world tilts and I can't tell which way is up anymore.

Someone knocks on the door. "Hurry up. There's a *line*."

It's too hard to pull my tights back up, and I poked my finger through them anyway, so I strip them off and put them somewhere near the trash. I fuss with my skirt until I think it is covering me again. The walk home will be cold, but I don't want to leave yet anyway. I want the music and its magic back.

The hallway is tilted and labyrinth-long. "'Bout time," says the cat-eyed girl who was pounding on the door.

"Sorry," I mumble.

My hand traces the wall. As long as the music is getting louder I am moving in the right direction.

"Hey, baby," Noodle says. "You looking for me? I'm here."

He's here. In front of me like a wall. His arm slides around me and suddenly we're walking again. But the music is getting softer, more distant.

"Music," I say. "I want to dance."

"We're gonna dance, baby," he says. "You and me." The arm that's around me is holding me up and also kind of cupping my boob.

It's funny. Usually getting drunk makes me want to lean into him. Not tonight. Here and now I see him for the slithering snake he is.

No.

It's funny, but not.

A soft click of a door latch and the music is muffled even further. My back is against the wall and Noodle presses up against me with his whole body. His hands push up my skirt. His mouth is on my neck, my chest. When I try to wriggle away, he takes hold of my wrists, pinning them beside my head.

"Shh," he says.

Manhandled. I know what this means now. What it means to be up against a wall with no power and no recourse.

No. The word echoes in my brain. Maybe it has always been there, straining to break free.

"No!" When it comes out loud it feels like something should shatter. But nothing does. Not his grip on my arm. Not the look in his eyes.

"Stop!" I shout, but maybe it comes out like a whimper.

"You used to like it when I did this," he says. "I know you like it."

"No. Please." There is nothing I can do. There is no fight in my body. I think about pushing against him but my arms are limp. I close my eyes. Maybe I can pass out and it will be like it never happened. He has been in me before. Maybe I won't know the difference.

"Let her go." Brick steps in and thrusts his arm like a bar across Noodle's chest. He shoves him back. The front of me goes cold, now exposed to the room.

And then Noodle is gone, and there's only Brick. Standing in front of me, holding me up. Someone has to.

"I have to go," I mumble. "I have to get home now." Somewhere, I have a purse, and phone. Kimberly—

"Nope. You're staying here tonight," Brick says. He lifts me up in his arms and carries me from this room to another one. Blue-gray walls, silver fixtures. Brick's own bedroom.

He sets me down near the edge of the bed. He straightens my clothes and pushes back my hair. His face is so concerned. He's sweet to me. Always has been. It would be easy. So easy to . . .

"Don't," he says. "Don't come at me like that unless you mean it." He puts his hands on my wrists, real gentle. My skin still stings there from Noodle's grip. I want to erase everything that just happened. Put myself back in the column of good.

Brick pushes me back a step. But his eyes say different. His fly says different. I wrench my hand away, slide it down his front. Kimberly might walk away from me but Brick won't. He'll always be there for me.

He catches my hand again. "Jennica, you're drunk."

"You wanna prove you're some kinda good guy?" He sways, or maybe it's me. "Bullshit. You run this neighborhood. There's nothing good in that."

"Jennica—"

"You're no good," I shout.

He stands silent. Dizziness rises from somewhere behind my knees. My hands find the edge of the mattress. Toss myself against it. My shin cracks against the baseboard. "Ow."

"You okay?"

He kneels beside me, massaging the sore spot on my leg. His hands feel good, like they could cover all of me, make the hurt go away.

He slides my shoes off. "Get some sleep, okay? I don't know what's going on with you, but we can talk tomorrow."

Screw that. I reach for him, pull him in. When our mouths meet, I taste salt and beer and breath.

It's one quick moment, or it lasts a hundred years. Something like that. It's gentle and wet and, honestly, why is it always so hard to get ourselves together?

He tears his face away. And that's what it feels like, a Band-Aid being ripped off, a curtain being torn from ceiling to floor.

"Jesus, fuck," he says. "Jennica." He's somewhere else, not up against me. Why? I blink until the room comes back into focus. He's all the way over by the windows.

I come up on my elbows. "What? Isn't this what you've always wanted?"

He comes closer, sweeps my hair to the side. "For once in this fucking life, I'm gonna do the right thing," he says. "And I'll probably regret it."

MELODY

Brick comes out into the hallway, looking stressed. And furious. All at the same time.

"She okay?" I ask. He's been in the bedroom with Jennica. I want to make sure I did the right thing. When I saw Noodle carrying her off to a bedroom . . . something about it ain't feel right. I'm not some kind of tattletale. I hope that ain't what he thinks. God, it probably is. He tells me he wants to go militant, and I bring him Zeke and Kimberly. I see a known asshole bringing a wasted girl into a quiet place, and I tell Brick. Maybe I am a tattletale.

"Do me a favor," he says. "Help her get in the bed."

"Noodle took off," I tell him. "Don't go looking for him." Great. To top it off, now I'm the weak-ass chick who doesn't want to see Brick in a fight. He's never going to trust me. But why do I even care?

Brick nods. "I'll wait here." His voice is strained. "Just, make sure she's okay, would you?"

"Yeah, sure." Maybe I should have gone in there with him to begin with. But the look on his face was worse than thunder. And it all happened so fast.

The room is dimly lit. Jennica is already on the bed, asleep or passed out. Either way, not much for me to do. I prop a pillow against her back so she stays on her side, then I slip off her shoes and pull the sheet and blanket up over her. Tuck her hair back, out of her face, real gentle. Like a good friend would do. She's breathing soft and even. I ain't sure whether to wish she'll wake up remembering or not.

True to his word, Brick is waiting in the hallway. "Thanks," he says, when I emerge. "I owe you."

No good way to respond to that. I shouldn't get extra credit for doing a good deed. "Nah. I tell it like it is, right?"

"That's only what I like most about you." He touches my shoulder, his thumb kinda skating along my collarbone. My mouth opens, just a little. Brick's eyes go cloudy. His hand's up behind my neck and I'm not sure what to make of being caught this way. No time to think or to plan. He leans in and I don't stop him. Why would I? He's fine. He's the king of all in sight and here he's chosen little old me. He could have any woman he wants.

The unexpected thing is, it's not just a hookup, either. I stepped to him and he liked it. He needs someone like me to keep it real with. I'm good for him. We balance.

Melody Jacquard, coming up in the world. And it feels great.

DeVANTE

"Listen," Robb says. "You gotta talk to Tyrell and get him on board. I'm sick of tiptoeing around his studious ass. You gotta tell him."

I pause my game. "What makes you think I can do that?" Because we're both black?

"You can speak his language, right?"

I pretend not to hate that. "His language is Excel spreadsheets." I struggle to inject lightness to my voice. "Who else speaks that?"

Robb laughs. "I don't know. Just try, okay?"

It's easier to agree. "Okay."

"Thanks," Robb says. "You wanna walk down to the Black House together?"

I glance at my screen. The meeting doesn't start for an hour. "Gotta hit the books a little longer," I tell him. I hold up the controller. "This was my ten minute break, but I should read another chapter of Econ."

"Okay. Just try to get T to come, for once."

Pause. Save. Power off. "Why do you care so much if he comes with us? It's not like you're best friends to begin with."

Robb pauses. Shrugs. "It's where he's from. He should stand up, don't you think?"

"I think it's his business."

"Fixing the damn world?" Robb slaps the doorframe. "It should be everybody's business."

EVA

In my room I can pull up my sleeves and examine my bruises. When I am not looking, other kids reach out and pinch me as hard as they can. I say nothing. Like I'm supposed to.

In my parents' bedroom, Mommy thumps something down on the dresser. Probably her hairbrush. Maybe her fist.

The walls are thin. I hear everything. But I say nothing, like I'm supposed to.

"You need an attorney, Darren. With this money we can afford the best."

"I can't accept their money."

The floorboards creak as Mommy paces. It is always Mommy who paces. Daddy holds still, like a coiled spring.

Mommy says, "No one will know."

"They'll know. What does it say if I accept it?"

"It says you're a father with a child to feed and a mortgage."

Daddy's voice is tight. So tight. "People already think I did it on purpose."

"No one will know."

There is no such thing as silence, but for a moment the air is still.

"I'll know."

@Viana_Brown: Why do they always call her "the slain black girl" on TV? #HerNameWasShae

@BrownMamaBear: IT COULD HAVE BEEN MY BABY. #EveryBlackParent #BlackParentFears

> **@Momof6:** Teach your kids to listen to police. End of story.

> **@WhitePowerCord:** Criminals get what's coming to them. Underhill PD FTW!!!!!

@UnderhillSCORE: Curfew's up. So are we. It's time to take a stand. We know who's against us. Who's with us? #Underhill

> **@BrownMamaBear:** All you kids go on home now. Stop your foolishness! They're coming for you.

@WhitePowerCord: SHOOT THEM DOWN. SHOOT THEM ALL. CURFEW'S UP. WHAT ARE YOU WAITING FOR #UnderhillPD ?

> **@Viana_Brown:** No officer with a shred of humanity would fire into a crowd of peaceful protestors. #Underhill

> **@WhitePowerCord:** Then maybe private citizens need to take matters into our own hands. You'll see us up close tomorrow. #WhiteOut #MakeItKnown

@KelvinX_: Tear gas goin up! Say your prayers and make your stand, Underhill. #UnderhillRiot

DAY SIXTEEN: TORCHES AND TERROR

PEACH STREET

This street stretches to the other side of town. Bends and curves with the whims of the city. Feel the ripple effect? We are all connected, pebble by pebble, block by block. One smooth double yellow line.

When the torches light up across town, people feel the ripple effect in Underhill. The street shivers in the light of the flames, and the city stands up to take notice.

WITNESS

You try to explain to your daughters what it means to be hated. They do not understand.

There are bows in their hair. As they look up at you, their eyes bear everything fragile in the world.

They do not understand. You pray they won't ever.

It is hard to say the word "hate" in their presence. It is impossible to convince them they are any less than loved. They feel safe and happy. You want to be proud of yourself for gifting them peace, but you are fearful of their naïveté. Their small hands hold yours. They can see that you are sad.

They do not understand. Today, you are the scary one, telling tales of a nation out to get them. You squeeze their little knees and promise to protect them. Try to forget that it is out of your hands.

There are bows in their hair. Placed by their mother's swift and gentle hands. The strongest hands you've ever known.

STEVE CONNERS

Every news outlet carries the footage of the White Out protest. Neo-Nazis and their families stand in Griffith Park. I can almost see it from here, but not quite. Out my window, down at the street level, the city looks peaceful. The corner of the park I can see is not the part with the bandstand. It's not that I want to see it firsthand. Not exactly. It's more about how unsettling it is to have it happening out there, out of sight.

John strolls into my office. I'm leaning back in my chair, online footage running on-screen. It relates to my job, so I don't bother to mute the screen or punch it off.

"You're watching this?" I ask. He's here to discuss the Henderson account, no doubt. It's what I should be thinking about. How this white power demonstration relates, how we should react. Instead, my mind is scattered.

"The full storm hasn't hit the media yet," John says.

"How so?"

He plops two typed pages onto my desk. A press release. I recognize the logo of the news outlet, a fringe conservative site with questionable judgment regarding content and sources and, well, questionable everything.

"What have they done now?" I muse as I skim. The press release is poorly written, but the salient details are clear enough:

White-nationalist organization White Out, in conjunction with the White Might, White Rights demonstration today, has announced that they've raised $$$ for Officer Henderson's family, to offset the loss of income during his time on administrative leave . . .

"Well, that's some crazy," I say. "What kind of respectable journalistic outlet uses the money symbol instead of spelling out the word?"

John chuckles. "Tell me about it."

All joking aside, this development will open up a whole new mess for us. "What's Henderson saying about this?"

"This is where it gets interesting."

My brows go up. "Uh-oh. Is he connected to the group? Did he ask them for money?"

"No, nothing like that. It was out of the blue."

"Good. So, clear deniability." I set the press release aside.

"But still an optics problem."

"Everything about this is an optics problem." I toss my pen onto the desk. "We have to be simple about it. We announce that he's not connected to these groups and isn't accepting their money."

"There's the rub," John says.

"What?" The pieces come together in my mind, drop like a stone to my gut. "No."

"Yeah. Henderson wants to accept the money."

"He can't." Out of the question.

"He is."

My feet press against the glide mat, roll my chair back. I need space. Need air.

John tosses himself into my corner chair. "So . . ."

Loosen my tie. "He can't. Come on. He's being investigated for the death of a black child, and he's going to take money from white supremacist groups now? The press will have a field day."

"I know, but it turns out a fair amount of it was delivered in cash. There's no easy way to return it. Frankly, I think he's already using it."

"Great."

"He didn't report receiving it. Didn't know it was going to become public. Thought it would be his little secret, I guess."

"Not the brightest bulb in the box, is he?"

John props his foot on his knee. Bounces it. I would swear he's enjoying this. "To be fair, he's facing some hefty legal fees, even with the police union involved."

"He doesn't know better than to get in bed with these people?"

"He claims he doesn't know for sure where it came from. It was an envelope, with a note."

"Does he have the note?"

"Says he threw it away. Didn't think it mattered."

Brighter bulb than I thought, maybe. I don't know if I prefer him to be a bumbling idiot or someone capable of calculation. Bleak pictures, both. "Maybe that was something separate, and he can still refuse the White Out contribution. It might still be coming."

Silence falls between us. The moment is long, both of us working the problem.

John finally speaks. "Does it offend you, as a black man?"

My face wrinkles of its own accord. "What kind of question is that?"

He shrugs. "Optics."

"It offends me, along with every black and brown human being on the planet, and hopefully a good portion of the white ones."

John sighs.

"Look, it's cash in exchange for a lynching. They're essentially saying that Shae Tatum deserved to die because of the color of her skin. No due process. They want to reward Henderson's extra-legal judgment solely on the grounds of race."

"It makes him look guilty."

"He is guilty!" Whoa. Breathe. Objectivity has left the building. "You wanted my opinion, as a black man."

John nods. Lets it slide. He has his reasons for everything. You won't see him fly off the handle. And I can't afford to, as a black man in the corporate landscape. Can't afford to be labeled "angry."

"What would you like to see come of it?" he says. "What would take the edge off?"

Honestly? To see every person with white supremacist leanings scorched off the planet. But John is asking from a PR perspective. "I don't know. He could donate it. Preferably to a black charity."

"From a damage-control standpoint, that would be best."

I nod. "Something camera-friendly. An after-school program. Probably not SCORE."

John laughs. "Something more neutral."

"He can't keep this money. It is the height of stupidity to think otherwise."

"From a PR perspective?"

I shrug. "That, and more." John looks expectant. "Legally, it opens up the door for him to be sued successfully in civil court. He's accepted money from a group that thinks black people deserve death for existing. It's perfectly legal to hold that ideology, in theory, but it's not legal to actually kill someone for the color of their skin."

John frowns. "If he acted in the line of duty, feeling his life was under threat, and those actions were made free of bias . . ."

Now he's getting it. "Right. It could be argued that accepting this money is an admission that that might not have been the case."

"The legal side is not our problem. But if Henderson's legal trouble gets worse, it becomes our problem."

I raise one shoulder. "Tell him to pick a charity and give generously, without being splashy about it. No one has to know how much he was really given, if it's coming in cash." My solution is rife with guilt, complicity, compromise.

John leaves, and I lean back in my desk chair. Pivot to the window. Insulated glass.

I prop my feet on the corner of the desk, a well-worn spot. Peer at the tiny vehicles, crawling far below like ants. The people, even smaller.

Thinking about where the money ever comes from. Thinking about complicity.

EVA

Eddie Johnson draws eyes and ears and a snout on my folders with a permanent marker. Everyone laughs.

"Pig!" they whisper when the teacher is on the other side of the room.

There is no one I can tell, so I don't. The teachers are not better anyway. They whisper, too.

That's the daughter.

Apple, tree.

I'm supposed to know what to say. I do know what to say. Nothing.

Eddie Johnson says, "I bet he beats your mom. All cops are beaters."

There is only so much a girl can take. My brain snaps, taking my mouth along with it. "He's a good person. A good cop." My fists clench. *No, no, no.* I broke the rule. Say nothing.

Eddie Johnson shakes his head. "Good at beating people up, all right." He pounds his knuckles into the other palm.

The smack of skin on skin. Beer bottle against the wall. The boxing bag hanging from the garage ceiling.

This time it's not so hard to keep my silence. I don't have to say anything at all.

I know how to throw a good punch.

ZEKE

I smooth my blazer, second-guessing my shirt choices. Ha. And I thought I was nervous about dressing for my first date with Kimberly. This is some other level.

I hover near the front door of the community center. Can't stop myself from eagerly peering out the window every few moments.

The Reverend Alabaster Sloan is a living legend. He's been organizing since the seventies, when he was a teenager. He marched for civil rights as a child before that.

"He should be here any minute," I tell Kimberly.

"I know," she says. She's bustling around doing our actual work, while I stand here like a fool, vaguely practicing the moment when he walks in and I extend my hand in greeting. Wow, I'm such a dork.

I turn back to our task, which is inventorying the materials we've packed to take to the protest. "Is that everything?"

"Think so," Kimberly says, examining her clipboard. She waves over two teen volunteers. "Let's load it up, guys."

The boys start loading the boxes into the rental van parked in our lot. They're full of flyers about police shootings, SCORE pamphlets, "Know Your Rights" and "What to do if you get arrested" cards. Packs of black Sharpies for people to write our lawyers' phone number on their skin in case those cards are confiscated. Two cases of three-inch, baby-pink buttons that say in bold black letters, UNARMED. Poster boards painstakingly hand-lettered with messages like #TODAYFORSHAE #TOMORROWFORALL, RUNNING WHILE BLACK IS NOT A CRIME, LOVE NOT HATE, EQUALITY IS JUSTICE, and BLACK IS BEAUTIFUL.

The boys walk back in after a trip to the van. "Yo, I think your dude is here," one of them says.

"*My dude*?" I echo, cuffing him on the shoulder. "Have some respect."

He grins. "Your boy?"

I can't help but grin, too. "Okay, okay."

I pull open the heavy front door. Sure enough, there is Alabaster Sloan. "Good afternoon, sir. Welcome to Underhill Community Center."

We shake hands. He has a firm, comfortable grip. He's perfect. I hope my return handshake comes across as half that cool and confident.

"Ezekiel?" he asks.

"Yes, sir. But you can call me Zeke."

He nods.

The boys appear for another load, and I motion them over. "Senator, these are two of our best volunteers, Lemanuel and Ricky."

They perk up, standing straight. "Hi, Senator," they mumble. They look both flattered and unsettled to be called out.

The senator smiles and shakes their hands in turn. "Thanks for what you're doing. It's important work."

"Uh, thanks," Ricky says.

"Happy to help," Lemanuel adds.

They look at me, clearly unsure what to do next. "Finish the van, okay?"

"Yup, yup." They grab more boxes and flee.

"Come on in." I spread my hand out, inviting Senator Sloan deeper into the room. He moves past me comfortably, and weaves around the chairs to greet Kimberly. I flounder in his famous wake.

"Hello, Kimberly." He knows her on sight. That's impressive. They've met before, she told me. I assumed it was in passing.

"Hello . . . Senator." She pauses in the middle of speaking. Maybe she, like me, isn't sure what to call him. Senator? Reverend? Sir?

Senator Sloan grasps Kimberly by the shoulders and kisses her on the cheek. "Nice to see you again."

I'm confused, but there's no time to focus on that.

Yvonne flutters toward us. "Oh, hello, Senator." She enfolds him in the wings of her long, flowing dress thing. "Welcome, welcome."

Senator Sloan embraces her in kind. "Good to be back. Wish the circumstances were different." Somehow, he makes the perfunctory comment sound warm and original. He's a master communicator. I prepare myself to pay close attention to his every word, every gesture.

Yvonne says, "If you have a minute, I'd love to show you some of what's been done with your most recent generous donation."

"Of course, Yvonne."

His mere presence in the room makes the space zing to life. People drift toward us, as if drawn by an invisible tide. As long as he's here, it's a master class in organizing. Inspiring people.

I hover in his wake. Behind his back, I mouth to Kimberly, *Oh, my God.*

She smiles only slightly.

It's almost time to go. The van keys are still sitting on my desk, I remember. I go pick them up, double-checking that we got everything.

I return to find Kimberly standing in the community room with Senator Sloan. Something about it trips me up. My feet pause halfway there, my eyes fixed on their exchange. The pose between them. Yvonne is nearby, butterflying around the senator, and yet his gaze is on Kimberly.

She's shy around him. She lowers her head, in a way I haven't seen. Except once. When we were talking about our history. About how she's never had sex before me, and only been interested in one man. It's weird that my mind goes to that place, but it does.

He's familiar with her, too. He puts his hand on her shoulder like they've known each other forever. Or else he's just that kind of guy, smooth enough to get away with it. Does she want him to be touching her? When his hand goes out, her eyes go down.

My gut tugs and flutters. Some kind of warning. Or . . . I'm jealous. Is she *into* him? He's godlike, I know, but he's so old.

Kimberly shrugs away from Sloan's touch, turns her body at an angle and focuses on her clipboard.

I stroll toward them, like I belong in the conversation. Which, technically, I do.

"I'm here to support you," the senator's saying. "I don't have to speak. I can just be a face in the crowd."

"You've come all this way," I interject. "We'll make sure the cameras find you." It's great for our cause, that he's here.

Kimberly shoots me some side-eye. Damn. I totally just did a jerky guy thing that girls hate. And with reason. I shouldn't be butting in like that. She had this.

Senator Sloan laughs. "The cameras will find me. Don't worry about that."

"It's about time to go," I tell them. "Everybody ready?"

"I have my car out front," Senator Sloan says.

We walk him back toward the door. "I'll be driving the van. Would you like to have your driver follow me?"

"Kimberly can ride with me. She'll make sure I get to the right place." He smiles fondly at her and my spidey-sense tingles.

JENNICA

My eyes grog their way open. I am cozy and cotton mouthed, deep-settled and unsettled all at once. The comforter is gray and blue and thick. It goes on forever. This is not my bed.

Where am I?

I struggle upward, blink into the near dark.

"Hey," Brick says. "You okay? You're okay."

Oh, no. Oh, God. It all comes back to me. The shots, the kissing, him pushing me away.

"What happened?" I whisper. "What am I doing here?"

He sits up. He's rubbing my back. "You don't remember?"

All I can do is stare at my hands. I remember. And I'm humiliated.

I shake my head. "I drank too much." Maybe this is the best course of action.

"Oh." Brick scoots closer. I can't tell if his voice is disappointed or relieved.

"I probably did something embarrassing," I admit. "And I'm in your bed, so . . ."

"Nothing happened," he assures me. His arm is around my waist and it shouldn't feel this good. It shouldn't. He's warm and close and his hand cradles my hip. I'm still in my clothes, so it feels safe enough to let him hold me. I turn my face into his shoulder.

"I can't have you walking around drunk, trying to get home after curfew is all. You always have a place here."

"Why are you this nice to me?" It's like I want him to say it. Even though I'd have to shoot him down.

Or would I?

"I'm worried about you. You're not acting like yourself."

"I'm fine. Really." I let my face rest on his muscled chest. He's so broad, unlike Noodle. He feels like a wall around me, like nothing can touch me here. Safe.

"My boys . . . We're all going to this demonstration in a little while."

"Zeke and Kimberly were here," I recall. "You made plans with them?"

"Yeah." Brick strokes my hair. "You wanna talk?"

I lean into him, without answering at first. Maybe I've misjudged the whole situation. Maybe it doesn't have to be so black and white.

"I messed up," I whisper. "Noodle—"

"That's nothing," Brick says. "He done you wrong."

It's not so easy to see it that way. I came here. I wanted . . . something. Just not Noodle. Not like that.

"Listen," Brick says. "You're perfect. You're beautiful. I—you just say the word, and I'll mess him up so bad—"

"No, no." My hand cups Brick's bicep. Oh, wow. An uninvited laser of YES shoots through me. Those muscles. I'm kinda turned on and I hate it because it reminds me of last night. Of Noodle's hand going between my legs.

"No," I whimper. With my face in Brick's chest, I can't stop the tears. "I'm sorry. I'm so messed up."

Brick hugs me gently, whispering nice words.

When I'm quiet, when I'm trying to figure out what to say next—in other words, right when it starts to get awkward—Brick shifts slightly, reaching for something. Then comes the blinking, sucking sound of the TV powering on.

I straighten up, wipe my cheeks.

"*Members of the white-supremacist organization White Out have begun to gather in Griffith Park this afternoon . . .*"

"You wanna see messed up?" Brick says. "Check out these motherfuckers."

TINA

On paper
white out means
all you see is white
black type covered up
erased.
It is usually exciting
a clean slate—
the whole point of white out is
to make room for more black.

On TV, White Out means
erasing all the black in the world.
Their sign is a big paintbrush
dipped in white
because this is a white country
for white people.
They seem excited but
they do not make much sense—
white people are not
the only ones here.

BRICK

The first thought in my head is to laugh. There they stand, hundreds of white men, carrying flaming Tiki torches. It is mid-afternoon on a cloudy winter day, but it is still daylight.

The second thought in my head is that their torches are small. They don't have the first clue what it means to be on fire. No understanding of the scope and depth of rage.

The third thought—they are pitiful, like children at play. They should be comical, except they aren't.

"It's okay," Jennica says. Her hand is on my elbow. "They can't hurt us."

I don't understand how she reads distress in me. I am stoic. These thoughts do not play out on my face or in my words. She strokes my arm anyway.

"It's okay."

"It's not," I murmur. "These assholes." The crowd is bigger than I expected. This white supremacy thing is supposed to be fringe, a fad. But there are hundreds of them. I can't see the far edges of their gathering. It is torches from here to infinity.

A thin blue line between us and them. Think oil and water, fire and ice. Things that react, things that destroy each other in the process of failing to mix.

Back in her room, Sheila must be watching this coverage. It has been hard to tear her away from the TV ever since Shae. My mini news junkie.

If she sees me, will she be happy, or will she be scared?

MELODY

"Big protest." Sheila points to the TV the moment I appear in the doorway.

"Sure is." I walk into her room and jangle her beaded braids. She's been hooked on the news since Shae died. Baptism by fire burns hot. Sheila has never been one for news before. She likes to watch things that make her laugh, but I s'pose it's hard to think of laughing when your best friend is dead.

The mattress dips as I take a seat next to her on the end of her bed. She has a blanket over her knees and I pull it to share the warmth. Wrap my arm around her. Sheila leans against my shoulder.

"White people think they're better than us," she says.

"Not all white people," I answer, stroking her hair. It's what you're supposed to say, right? Sometimes I'm not so sure.

"I'm going," I tell her. "I'll see your brother there." My heart flutters at the thought of Brick. My memory rings with the sensation of his muscles against me. His breath on my cheek. The quick, hard rhythm as we rise together. The way his arms wrap me tight as we lay together. His sweet whispers. He is so much more than meets the eye. We both are.

I imagine him waking, wonder if his first thoughts were of me. Like mine were of him. Wonder if he will take my hand when we meet. Or kiss me in front of his friends. Wonder if instead, he will want to keep me a secret of his own. For now.

I shake my head to clear away the doubt. He likes me. More than likes me. I could see it in his eyes, hear it in his words. He could have any woman he wants, and he chose me. I was chosen.

My body flushes at the very thought. Not appropriate thoughts for work, with his baby sister under my arm. I am tempted to tell her, *we might be sisters soon.* But it was one night. It is too soon, and she is too fragile.

"Everything is always breaking," Sheila says.

It jars me, the way she can somehow read my mind. "What? No, nothing is breaking." We are fine. Even when it doesn't seem it. We are fine.

"The news," she says. "It is always breaking."

Oh. "I suppose so," I answer. "Sad and difficult things are happening all around us."

"And to us," she says. "We are breaking."

I hold her close. "We are strong," I tell her. "All the bad things in the world cannot break us."

KIMBERLY

"We need to get a response chant going." Zeke tries to hand me the megaphone.

"Me?" No, no, no. Not me.

"Sure," he says. "You're good with words."

"Uh . . ."

Zeke kisses my cheek, whispers, "And I know you've got rhythm."

A totally inappropriate giggle sneaks out of me. I smack his chest. "You're so bad. We're at a protest, for crying out loud."

He's grinning and he's just so, so cute. The megaphone is still in his hands, pushing toward me. "Take it," he says. "There's no one better."

No, no, no. Not me. I've never wanted to be the one standing at the front of the crowd. The one with the megaphone, leading the people in chants. I'm a crowd-dweller, a stagehand. Never the leader, never the star. I wouldn't know what to do with all these eyes on me. *Step up, K*, those looks say. *Start talking.*

"Maybe later," I suggest.

"Okay." Zeke raises the bullhorn to his own lips, turns to the crowd. "We will not stand for bias. We will not stand for white supremacy. We will not stand for police brutality . . ."

Zeke is the best spokesman. It's good, it's right for him to have the loudest voice. I pull back, standing shoulder to shoulder with others, a handful of UNARMED buttons at the ready.

"He's not wrong." Al's voice comes soft in my ear. It cuts right through the noise of all the people around us. Like a laser. Like a knife.

I glance over my shoulder.

"There's no one better." He smiles at me. Warmly, and yet I find myself pulling my ear wrap more firmly over my ears.

It could be Al—Senator Sloan—taking the bullhorn. But he's made remarks already. He'll make more later, I'm sure. For now he's one face, tucked deep in the crowd where the cameras can't focus on him.

"It's not what I want," I tell him.

"How do you know, unless you've done it?"

What is this about? Does he want me at the microphone? Why does he even care?

He raises his eyebrows.

"I don't have to hit myself on the thumb with a hammer to know it would hurt."

He laughs. "Well, you've got me there."

Senator Sloan's hand finds the small of my back. It feels good and comfortable, and familiar and terrible all at the same time. Why is it like this with him? Why is he doing this to me?

I turn to face him such that his hand slips away. My body hums with something between indignation and fury. I've never felt this urge before. It's strange and otherworldly. There are things I want to say, want to scream.

I grab the megaphone from Zeke. He's startled.

"Sorry." Too impulsive. Unlike me. My heart rattles inside my rib cage. I don't even know what I'm doing.

"No, it's cool. You want to try now?"

"Today for Shae!" I shout.

"Tomorrow for all!" respond the people before me.

"Today for Shae!"

"Tomorrow for all!"

EVA

"This is not what we need right now," Mommy says. She drives with her fists clenched around the steering wheel. Her shirtsleeves taper smoothly to her wrists such that everything is covered. There are bruises on my arms, from all the pinching. Maybe I need to get sleeves like hers.

She studies me in the rearview mirror. I can sense it, even though I do not meet her eyes in the sliver of glass.

"Everything we do right now reflects on Daddy," she continues. "We have to be responsible."

She doesn't understand. She gets to sit home all day and hide. If I could hide, then nothing would be a problem. I don't know how to tell her. Long sleeves are not the answer to everything.

"Do you hear me?"

I nod, staring out my window.

"Eva Denise Henderson, do you hear me? What do you have to say for yourself?"

"Nothing," I mumble. I already know. I am supposed to say nothing.

Host: *And we're back, with our guests: Jamal Howard, author of* Black Power in the Twenty-First Century, *and Brad Carter, author of* The Economics of Freedom.

Howard: *You're quick to defend the rights of white supremacists—*

Carter: *People have the right to demonstrate for their beliefs. It's a foundational principle of American democracy—*

Howard: *That's also what's happening in Underhill, and yet—*

Carter: *That's a riot. There's a difference between a peaceful demonstration and rioting.*

Howard: *Calling for the blood of black Americans is a riot.*

Carter: *It's peaceful. I don't like the ideals of white supremacy any more than you do, but—*

Howard: *You probably like them a little more than I do. (laughs)*

Carter: *You're twisting my words—*

Howard: *How can you draw a parallel between the rights of black Americans to protest for equal treatment and the rights of white supremacists to march demanding their own privilege be heightened?*

Carter: *It's a fundamental right to demonstrate for your beliefs.*

Howard: *Yet when black people demonstrate, you call it a riot.*

Carter: *It was a riot.*

Howard: *If a thousand black men marched down the street with torches, it would be called a riot.*

Carter: *It would be a riot!*

Howard: *So, you agree that the white supremacist rally was a riot?*

Carter: *They were demonstrating their beliefs.*

Howard: *And, we're back where we started.*

Carter: *In Underhill, there was looting. Vandalism. Assaults on police officers.*

Howard: *We've all seen worse in the wake of a major sports upset. "Happy" white citizens tearing up public spaces.*

Carter: *That would be a riot. But tonight's White Out march was peaceful. Don't muddy the water—*

Howard: *The media coverage skews in favor of white people expressing extreme emotion in public.*

Carter: *Emotion does not equate to violence!*

Howard: *It does when it's hate speech.*

Carter: *It's not inherently—*

Howard: *The more you defend a white supremacist's right to protest, the more complicit in those beliefs you sound.*

Carter: *Ensuring White Out's right to protest ensures all our constitutional rights.*

Howard: *White Americans should stop paying lip service to* *values of equality and diversity if they're going to also defend the values of white supremacy.*

Carter: *White supremacy is a fringe ideology—*

Howard: *You wanted to talk about the Constitution? I'm three-fifths of a person. That's not fringe ideology. It's foundational.*

Carter: *The legal reality of equality can't be erased by a small group of citizens expressing their beliefs.*

Howard: *"The legal reality of equality?" Are you kidding?*

Carter: *Plenty of people believe in things that aren't supported by the law.*

Howard: *The image of white people marching with torches by night evokes more than a belief. It evokes intent. Historically such images are associated with lynchings. The Klan and its members passing extra-legal judgment on any black people they had it in for. The image evokes hatred and represents an absence of due process. Forces that this country has been working for a century to overturn.*

Carter: *Freedom of speech still—*

Howard: *A citizen's right to freedom of speech ends at the place where that speech begins to harm others. Hate speech is not protected under the First Amendment.*

Carter: *In their view, they are seeking white power. They're not against anyone—*

Howard: *White power comes at the expense of everyone else.*

Carter: *And black power doesn't?*

Howard: *It doesn't. Black power is about achieving equality. White power is about continued dominance. This isn't hard to understand. Study your history.*

Host: *The takeaway? Keep history in mind. Free speech and protest have been part of America since the days of the Constitution. We're live with authors Jamal Howard and Brad Carter. We'll be back after this.*

TYRELL

There's a picture on TV. White men with torches, walking down the street. Real calm. No frothing at the mouth or anything, unless you count every racist breath.

"This is a mess," Robb says. "I can't even believe this is happening in America."

"The America you come from," I mutter.

Robb looks at me. Dang. I don't want to get into a whole thing. This is why I never engage. "They look like the frigging Klan," he says.

"They are."

"Out in the open like that? Can you even believe it?"

Is it better when they're not out in the open? "Well, yeah. This is the America I come from."

"I thought you grew up in the city. Are there white supremacists in your neighborhood?"

I shrug. *You mean like the cops who put us into walls, the teachers who tell us we won't amount to anything, the cabbies who won't stop for us, the bankers inside their bulletproof glass cages? You mean like the guy who shot my best friend?*

"You see that?" I point at the screen. "No one's getting arrested."

"It's a peaceful demonstration. They're allowed to speak their minds." Robb sounds . . . almost . . . excited? On the edge of his seat, like he can't wait to see what horrors happen next.

I want to talk to him about police dogs. Fire hoses. A Snickers bar and a spilled gallon of milk. But I don't know where to begin. I don't want to know what I know, let alone repeat it. Let alone *believe* it.

ROBB

There's only one America. And these assholes don't belong in it. This is not my country. It can't be.

Look at them, with their torches, talking about white power. Everybody's supposed to be equal, that's real American values. This racist shitshow is a performance by some fringe element from a cornfield in the middle of nowhere. It's not real. It's not mainstream.

These skinhead jerks get to have their say. I mean, I know that. Free country and all. But it's so messed up. Nobody has to listen to this mess. Why is anyone even paying attention?

Come on, they're literally flying the US flag and the Confederate flag at the same time. Do they not get the irony? The whole point of the Confederate flag is that some states didn't want to be part of this union. Duh.

I don't even get why the press is covering it like it's normal. Just another day in America? Hell no. This isn't America. Not even close.

DeVANTE

"Get back under your bedsheets!" Robb shouts at the television. "This is such bullshit."

I tap my highlighter against the edge of my *Classic Shakespeare Reader*. Methinks Robb's enjoying this circus a little too much. Forsooth.

"Not sure we want to encourage the bedsheet model, either," I suggest.

"This is supposedly progress, right?" Robb says. "They can't just run around lynching people like they used to."

"They don't have to," I argue. "Now they've got cops to do the dirty work."

Robb rolls his eyes. "You know what I mean."

It's not worth arguing further. "Sure."

"We should've gone down for this," he says, when the footage flips to the counterprotest. "It's not a far drive."

"To go look at a bunch of white supremacists." *No need to travel—I can do that from here.* I laugh to myself.

"What's the most racist place you ever went?" Robb asks.

Is he for real? I shake my head. "I don't even know what that means."

Robb waves his hands like he's trying to work on a rephrase. "You know, like have you ever gone someplace where people were, like, 'Oh, you have to be careful around there' and stuff?"

My brow goes up. Like the other end of a seesaw. Can't stop it. "I have to be careful everywhere."

"No, but, like . . . I don't know. A neighborhood where people fly Confederate flags and stuff. Where there's actual racists."

"There are actual racists everywhere."

"Not en masse like that." He points at the TV.

Says you. "You don't know what it's like."

"I do, man."

I could shake my head. But it feels like a waste of energy?

OFFICER YOUNG

The volume of the White Out crowd is surprising, as is their persistence. The torches cast an eerie glow across their faces as the sun goes down.

It's hard to stand here and not think about what makes people hate. What they do with the hatred. There is no one I hate enough to bring a torch to a park and chant in the dead middle of winter. I think hard about it. There's no one. Well, terrorists, I guess. The kind of man who straps a bomb to his chest and walks into a school to set it off. I hate guys like that enough to set them on fire. That's not the same as hating people for their skin color. Thinking white is always best. It should be about what you do, not who you are. I get that.

These White Out fools, they're angry. As angry as the crowds we've been patrolling in Underhill. We wear our same helmets and shields. We stand in our rows and our clumps, watching each other's backs. The vibe among us is alert, as it should be. We're on point. We pay attention, but the difference is palpable.

This crowd, they're angry. The difference is the certainty that they're not angry at *us*.

JENNICA

Kimberly rises a head above the fray, shouting into the bullhorn. She is fierce, she is huge, she is amazing. The whole crowd responds to her words. She holds them in sway, within her raised fist. I can't tear my eyes away. The blood in my heart tugs forward and back in a raging tide. I am so proud of my friend, and yet I can already see it. The same strong tide will carry her away from me.

Brick removes his arm from my shoulder. "I have to try to take this call," he says. "I'll be back." I shiver. He slips away without waiting for my answer. What would I even say that didn't sound stupid?

I'm safe enough, amid a sea of Kings, with Noodle nowhere in sight. But I still feel the chill in the air as Brick moves away. One thin blanket of comfort removed, I'm that much closer to the cold. That much closer to standing alone.

"Hey, Jennica."

"Hi, Melody."

"Are you okay? I was worried about you last night."

Her face forms within my slivers of memory. Right. "I'm fine."

"Brick was here a minute ago, wasn't he?" She strains her neck around, trying to catch sight of him.

"He'll be back. He had to take a call."

"Oh. Okay." She seems relieved, like she's been hunting for him for ages. She also seems kinda worked up about something.

"How are you?" I ask. "Is everything cool?"

From across the barricade comes the sound of smashing glass. We flinch. A man's voice shouts, "Oooh oooh ooh! Go back to Africa, you motherfucking apes!"

A great jostling of the crowd tumbles us like an ocean wave. Melody and I press closer to each other. "Uh, I mean, is everything cool . . . apart from the white supremacy . . . ?"

We laugh. It's not funny, but you gotta get through it somehow, I guess?

"Yeah," she says. "I think things are cool." Pause. "You're good friends with Brick, right?"

We're good . . . somethings, yeah. "Sure," I say out loud. "We go back a while."

"So, I mean. He's a good guy, right?"

The million dollar question. "He's complicated." That seems like a safe answer.

She nods. "Underneath all the Kings stuff? That's just one layer. There's more to him."

"Untold depths," I can say honestly.

Melody smiles. "Yeah. I mean . . . yeah. He's really sweet with Sheila."

"Sheila?" A switch in my heart flips. Anxious.

"His sister."

Right. I forgot he has a sister. She's just a kid, I know that much. He keeps her far from the world of the Kings, with good reason.

"That version of him feels real to me. The Kings stuff, it's weird, right? Like putting on a suit to go to work?"

Where is she going with this? "The Kings are as real as it gets." Can't be getting confused about that.

"He dates a lot of women, though?"

"He sleeps with a lot of women," I say. Dating, I don't know where you draw the line on that.

"He's not just interested in sex," Melody says. "We talk about things. He cares about real stuff." She cranes her neck. "I mean, he's here, right?"

"I'm sure he's still here, yeah." He wouldn't leave without me . . . would he? And just like that, I'm craning my neck, too.

"I mean, we've hung out a bit lately, and he never acted like it was all about going to bed. Last night was the first time."

Last night? My head spins. So does my stomach. I'm already hang-over dizzy, and now the whole world feels off balance.

It's not hard to put the pieces together. Brick says no to me, after all this time, because there's someone else. Of course there is. Why would I think he was ever into me?

I shake my head to clear it of all the wrong thoughts. "Um."

"You okay?"

"I have to get out of here," I murmur.

"What?" Melody leans closer to me. She can't hear me over the chant-ing, which has intensified.

Today for Shae! shouts Kimberly's voice, amplified.

Tomorrow for all! answers the crowd.

Today for Shae! I can no longer see her, but Kimberly is around me, above me, within me. She is a bright, shining, glorious star and the whole world answers her call.

Tomorrow for all!

I push my voice hard, right toward Melody's ear. "I have to go."

Today for Shae!

I can't breathe. I can't think.

"Are you okay?" Melody asks. Her arm goes around my shoulder. I shrug free.

Today for Shae! Kimberly's voice is everywhere. I can't follow it to the source, and even if I did, she'd be too busy to talk.

Tomorrow for all!

"When you find Brick, just tell him . . . Tell him I had to get to work." I stumble away, pushing people aside to get toward a bus stop. I rode over here with Brick. He was supposed to bring me home, but I can't face him.

Today for Shae!

Tomorrow for all!

I can't face Kimberly, either. The world spins as I rush to get more distance. When I reach the sidewalk, the first thing I see is a sewer grate along the gutter. It's like my body was waiting, holding itself in check.

Vomit rushes up my throat and out in a coughing rush. It's gross and achy, and somewhere behind me a kid goes, "Ewww, Mom, look!"

My knees hit the curb. My whole body is shaking.

"You okay, baby?" says a woman, probably the kid's mother.

I hold up my hands, as if to make a wall. A good wall. It will be a fortress, with possibly a moat. Your concern will not get through, stranger-lady. Force field: engage.

"I'm fine." I cough, wiping my mouth. Never better.

BRICK

The torches burn brighter as the sun goes down, and there is nothing subtle about it. Their chanting continues. For a fleeting moment, I imagine crossing the barricade. Gun in hand. Strolling straight into the white-hot center and popping them one by one. As many as I can get to before I'm taken out.

Maybe the thought is not so fleeting.

My boys are packing. I'm not. The cops are gunning for me already. I'm not about to get picked up on a weapons charge. They'd find a way to spin it hard. I know they would.

So I'm not carrying. A rational decision I don't completely understand. Because . . . this rage. I'm on fire.

Maybe I'm a coward at heart.

It does nothing but stoke my rage, knowing that.

I'm not about to set myself up for prison. That's rational. But the core of me defies logic. Wants to. A blaze burns around me, consuming me. I can barely see myself within it.

"We have to pack it up," Zeke says. "Our permit ends soon."

"Fuck that," I answer. "We're not leaving till they do."

"There are more of them than there are of us," he says. "Who do you think is gonna get arrested first?"

"So we get arrested." I smack my fist into my palm.

Wait, what? No. No. NO. But I can't stop myself from fronting.

I'm right in Zeke's face. "These motherfuckers need to know who we are."

WILL/eMZee

I can't, with the hypocrisy. I take it to the wall:

> WHITE PEOPLE: WE MATTER MOST!
> WE DESERVE PREFERENTIAL TREATMENT!
>
> COPS: YOU HAVE THE RIGHT TO
> EXPRESS YOUR OPINION. HERE'S A PERMIT.
>
> BLACK PEOPLE: WE WANT EQUALITY!
> WE DESERVE JUSTICE!
>
> COPS: YOU'RE OUT OF CONTROL.
> HERE'S A BULLET.

MELODY

"We do not back down!" Brick is shouting. "We're just supposed to walk away? While they're still out there? Hell no!"

Zeke pulls himself up big. He's tall, like Brick, but thinner. "Peaceful protest. We abide by the law."

"Fuck that! We need some civil disobedience up in here."

"Not now, not here." Zeke's one calm-ass brother. Between their shoulders, uniform fabric, coming closer. I crane to look.

"It ain't right!" Brick's raised voice draws the attention of the cops at the perimeter. Clusterfuck. They staring us up.

"Pigs at ten o'clock," I say. "Simmer."

"Listen," Zeke says. "If we get rowdy, they'll start arresting us. That'll be the news tonight."

"That's the news every night, goddammit," Brick thunders.

"Exactly," Zeke explains. "Tonight, we want it to be different. We walk away, in keeping with our permit." He points toward White Out. "They won't. We need to see what happens. We have footage of tanks rolling up to peaceful protests in Underhill. If the same thing doesn't happen here tonight, it's evidence of discriminatory police tactics."

"I feel you," Brick murmurs. But it's still fire.

I can't lay claim to Brick, not even. It's not like I'm his girlfriend. I mean, I don't rightly know if I am. I do know he doesn't want this fight. Not on the inside.

My hand on his sleeve, and he flinches. His body's all tight and poised. Tense, like a finger on a trigger.

"I need a ride home," I tell him. "You ain't gonna ditch me here, are you?"

Brick lets me pull him away. Can't keep my eye on the uniforms while we move, but they're out there. Clinging to our trail like a shadow.

KIMBERLY

It's only a twenty-minute ride, from the park back to the community center. It won't be the end of the world. Only staff can drive the van, or I'd send Zeke with Al instead of me. He can't get enough of the senator.

It's growing dark, and the demonstration permits end at sundown. Today we follow the letter of the law, to make a point. The police say when we are gone, they will move in and clear the White Out protesters, too. Time will tell.

There's not much to pack. We've given out all of the UNARMED buttons and most of the flyers. A few Underhill volunteers collect what remains of the poster board signs, while others walk around urging the crowd to disperse. They hand out "What to do if you get arrested" cards. It's unlikely that everyone will actually choose to leave.

It's hard to leave, to shut off our railing against the ongoing chant. *White might! White rights!* The torches seem to hiss against the gathering dusk.

I securely tuck the flyer box flaps under each other. It feels like giving up.

"Ready?" Al says. Senator Sloan. I keep slipping. "Our ride is here." What he means is, *Let's step into the car, where we'll be alone.*

I already feel a way I don't want to feel. There's something masochistic about making yourself gaze directly at open hatred for hours on end. It's like staring into the sun. You take damage. Even if the white spots fade and you can eventually see again, your eyes will never be the same.

The police hover and nudge people along. They can see that we're leaving. It's amicable. Remarkably so, considering how this moment tends to go back in Underhill. I snap a picture of a cop standing with his arms wide, smiling as he directs people across the street. I will tweet about it, when I can find the right words. #ObediencePays, maybe. Except plenty of people would fail to see the intended irony.

Al's—the senator's town car pulls up to the edge of the thinning crowd. He ducks inside immediately. The gathered photographers snap images of him until he disappears behind the tinted glass.

The police move barricades, to clear a lane for him. But the town car waits. For me.

Zeke squeezes my arm. "See you back there." I wish he would lean in and kiss me goodbye, right in view of the senator, but he probably won't. And I won't. We're working.

I cross to the door behind the driver's seat. Breathing deeply. Twenty minutes, and I'm home. And maybe I'll never have to see the senator again.

Wow. It feels good to sit down. I lean my head against the seat. Close my eyes. Breathe. For a moment I dare to hope we'll pass the ride in silence.

"How did you think it went?" Al—Senator Sloan—asks. What he means is, *Tell me nice things about what I've done for you today.*

"We had a nice turnout." I open my eyes. "We were peaceful. We were loud."

There's a silence. I've failed to answer the implied question.

"Your speech was good," I add. "Two clips have already gone viral. I'm sure it will continue to get great coverage across platforms."

"Anything for the cause," he says. What he means is, *I will do whatever it takes to get re-elected.* He pulls his phone out of his jacket pocket, presumably to confirm that my information is correct. He should just believe me. I've been tracking it all day.

We glide by rows of upscale housing. Uniformed doormen. Lycra-clad, down-vested joggers. SUV strollers, and everyone with a name-brand coffee cup in their hand. Sparkling sidewalks—literally, do they put glitter in them, or something? Stately brick, modern metal, walls and walls of windows. Who are the people behind all that shiny glass? Did they watch us on TV today, or will they tonight? Are they walking on treadmills and reading iPads and watching sitcoms while our world burns? Were they out in Griffith Park with torches? Did they want to be?

"It's been nice to see you, Kimberly. You look well," Al says. What he means is, *You look pretty, or sexy, or something in that vein.*

"I'm good."

"I'm glad to see you're still involved in the work." What he means is, *I was right to pluck you from obscurity so you could carry my briefcase.*

"It's become important to me."

"You're a natural." What he means is, *I made you from scratch.*

"I don't know about that." Out the window, the buildings grow shorter, closer together and more worn down. We're almost home.

"Nonsense, Kimberly. You're a leader."

The town car is generously sized, but so are we. It doesn't take much for his hand to move closer to mine. Too close. His fingers walk and talk at the same time. Maybe I imagine them stroking slow circles over the back of my hand, where it rests on the seat between us. I'm still watching the city go by.

"I still think about that week," he says. What he means is, *I wouldn't mind getting in your pants this time, if you'll let me.*

"I don't," I lie. "So much has happened since then." I cross my arms over my stomach, even though it presses my boobs together, and I'm sure that is where his eye goes.

"You're an amazing woman," he says. What he means is, *Who do you think you are? No one says no to Alabaster Sloan.*

"I'm doing my best," I answer.

"I'm proud of you." There's something about his voice that I never noticed before. Every word is full of so many things all at once. Layers and layers of meaning. Maybe it's why people find him so pleasant to listen to. Why he moves them. It sounds like he is speaking with the voice of millions, and what I hear them all saying is, *You are small.*

ZEKE

I'm kinda wishing I'd taken time to clean up the SCORE office. It looks like a cyclone hit it. An anti-white-supremacist cyclone. *This is what organizing looks like,* I remind myself. *We worked hard today.*

Senator Sloan loosens his tie and settles back in the armchair in the corner. He takes a long swig from his can of Diet Coke. I slouch in the chair behind my desk. We're silent for a while. It's comfortable. Just two guys, hanging out. My brain can't quite wrap itself around the fact of who he is anymore. Every once in a while my mind kicks me, like, *Dude, you're chilling with Alabaster Sloan!!!* And then it goes back to feeling normal.

Senator Sloan glances around the room. I fight the urge to bustle around and straighten things up. It's only a tiny mental fight. I'm too exhausted.

"Your work with SCORE is volunteer?" Sloan says.

"Yes, sir. We have a couple of grants but nothing that would cover an actual staff position."

"Who writes your grants?"

"I do." I grin. "Most of the behind-the-scenes work is me."

"Impressive," the senator says. "I know how much work goes into something like this."

That's not fair. Don't be that guy, I chide myself. There's a temptation, for sure, to puff myself up in front of Senator Sloan. I add, "At least, it was all me in the beginning. Kimberly has really stepped up in the last few months. I wouldn't be able to do nearly as much without her."

"And when you graduate? Nonprofit sector, politics? What do you envision?"

When anyone else asks me this, it feels like a can of worms. Like there is something squirming inside me yearning to get out, and I can never put words to it. The question itself feels like a game I can't win. But when Sloan asks, it's not hard to answer honestly.

"I don't know. I want to do a bunch of things. To make a difference. Is that corny?"

"What's the point of anything, if not to make a difference?" he answers.

"Yeah." I muse on that. "I'm not sure everyone sees it that way."

"Then they're wrong," he says, in that definitive, resonant preacher voice. His certainty fills the small space.

I riffle the corners of a stack of paper on my desk. "I'm supposed to want something concrete. Something simple. To be a lawyer. An accountant. A teacher."

"Do you want to teach?"

"Not per se." I pause. "But leadership is teaching, isn't it? From a slant, maybe."

Senator Sloan swigs the Diet Coke. Studies me. "You have a vision," he says. "You just don't know how to realize it yet."

"I do realize," I say quietly. It's strange, that it feels like a secret, something to place in a vault, or to be ashamed of.

"Mmm." He shakes his head. "I mean realize, in the sense that you don't know how to bring it into fruition yet. How to make it real."

"Oh. Yeah. For sure." I shrug, smile as brightly as I can in the face of the uncertainty that is my future. "All things in time, or something like that?"

"Mmm. They do say that, don't they."

He is wise, beyond what I even knew. Even in his quiet moments, he exudes something loud. His very presence speaks. He knows how to realize his vision. I wonder what it feels like, to know who you are, and to stand in it.

"I have an opening in my congressional office staff," he says. "Legislative Aide."

"Legislative Aide?" I echo. My ears ring with it. Legislative Aide Aide Aide Aide. . . . Is this really happening?

"That's the title," Senator Sloan says. "In terms of role, you'd function as a community liaison, between my office and my constituents, particularly around organizing."

I don't entirely know what that means, but it sounds amazing.

"Wow. Senator. Thank you, I—" I have no words. Thunderstruck doesn't begin to cover it. But— "I don't graduate until end of May."

"You'd start in August. Plenty of time to transition leadership for SCORE and get settled in Washington."

Right. SCORE. This thing I've given my time and life to for the past two and a half years. Right. Washington, DC. The congressional offices.

"Um . . ."

Sloan chuckles. "You don't have to decide now. Let me know next week."

Right. I don't have to decide now. "Sure, of course. Thank you for the opportunity. I'll let you know by then."

My ears are still ringing. Is there a decision to be made?

Senator Sloan sips his Diet Coke. As we settle into silence again, the SCORE office grows more cluttered and cramped by the second. I imagine myself in a classy suit. Strolling through the US Capitol. Casual, like I belong.

EVA

It's hard to sleep. My knuckles ache. It hurts a whole lot to punch someone.

But maybe it hurts more not to punch them.

Daddy cries through the night. I put my hand on the wall and listen. There is nothing I can do.

In the morning, when I say, "I'm sorry you're sad," he pretends he doesn't know what I'm talking about.

"It's complicated," Mommy says.

@KelvinX_: Have you seen these mofos with the torches? #HelloLynchburg

> **@WhitePowerCord:** You can hate on us all you want. But you can't touch us. We have a right to be here.

> **@KelvinX_:** *scratches head* Huh. That sentiment sounds awfully familiar . . .

> **@WhitePowerCord:** We are taking this country BACK.

> **@KelvinX_:** We are taking this country BLACK.

@BrownMamaBear: #TodayForShae barely scratches the surface. When are black people gonna get serious about taking care of our communities?

@TroubleInRiverCty: Keep on coming, Underhill PD. You can't arrest and kill all of us. The whole world is watching.

@WesSteeleStudio: The press refuses to mention Henderson's impeccable service record. Why? Could it be BIAS AGAINST WHITE AMERICANS? Racism is alive and well in Underhill. #SteeleStudioExclusive

@Viana_Brown: Told a white friend about Shae Tatum. She said "That doesn't happen." #DifferentWorlds

PEACH STREET

There is something worse than spilled blood. The poison in their voices ricochets for days. People travel the sidewalks wary, wondering what is in each other's minds.

Two black men pass a white man in front of the hardware store. Their eyes ask, *Was it you, with the torches?*

His eyes say, *You'll never really know.*

WITNESS

It is not enough to watch the coverage. Pacing the living room carpet, you are stuck in the middle. Too close and yet too far.

What you've seen surges to the forefront, again and again.

The past is not past. The future is cast in shadow. The present—this moment, now—bears its own kind of peril.

You wade through the helplessness of all you know and all you cannot say.

STEVE CONNERS

"Will's out again," my wife says. She stands at the kitchen window of our condo, looking down at the street. From my spot at the kitchen table, my view is the twists in her hair, the curves of her back, the hasty bow on her apron. Chicken sizzles on the stovetop. The rice lid pops and clatters as it simmers in the background. Greens in a bowl wait to get tossed in the chicken grease.

"He's supposed to be home for dinner," I remind her. "We've talked about this."

"He won't be," she says. "He's out there. I can feel it."

Sigh. Far be it from me to question mother's intuition. "He's angry. You—I mean, I can't blame him for that."

"I don't—I can't rest—" She clutches at her chest and fumbles over the words. I get up, to go to her.

My cell vibrates, gliding across the kitchen tabletop. The screen glows, JOHN LANSBURY. Impeccable timing, as ever.

"Hi, John?"

My wife turns back to the window. I go over and put my hand on her shoulder, but she shrugs away from me, returning to tend the chicken.

"You watching the news?" John asks.

"Not yet. We're making dinner." My wife shoots me a glance. Okay, "we" is a stretch. I chopped the greens. And since then I've been sitting here. I shrug an apology at her. She sticks her tongue out.

"They're pushing toward a verdict," John says. "Tomorrow or the next day."

"The grand jury?"

My wife stops stirring and turns. I look away, because I have to.

"Yes," he says. "We'll need to be ready when they come back. Whichever way it goes."

"We will be." And now it's me at the window, staring down into the dusk. The chicken smell, rich and amazing, wafts up stronger behind me. She's taking it off the pan, putting in the greens. Dinner soon, and Will's not home.

John is on a roll. "We need talking points, press releases, and a revised media plan for the commissioner and the union reps. Henderson should continue in silence, don't you think?"

"Of course. It helps nothing to hear from him." This conversation is pointless. All of this could wait until tomorrow. I've already worked up the talking points. I don't know why he even called.

"Right, right. Anyway . . ." John rambles loosely about our agenda. My wife absently stirs the greens. She glances over her shoulder at me. Our eyes meet and it's everything at once. Why we hate my job right now, what we fear for our son. She stretches her free hand toward me and I take it. A lifeline.

The front door lock clicks and the door opens. Relief floods me. I squeeze my wife's hand gently. He's home. We're okay. Another day behind us, clean and safe, with all three of us home together for dinner. Nothing we take for granted anymore.

"Will, baby?" my wife calls to him. "Wash up for dinner."

There's no answer but the shuffle of sneakers in the hallway, the slamming of a bedroom door. My wife's face crumples. Her relief drains away, replaced by annoyance.

Will's such a good kid. Loving and cheerful, artistic and brave. But lately there's no reaching him. He's pulled so far away from us.

John's still talking. "Steve? What do you think?"

"Um—many thoughts. Let me reflect on things and give you a report in the late morning tomorrow."

"Which way do you think it will break?" John's voice goes

energetic. I have nothing left for him. Nothing left for any of it tonight.

I press my palm more firmly against my wife's. She looks at me. Everything at once.

"The way it always breaks," I answer.

Our job only gets harder from here.

EVA

Tomorrow or the next day, we find out if Daddy has to go to court.

Today, we have new clothes, new toys, and the promise of a family vacation. "You're still on leave," Mommy says. "We could get away for a while."

"I can't leave the state," Daddy says. "It will look like I'm running."

"There's plenty to do nearby."

"You're pushing it," Daddy says. "Give it a rest."

"Can we move? I'm never, ever going back to school." I sit with my arms crossed. I'm suspended for a week for fighting. It won't be long enough.

"Well, aren't you two in a mood." Mommy huffs over to the computer. For a while there is no sound except a lot of clicking.

"Look," Mommy says. We look. She shows us some websites. Museums. Restaurants. "And this is where we could stay."

A tall, shiny hotel with room service, movies on the TV, and a nice swimming pool.

"Jesus Christ," Daddy says. "It's how much per night?"

Mommy turns away from the computer. "I will not let you punish yourself for the rest of your life. Not for one tragic accident." The words drop like anvils. Tragic. Accident. I picture them falling off a cliff, like in a Road Runner cartoon. Mommy is like the coyote, trying to kill the bad feelings that are running all over the house.

Mommy spins back to the computer. "I'm booking it."

"No." Daddy drops onto the couch, head in his hands. "How am I supposed to just . . ." His voice zips off, leaving a cloud of dust. The Road Runner is alive and well.

More clicking.

Mommy doesn't stop me when I slide into her lap. She types in our address and credit card numbers. All the while, the images of the hotel blink by, all shiny and clean. I learn a new word.

"What is 'amenities'?"

"What *are* amenities," Mommy corrects. "It means good things."

We will have amenities. The worst thing that ever happened to us has turned into something not so bad. Every cloud has a silver lining, Mommy always says.

ZEKE

Even the old, boring day-to-day work feels different with Kimberly around now. I've never felt this way about anyone. I just want to make out with her all day, I feel like, even though making out is kind of exhausting after a while. We wouldn't even have to make out the whole time. Just spend the day lounging in the same space, so that we could be touching. But who has time to lounge?

"You okay?" Kimberly smiles at me. It's been quiet between us for a while, which is unusual.

"Sure, yeah." Nothing to do but smile back. What will she think when I tell her about Senator Sloan's offer? Washington, DC, feels distant and exciting. My whole self comes alive in a different way, thinking about it. But it also means the end of this thing that I've built. Saying goodbye to SCORE.

SCORE would be fine in Kimberly's capable hands, of course. It's not totally about the work, it's . . . something different. If Kimberly's here, and I'm there . . .

I don't want to think about it. My hands cap and uncap the colorful markers before me.

The grand jury has been hearing the Darren Henderson/Shae Tatum case. Their pronouncement is due any day now. Maybe tomorrow, but probably the day after. That's what they've told us, anyway. When it comes, we'll be there. Kimberly and me, and a whole lot of others.

Look at her now, punching out UNARMED buttons on the button maker. She makes mundane things seem incredibly sexy. How does she do that? I peek at her out the corner of my eye, occasionally bumping her knee with mine.

I'm hand-lettering yet another poster with her catchphrase on it. "'Today for Shae, Tomorrow for All' was a stroke of genius," I tell her.

She grins. "So you've said."

For the thousandth time, probably. "What can I say? I'm a fanboy for your brain."

Kimberly tosses a finished button in the box, flexes her wrist, then reaches for a poster board. "What other signs do you want?"

"No Justice, No Peace."

"I don't know if we should use that," she says.

"No justice, no peace?" But it's so simple, so powerful. Easy to chant.

"Yeah. We're supposed to be advocating nonviolence."

"That's not what it means."

Kimberly frowns. "No justice, no peace. As in, if we don't get justice, we won't be peaceful?"

I shake my head, lean into it. This is exactly the kind of discussion I love. "No, no. It's a much more complicated idea of peace. It's drawn from a quote from the Reverend Dr. King."

"Really?" I swear to God, she leans in and bats her eyes at me. I totally thought that was some made-up thing from fiction. But it's super hot.

"Yeah. He has this quote about the relationship between justice and peace, that you can't have one without the other. It's—" I pause. "Well, you know?" I don't want to be the guy who always explains things. I know I get overly detailed about stuff like this. Other people get bored with it.

"I don't know that quote," she says. "I guess Dr. King said a lot of important things, huh?"

I smile. "The thing is, they do go hand in hand. Justice and peace. In reality, if we don't have justice, we already don't have peace."

Kimberly frowns, mulling over it. "How so?"

"Well, think about what the justice system is supposed to do. It's supposed to uphold the moral ideals of our society, right?"

"Thou shalt not kill, and such."

"Right, so when you break the social code, there are consequences."

She nods. "I mean, I get that. We send people to jail for murder."

"So, to look deeper, what happens when the system is built to uphold a moral code that is skewed from actual fairness? Or, when people have different ideas about what is fair?"

"Isn't that why we have courts in the first place, to keep everyone honest?"

"Sure, but it requires integrity of the system." I tap my fingers against my lips. Is this making sense to her? Does she think I'm a giant nerd?

"And the system is broken."

"But also, in a sense, if there is no justice for us, what is our obligation to create peace?" I'm super excited now. No one ever wants to get this far into this. I love her.

Um.

Swallow that thought.

Try again. "What I mean is, black people basically live outside the law already, because the law doesn't serve us fairly."

"And so . . . ?" She's clicking through the pieces of the puzzle in her mind. I can tell.

"So, it's possible that the only way to achieve actual justice, the only way to change the system that is acting against us, is to act outside the law."

"But that would be illegal." She blushes. "I know that sounds super obvious. I don't understand."

"It's hard stuff. Think back to the 1960s. Organizers used civil disobedience to great effect."

"All the sit-ins and marches."

"Yeah, technically they were breaking the law. Black people would go sit in at Whites-Only lunch counters, knowing that they'd be arrested."

"And the laws eventually changed."

I nod. "In part because black people proved to lawmakers that the laws were unjust."

Kimberly shakes her head. "Well, but more so because we disrupted the economic structures of those businesses. They couldn't sell lunches to white people while black people—who they refused to serve—were occupying the counters. They couldn't make money."

I'm totally impressed. Hardly anybody knows that. Is it weird that it makes me want to jump her bones? Yup, totally weird. I'm hopeless.

Kimberly goes on. "Not only was it bad PR, it was damaging the actual business. So, really, we never had a moral awakening on race. There was no great change of heart in America after the 1960s."

Ding-ding! Jackpot! "And that's why we're still stuck making signs and marching. In the twenty-first century." I hold up the NO JUSTICE, NO PEACE poster board. "Sucks, doesn't it?"

Kimberly's quiet for a minute. She traces her finger along the bottom of the words. "Does everybody know that's not what it means?" she asks softly. "Was it just me?"

Crud. I've accidentally made her feel stupid. I rush to correct it. "Oh, gosh, no. Most people don't fully get it. It's a really good question. And you really know your history. I'm so impressed. You're really smart." And now I'm a babbling idiot. Perfect.

"It's just . . ." She hesitates. "I still don't understand why we should use it. Isn't the point of slogans to be really clear?"

"It's clear enough."

"But it's not," she argues. "We just had a whole conversation about how it isn't."

And you know what, she's right.

DeVANTE

Robb's left their door open. I know from history that Tyrell hates when he does that. I knock at the jamb. Tyrell pulls out his earbuds and turns around.

"Hey, man," he says.

"Hey."

Tyrell is not enamored by throw pillows. He's the only guy in our suite, one of the only guys on the whole floor, who's never been by to see Doc DeVante and lie on my "couch." Maybe he's shy. Maybe he doesn't have any problems. He doesn't seem to have any friends, either.

A shot of guilt pierces me. Maybe I should be making more of an effort.

"So I'm going with Robb down to the Black House. You wanna come?"

Tyrell shakes his head. "I need to focus on my studies."

"We're talking about protest responses after the White Out march."

"Not interested, thanks."

He barely has the time of day for me. I don't get it.

"Doesn't it upset you?"

He looks at me, full on, for one long second. "What?"

Is he kidding? My fingers spring out wide. "White supremacists marching in the streets of an American city."

"Oh." Back to his math books. "Yeah."

Forget it.

This punk comes from some entitled place. He doesn't know what it's like to live the streets. Bro lives his life according to some spreadsheet. I want to shake him. Get out in the world. Know what we're up against.

How do I make him understand?

ROBB

"SCORE is planning a demonstration at the courthouse, during the grand jury deliberations." I scroll through my phone as DeVante and I walk along the campus path toward the black student union. "We should go to that."

"All the way in Underhill?"

"It's only about six hours." I grin. "Sometimes five, the way I drive."

A fleet of bikers zooms toward us. "Not sure," DeVante says.

"Come on. We have to be there." At least, I do. I have all this privilege, everyone is always saying. Because I'm white and male and my parents have money. So I want to use my power for good.

It's just, I'd rather not go alone. Plus, what's the point of protesting to support your black friends if your black friends don't even show up?

"I don't know." DeVante sounds less excited than I expected.

"Come on. What's the point of campus organizing? We live in a bubble."

DeVante cuts me side-eye. There's something he's not saying, like usual. Apparently there are things I don't get because I'm not black. Whatever. I've studied the issues. I do get it. Black people are oppressed and racism is alive and well in the twenty-first century, which sucks. But personally I think everybody's equal and I don't judge people on race. What else am I supposed to do?

"It's a weekday," he says. "That means missing class."

"One day of class, maybe. Who wants to be cooped up in a classroom talking theory when we could make a difference in the actual world? No-brainer."

DeVante moves behind me to let the bikers pass. We are subsumed by their wind. "Let's wait until we get to the Black House," he says. "We'll have to talk together about what is the best plan."

Blah. All they ever do is talk. Someone has to step up and take some action. It might as well be me. I know what's right.

DeVante comes side by side with me again. He grips his backpack straps in his fists and stares at the pavement ahead of us. In this moment, he looks like Tyrell to me—calculating the logistics. But it's not that complicated. I can do my part to help.

"I don't care," I tell him. "I'm going. I have a car. You can come if you want."

BRICK

I've gotta get smarter about things. Sun streaks in through a gap in the blackout curtains. Melody cozies up against me, still half asleep.

I'm slipping.

This bed has a "no overnights" policy. Or, it used to. Can't get comfortable with this kind of arrangement. I like sleeping alone.

But I liked waking up next to Jennica more. That night, the morning after, those memories are planted in my mind like a flag. Every thought is a breeze, stirring it. I can't be awake, can't move, can't think without stirring it up.

I don't mind waking up next to Melody, either. Any warm body is better than none, it turns out. But I can't go making promises to women I can't keep. I'm not into leading people on. My usual dates know how I roll. We screw, we snuggle, then we go our separate ways. No hang-ups. I sleep careful. I sleep smart. No drama.

"Morning," Melody mumbles. "You good?"

Till now.

"I'm good. You?"

I reach for my phone on the nightstand. Two missed texts from Jennica.

He's stopped coming around. At all.

You didn't do anything, right?

She might as well have walked in and poured some gas on the embers of my fire. I just got myself down to a simmer, and now this. Damn it.

I toss off the covers, startling Melody. Storm into the bathroom to deal with my situation alone.

What do I have to do? Jennica says she wants away from him, but it's like some weird obsession. He fucks with her, and she's pissed one minute and the next it's like *Come fuck with me some more.* It's messed up.

Melody's sitting up in the bed when I return. Her shirt is off and the covers are pulled up right underneath her excellent rack.

Damn it. I have no resolve. She's right there, and willing, and it feels good. I got nothing to apologize for.

Afterward, she says, "I have to get to work. Can we meet for lunch, maybe?" She strokes my cheek. "I want to see you."

"I've got some things to do today," I tell her. "You wanna come by tonight instead?"

"Dinner again?" she asks.

Right. Last night I took her out for dinner. Two nights in a row? I'm really slipping.

"Come over to my place. I can make you my paella."

"Why don't we do it here?" I suggest. "Leave me a list and I'll send someone out for the groceries. I got pots and pans I never use. Gotta break them in sometime."

And I've got a party to throw after that. Gotta get back to business as usual.

"Sure," she says. When she kisses me, it is good and easy. Comforting. Not even confusing, in the moment. Not confusing until after.

●●●

The diner's not crowded. I'm not sure I'm glad. Jennica's face perks up when she sees me. "Hey."

"Hey." I lean across the counter and she pushes her cheek forward. I kiss it. She smells good, and I don't know how, after swimming in this grease pit all day.

"It's been a few days," she says. "You okay?"

I settle into my usual stool. "I been busy, that's all." Has it been a few days? Really? I didn't mean for that to happen. Time is slipping away.

"How about you? You doing okay?"

She smiles. "Same old, same old. You wanna eat?" She hands me the menu, as if I don't know everything already.

"Patty melt. Gimme some of that broccoli on the side."

"It's good today." She scrawls my order onto the pad.

Her smile is a world unto itself. Jennica is gorgeous through and through. That night we kissed, everything came alive. But she was in a bad place. She didn't really mean it. In the light of day, in the warmth of the diner, it's a kiss on the cheek, a touch of the hand. The rest is in my head. A fantasy, that we could ever be more than that.

I don't even know how much she remembers. I don't know how to talk about it with her. I don't know how to ask what any of it meant: *Were you lashing out in pain, or were you loose enough to reveal what you really wanted?*

We're friends. We may never be more.

If I keep coming here, I'll keep hoping. If I stop, I'm leaving her in the lurch.

KIMBERLY

"So . . . pizza night is not a thing anymore?" Jennica says. She's sitting on the couch.

Crud. I forgot again. I'm being a terrible friend and there's no excuse for it. I plop my purse onto the counter.

"We got really busy at the office this evening." That's a stretch, but what am I supposed to say? It'll hurt her feelings if I say I forgot. Again.

"You weren't at the salon?"

"I was, but my last appointment canceled. I went by the office after my shift." I slip out of my shoes and poke around the kitchen. Maybe I can whip up something that will feel kinda special. But nope. We've got nothing great in the fridge. Pantry, either.

"We can order in," I suggest. "We haven't done that in a while." The take-out menu drawer is nice and full. "My treat," I promise.

"Okay," she says. There's a pause while I riffle through the menus. "If you really want to," Jennica adds. "I mean, if you don't have anything better to do."

Oh, double crap. "I love hanging out with you. You know that."

Jennica's looking out the window, which is as close to turning her back on me as possible while sitting. "You never have time lately. But it's not a big deal."

"I'm sorry, okay?" I bring four choices over to her. All her favorites, including the pizza. "Really. It's just you and me tonight, okay?" Zeke was going to come over later, but I'll text him and tell him I'll see him tomorrow.

Jennica smiles. But there's something behind it that shatters my heart.

"Hey." I pile myself onto the couch beside her. She leans into me instantly. No hesitation. The shards of my heart pulse. "I know I haven't really been around much."

"You have a boyfriend now," she says. "I get it. I know what they're like. They want all your time and attention."

"No," I say. "It's not like that." Zeke's not asking me for everything. Not in the destructive, controlling way Jennica's used to. The thing is, I love him. I want to give everything. It's different. But I don't know how to explain. "This thing we're doing, with SCORE . . . it's bigger than us. It's only for a little longer. The grand jury will come back within a couple of days. Everything will settle back to normal."

It feels true, until I say it out loud.

Jennica lies very still in my arms. She doesn't say it, but I can feel her thinking it. I'm thinking it, too.

We won't settle. Nothing is normal. This thing with Zeke isn't fly-by-night. Neither is my involvement with SCORE.

We won't settle. The whole world is changing. No going back. There is no normal anymore.

WILL/eMZee

It's easier than it should be to sneak out of the apartment. My parents watch TV kinda loud, and if I just leave my door shut, they don't bother me. A closed door means I want to be left alone.

I tiptoe through the foyer and then wait with my hand on the knob. It's never long before a loud commercial comes on, and it covers the sound of the snapping lock.

I slip out, let the knob click back into place under cover of the same commercial. Scoot toward the elevator. Like clockwork.

Almost.

This time, the door clicks open behind me. "Hey."

Uh-oh.

Steve's in the hall with me. Busted. "Where are you going?" he says.

"What? No biggie. I'll be right back," I lie.

Steve pats his pockets, checking for his keys. He lets the apartment door close behind him. "Let me see your bag." He holds out his hand.

"It's only my books," I tell him. "I'm just used to carrying it."

Steve crosses his arms. "Would you rather talk to your mother about this?"

Hell freaking no. I swing my backpack off my shoulder and toss it at his feet. He unzips it.

My life is over. Being caught was always a possibility. I've known that. Caught by my parents, by a teacher, by the cops. I always thought I'd be mad when it happened. Defiant. It's different. It's worse.

Steve pulls out two of my paint cans, the gray and the white. When I see them in his hands, I feel like I'm crumpling, fading. Like I'm being dropped into a deep, deep hole from which I may never escape. Dirt walls and hopelessness, my very self stripped away.

"Put them back," I whisper. "Please. Please." There's something raw in my voice. Steve reacts to my words as if I did lash out, as if I sounded all defiant and enraged. I've burned him.

He places the cans back, carefully. He re-zips the bag. Does he know that I'm dying in front of him?

Steve pulls out his phone. Clicks around a minute. I'm not sure what to do with the silence. This moment is nothing like I ever imagined. It's all I can do to breathe. My bag is on the floor between us. I want to take it, but I can't move.

Steve holds out his phone. "This is you?"

He has eMZee art in his photos. It's kind of surreal. He thumbs through four images. The photos are taken through his car window, like he drove around looking for them. Not my best work, but . . . he's seen me.

"Yes," I admit. The fullness of the truth is refreshing.

Mrs. Nadinsky, our neighbor, opens her door. "Oh, hello, dears." She has her gray hair in rollers under a cap. She's carrying a small plastic trash bag.

"Hello, Mrs. Nadinsky," I answer, from the surreal space. Some things come automatically. "May I take that to the chute for you?"

"Well, aren't you the gentleman," she says, stretching the trash bag out to me. "Such a dear. Such a dear." She pats my shoulder, then retreats into her condo.

And suddenly I'm standing there holding Mrs. Nadinsky's trash. Silent in front of Steve, who is seeing the real me for the first time, my heart in a bag on the hallway carpet. I feel exposed and dirty and cold.

Words fail me. Steve stands silent, too. I grab my backpack by the top handle. Where I go, it goes.

The trash chute is down the hall, behind a little door. Near the elevator. When the chore is done, Steve is right behind me.

"It's beautiful art." Not what I expected him to say.

"Thanks."

"It worries me that you're breaking the law." Yup. Now he's back on the parent track.

"To make a point," I say. "It's resistance."

"It's vandalism."

"Call it what you want." I slide my arms into my backpack straps.

"Your mother wouldn't—"

"So don't tell her!" This isn't about her. It's us. Right here. Right now.

"I haven't. But I think you should tell her."

"Pssshhh." I move past him, toward the elevator.

"I can't let you keep doing this."

I spin around. "Let me? You're not my dad!"

Silence. There's no going back. It's been, I don't know, years now since I threw that at him. He is my dad, and we both know it. There's nothing I can say that will hurt him more. I didn't even mean it, but I'm too mad to take it back.

"I know that."

"I—" I want to say I'm sorry, but I can't. "I have to go."

"Come here," Steve speaks in this tight, controlled voice, like a spring pressed down hard. I know that feeling.

"Screw you. I'm outta here." I stride toward the elevator. Pound the button with my knuckles. With my fist.

"I said, come here," he demands. "Come here now." His voice fills the hallway like thunder. I turn toward the storm, because I can't help it.

Steve strides toward me. My whole body tenses. I didn't even know I had other levels of tightness left, but I do.

It's rare, one of those moments when I feel like he could hurt me. Like he becomes the black man the world fears, a vicious metamorphosis right before my eyes.

When he reaches for me, I'm actually scared. He's never truly scared me before, not once. My arms go up, protecting my face. He grabs my shoulders, and I punch my forearms outward, against his arms, breaking the grip.

"Stop," he says. "Come here."

His hug is strong and soft. If I was anything but stone, I could melt into it. But I am stone.

"We love you," he says. Bringing my mom into it is some ninja shit. But the warmth blows around me like wind. "You're not alone."

But I am alone. I am.

The elevator dings and the door slides open.

"You grounding me?" I ask.

"Is that what I should do?" he says. "Probably, yes. You're grounded."

The elevator door starts to close behind me. I wave my hand against the laser.

"It's not safe out there, at night. I want you safe. Not dead." His voice catches. "Not in jail."

"You want me to jail myself instead."

Steve's face falls. He moves in a small circle, turning himself away and back. He runs his hand over his neck.

"I hear that," he says.

The elevator door starts to close again. This time, Steve reaches over my shoulder and places his hand on the door, holding it open. I step back, into the opening.

"One way or another, a black man is 'safer' in an enclosed space. That's what you're telling me."

A jail cell. A casket. My room. If that has to be my whole world, what's the difference?

The elevator starts up its I-will-beep-until-you-make-a-choice alarm.

"Be safe," Steve says.

"What does that mean?" I ask.

Steve lets go of the door.

I get in, alone.

TINA

The TV is tuned to all the bad news.
My headphones do not help tonight.
Mommy says, *I'm sorry, baby.*
I need to see what happens with the grand jury.
I don't know what the grand jury is
or why everyone is waiting
to hear what it is going to say.
Everyone is angry and shouting—
that part, I understand.
When there was something scary on TV,
Nana used to let me crawl into her lap.
Now I only have pillows
and it's not enough.

TYRELL

Robb is persistent. I'll give him that. He is $y = -x^2 + 2x$. A firm equation, easy to solve but annoying. Insistent and committed to its trajectory, however misguided. When you graph it, it plunges toward negative infinity.

"You gotta come with us, dog. That's your hometown."

"Listen." I'm losing whatever patience I even have with him. "Just let it go, would you."

"Not till you say you'll go. Two nights, max," Robb insists. "You miss only one class. I'll get you back in time for the rest. It's for a good cause. When the grand jury comes in, there's gotta be a lot of voices calling for justice. We gotta stand up!"

It's a relief when my phone vibrates, glowing TINA over my homework.

Her voice is small. "Hi, Tyrell."

"Hey, baby. How's my girl?" I try to sound sexy. Won't make no difference to Tina.

Robb sighs and packs up his notebooks to scoot out of the way so we can have privacy. Good. I want him to think I'm talking to my girlfriend. That she's who keeps calling me.

Tina laughs in my ear. "You sound so funny on the phone sometimes."

The door closes behind Robb. My normal voice returns. "I know. It's because I'm happy when you call."

"You are?"

"Yeah. And the funny voice—it helps me with something."

"You sound normal now."

"Hey. Who you calling normal?"

Tina giggles. "You sound unique. You sound like Tyrell."

I smile. "Well, okay, then."

Quiet. I wait. Usually at this point she tells me about some thing or other that went on at school.

"Are you doing okay?" I ask her.

"I don't know what that means," she says.

Sometimes I don't know whether she misunderstood me or whether she's being insanely deep.

"Are you feeling sad right now? How are you feeling?"

"I have feelings cards," she says. "The sad card is always frowning."

"Are you frowning?"

"No. I am sad but I am not frowning."

"Frown is a funny word. Frowwwwwwwn." I draw out the *ow* sound until my breath runs out.

Tina giggles. "Frowwwwwwwn."

This kid. I wish I could do more for her. I wish there was some way to drop back in time and save her brother. I want that for myself all the time. I want it for her even more, somehow.

"There is another card for how I feel," she says.

"Which card is that?"

"The scared card," she says. "It has very big eyes and frowning eyebrows."

"Frowwwwwwwwwning eyebrows, huh?"

Tina giggles. "When are you coming home?" she says. "I watch out the window for you."

Oh, my heart. "You don't have to do that, Tina. I will tell you when I'm coming."

"When?"

"Tomorrow." It slips out, like a swear word. Like a tear gliding down my cheek.

"Tomorrow?" she repeats. "One sleep?"

My fingers press into my temple. "One sleep," I assure her. Goddammit.

The door creaks and Robb pokes his head back in. I toss him a thumbs-up. He returns to his desk and spreads out again. I'd have liked him to give me a little longer, but a shared space is a shared space.

"So, tomorrow I can watch out the window?"

"If you want to," I told her. "But you don't have to."

"I want to." She's bouncing in place. Her voice bobs with the rhythm.

"I love you, too."

I hang up. Squeeze the corner of the desk to keep from punching the wall. Keep my back to Robb until I can't anymore.

"I don't get you," Robb says. "If I had a girl waiting, I'd be trying to get home every weekend."

"You don't understand the situation." That might be the truest thing I've ever said to him.

"She gonna be at the protest?"

"Maybe."

"Gimme her number. We can meet up with her." He slides a glance my way. "Still saving you a spot in the car tomorrow."

I hate that he's gonna win this one. Or think he did.

It can't be helped. I've made promises.

I sigh. "Okay, *dog*. I call shotgun."

JENNICA

This is what I miss. Thursday night snuggles on the couch with the fuzzy green blanket and Kimberly's shoulder to lean on. She sits propped up by pillows with her feet on the coffee table and I curl against her with the blanket over both of us, tucked snug beneath my chin. Her laptop is stacked on a pile of books so we can stream.

The buzzer dings in the middle of our third episode. Kimberly flinches. She fumbles upright, flustered. "Oh, no. Oh, crud. I forgot to text him."

Our calm is shattered.

"Who?" I say, even though I already know.

"I'm so sorry," she gushes. "We made this plan hours ago, but then you and I were going to hang out. I forgot to cancel."

"It's okay," I say out loud, although my whole body feels like it is being crumpled inside a giant fist.

"No, no. Crud." She scrambles toward the door. "I'm so not ready for him."

I gather up the leftover food cartons as Kimberly buzzes Zeke in. The fuzzy green blanket clings to my shoulders and I will it not to fall.

"Yuck." Kimberly makes a face at her disheveled self in the wall mirror. She smooths down flyaway hairs. "Well. This is me. He knows what I look like, right?"

"You look fine," I tell her. She always looks good. Even when she's in the middle of betraying me.

Kimberly notices me bundling my way toward my bedroom. "No, wait," she says. "I'm just going to send him away. I promised you."

That's not what I expected her to say. I pause.

"I meant to text him, and I'm so sorry," she continues. "Come on, we're right in the middle of an episode!" She seems so earnest.

There's a part of me that wants to say okay, and make her do it. To find out for sure whether, when push comes to shove, she would really choose me.

But I don't want to know. There is only so much disappointment a girl can take. I tuck the blanket tighter around me. "That's silly. Don't send him away."

Kimberly chews her lip. "Really?"

"Really. I don't want to make problems for you with Zeke. He's a good guy."

She frowns. "No. It wouldn't make problems."

They haven't been together that long. She doesn't get it yet. "I told you, I know what guys are like. You should see him. I'll be fine." I offer my best smile.

See? I can be a good friend, even if Kimberly can't.

ZEKE

Kimberly turns off the lights in the kitchen and living room, except for the one they always leave on to discourage burglars. Then she leads me into her bedroom. Her roommate is going to sleep, she says. So we will tuck ourselves away quietly, too.

Kimberly is already dressed in soft clothes, these baggy pajama pants and a nicely fitting tank top under a thin sweater thing. No bra. I slip off my shoes and pants and climb onto her bed beside her. She's sitting cross-legged. I squeeze her knee.

"I don't want to have sex tonight," she blurts out.

I pull my hand back. "Okay . . ."

"Sorry." She picks at her fingernail polish. Glances at me through her lashes.

My hand finds her knee again. "It's totally okay. Of course it's okay." It's not like we have sex every time we hang out. But there's not usually a pronouncement about it. "I mean, are *you* okay?"

"Yeah. It's just . . . I don't want to bother my roommate tonight."

"Oh." It's a little weird, I guess. Thin walls and all. I try not to think about it. It's easier at my place, because my sister is so often out.

Kimberly leans toward me. I pull her close and we lean against the pillows. She lets her arm drape across me and leans her cheek against my chest. I become big in this moment, holding her under my wing and protecting her. The more gently I hold her, the more manly I feel, which seems odd. There are all these ways I'm supposed to be tough in the world, and yet this is the only place I feel strong.

"You said there was something you wanted to talk about," she says.

The settled feeling dissipates as all the questions ahead float back to me. "Yeah, I've got good news. Huge news."

"What?"

Deep breath. "Reverend Sloan offered me a job."

"A job?" Kimberly sits up, looking at me.

"In his congressional offices. In DC. When I graduate."

"Wow. That's amazing." She sounds somewhat less than amazed. "You must have really impressed him."

"I guess. I mean, I told him I couldn't have done it without you, of course." I kiss her shoulder.

Kimberly folds her arms beneath her breasts and hunches forward. "What, um, what kind of job is it?"

"I'd still be organizing, but on the national level." My fingers trail her spine. She's pulling away from me and I don't know what to do.

"Wow, Zeke, that's . . . I mean, you've been worried about what will happen when you graduate." She scoots her body a bit, turning toward me. I can't reach her now, but at least she's looking at me. "It's kind of perfect."

"I know. I was shocked when he first told me."

"When he first told you?"

"He mentioned it when he was here."

Kimberly folds her arms around her knees. "So . . . all this happened last week? Why didn't you tell me?"

"Um . . ." I've hurt her. Shouldn't have let that detail slip.

"I didn't tell you right away because I barely believed it myself." The email is already on-screen when I open my tablet. "Not until I got this."

Kimberly barely glances at the senator's formal employment offer. "So, you're leaving?"

"Thinking about it, yeah."

She goes quiet.

"It's an incredible opportunity. I mean, I can't turn it down." There's more to say, but I don't know how to say it.

Kimberly shakes her head. "Of course. Of course. It's amazing." Her voice is soft but strong.

"He's everything I want to be," I admit. "Since I was a kid, I've known about him. To learn from him, at the right hand . . ."

There's something in her gaze I don't recognize.

". . . I mean, he's everything."

"You're everything," she blurts out.

My skin flushes. Too many words flood the tip of my tongue. *I'm sorry. I love you. You're everything, too. But also not everything . . . I'm confused. I want you. I want this.*

Kimberly rolls off the bed, away from me. "You're amazing. You'll be so much more and better than Al ever could be. Of course you should go national." She crosses to the dresser, where she keeps her jewelry and perfume and makeup.

"I know there's a lot to talk about."

"It's Alabaster Sloan," she says. "What else is there to talk about?" She pulls a pre-moistened cloth—it looks like a baby wipe—from a small plastic pouch.

"I mean . . ." *talk about us.* Or . . . do we not need to? Can she just watch me go like that? I thought we were . . . Doesn't she care?

Kimberly runs the cloth over her face, cleaning it of her makeup. When it's all off, her eyes look smaller, less defined. The rest of her face looks exactly the same to me.

"So . . . you think I should take it?"

My iPad is still open on my knees. I touch the screen to brighten it back up. Kimberly switches off the overhead light and Sloan's offer screams up at me in the dark.

A few moments pass, while she fusses with tissues by the dresser. She blows her nose.

The mattress dips under Kimberly's weight. "You want the whole world," she whispers. Her voice is thick, and I realize maybe she's crying. "And you can have it. You're so good."

"We should talk."

"Sure." She sniffs. "But I know you're going to take it."

When she snuggles against me, I'm confused again. "We should talk," I repeat.

"We should rest," she says.

"Maybe it's better to talk in the morning," I suggest. "If you'll let me stay."

"Of course you can stay," she says. "I want you to stay."

There's so much weight to her words that I don't know what we're talking about anymore.

We slip under the covers. My mind is humming. It takes a while to calm it down. When I'm finally close to sleep, a stray thought drifts through my mind. *Did she call him Al?*

DeVANTE

"Let's giddyup and go," Robb says. "T, you ready?"

"Tyrell," Tyrell says, rather sternly. He shoulders his backpack. "I'm ready."

Sheesh. We've got six hours in the car ahead of us, and I've got a playlist fully programmed. All kinds of music. Hopefully some of which will help Tyrell become less of a wet blanket.

I bump his shoulder. "It's cool. This is gonna be fun."

"Road trip! Road trip! Road trip!" Robb chants, pumping his fist. Tyrell and I roll our eyes. At least we're together on that.

First thing I do when we get to the car is pop open the glove box.

"Dude, what are you doing?" Robb asks. "Tyrell gets shotgun. Roomie privilege."

"Just checking," I say.

"Checking what?"

"Never mind." I snapped the box shut. No errant weed, no tools. Just some papers, all white, and a black binder labeled with the make and model. The car manual.

I wouldn't have put it past Robb to have something that would land me or Tyrell in court if we get pulled over. Some of us don't have fancy lawyer dads or white skin to fall back on.

KIMBERLY

I wake up crying. I refuse to let it show, with Zeke in the bed with me. I blink back the tears, turn my face into the pillow to dry my cheeks. My sobs shake the bed. I don't want to wake him. I can't.

When I'm sure I can be quiet enough, I roll over. He's still sound asleep. Lying there looking all perfect. Except for how he's kind of drooling, which is perfect in a different way.

I ease the sheets aside and slip out to the bathroom.

Run the water hard. Sit on the tile and weep.

I put on the shower, because I'm getting wet anyway and I might as well. I tuck my hair into the shower cap. The room fills with steam and I sit in the tub with my head on my knees, letting the water pound over me.

The truth is like a drumbeat in the back of my mind. Zeke is leaving.

Zeke is leaving.

Zeke is leaving.

TYRELL

"Yo, man, slow down." It's hard to breathe, let alone speak.

The speedometer ticks toward seventy-five. Eighty.

Robb grins blondly, a poster boy for no consequences. "You chicken?" He guns it. Eighty-five.

"Please. For real."

Robb grins. "Chicken."

"I don't want to get pulled over."

"We won't. And we'll get there so much faster." He guns it harder. I should have kept my mouth shut.

I dry my palms along my jeans, then practice holding very still with my hands upon my knees.

Robb says chicken, I think head cut off. I think about what force it takes to separate a head from a body, the mass times acceleration of a knife across a throat. The cold, swift act that some would deign to call merciful.

Robb thinks faster, I think about a baton tapping a window. I calculate exactly how much faster we'll get there, and it's only a matter of minutes.

Seventeen minutes.

Those minutes and his fun. They're more important than me.

I keep my mouth shut. When in doubt, I run the numbers. Things in this car that could be mistaken for a gun:

My cell phone

Robb's cell phone

my wallet

Robb's wallet

my belt buckle

Robb's iPod, casually docked beside the gearshift

the gearshift itself

his camera tripod, tucked under the backseat

a roll of duct tape

my winter gloves

my headphones

the silver carabiner clipped to the shoulder strap of my backpack

the spine of my intro to physics textbook

a sports water bottle, gray

a plastic water bottle, clear

the turn signal lever

the windshield wiper lever

an audiobook CD case

the black registration binder in the glove compartment, which I would
be the one to have to open.

DeVANTE

"Fucking stop it!" Tyrell screams out from the front seat. My head jerks up, every part of me suddenly alert and uncomfortable. We're flying down the expressway, into the rising sun.

"I'm sleeping here," I blurt out.

"Stop!"

The terror in Tyrell's voice sets my heart racing. I blink. Robb laughs. My brain struggles to un-muddle the contrasting sounds. I scratch at some eye crust and try to catch up with the joke.

In the front seat, Tyrell is crying. Actual tears. What the—? Shit just got real and I slept through it.

"Guys?" I sit up straighter. The landscape blurs. We are seriously flying. I shift to peer over Robb's shoulder. Holy fuck.

"Slow down," I say. "That's not funny."

Robb grins. "Chickens."

"You think this is a fucking joke?" I reach up from behind and take his shoulder. Pinch my fingers as hard as I can into his soft tissue. Then I start naming names. *Sandra Bland. Philando Castile.*

"Ow. Jesus. Okay, asshole." He lets up off the gas.

Shae Tatum.

Many swirling thoughts in my still-sleepy brain collide. I release Robb's shoulder. "You're the asshole. You get where we're going today, right?"

"Oh, please," Robb says. "You're with me. Nothing's going to happen."

Tyrell wipes his eyes. He glances at me in the rearview mirror, grateful. I stare back at him, promising. I won't fall asleep again.

We're not friends. We've barely ever had a conversation. But we're together on this.

We are black men in America. We are trapped. We're stuck in this car, in this flying metal box, a restricted space where we have no control.

We are at the mercy of yet another white guy who thinks he gets it, but he doesn't.

ROBB

We are stopped at the side of the road. Tyrell kneels at the edge of the grass, trying to get his stomach back.

"Come on, let's take it to the next exit. There's gotta be a gas station or something."

I've used up all the paper towels in my trunk trying to clean Tyrell's mess. I really want to wash my hands.

"Give him a minute," DeVante says. "For crying out loud."

"I can't believe you peed my car seat," I tell Tyrell. It's mostly on his jeans, but still. My car smells like piss now and it's disgusting. We have to ride in there for another hour, and it's going to dry before I can get it properly cleaned.

"Whose fault is that?" DeVante says. "You're the one playing chicken with the highway patrol."

"I was just messing with him," I say. "I would have slowed down if I saw a cop for real." Of course I would have. I'm not stupid. "It's not like I actually want to get a ticket."

"You're worried about a ticket and we're worried about getting shot," DeVante says.

"No one is going to get shot."

DeVante grabs his forehead. "You think this is some fucking video game? After all that news you watch? It's just entertainment?"

"Of course not." I fucked up and I know it. I was trying to get a rise out of Tyrell, cold fish that he is. I took it too far, but everyone makes mistakes. "Can we move on now?" I say.

"You're taking us to a place where there are tanks in the street. Do you get that?" DeVante shakes his head. "White privilege at work," he mutters.

My skin stings. "It was my idea to go to the demonstration in the first place," I remind him. "I'm totally on board with the protests."

DeVante crouches beside Tyrell. "Come on," he says. "We have to go eventually, you know."

"Can't . . ." Tyrell whispers something else.

Oh, for the love of—

DeVante reaches toward me. "Give me the keys. I'm driving."

TYRELL

Underhill. It is home, and it is another world. All at once. That thing they say about college being a bubble away from the rest of the world is true, I guess. Perhaps this is how it feels to be an astronaut reentering the earth's atmosphere, free-falling, hoping your heat shield holds, hoping your parachutes deploy. You've been in a place so beautiful, a place few people where you come from can appreciate or understand, and now you must return . . . assuming the very sky will let you. The movie they showed in the dorm lounge last Friday was *Apollo 13* and all I can picture right now is that moment at the end of the movie when everyone is holding their breath. After everything they've been through, will they survive reentry?

Will I survive?

I don't know.

I don't know.

We roll through the familiar streets, and my stomach clenches tighter with each block. "Right on Peach," I instruct DeVante, who's still driving. We're almost home.

"Are we almost there?" Robb wants me and my urine stench out of his car ASAP. I get it.

"You can let me out anywhere," I say. It's easy walking distance from here.

"Naw, man. I got you," DeVante says. "Door to door."

We make the turn onto Peach Street and . . .

"Oh, shit." Robb grabs both front seats by the shoulder and pulls himself forward. "What the fuck?"

Underhill is not home. It is another world. It is a police state, a war zone, a corridor of barricades and patrol officers. We can't even drive all the way down Peach. They've re-routed the traffic around the section of blocks where the protesting has occurred. Across the concrete barricades, it is clear that storefronts have been burned out and looted. The sidewalks are littered with broken glass and debris.

"Just drop me on the corner right here."

"Are you sure, man?" DeVante's voice echoes my feeling. "You could come with us."

No, I'm not sure that I want to walk these streets tonight . . . but I'm equally sure that I live here. And accordingly, I have no choice.

"We're not staying in Underhill," Robb says. "DeVante has an uncle who lives across town."

"A better part of town, you mean."

Robb throws himself back in the seat. Says nothing. Whatever. I can't help it. Everything Robb says is like needles to me at this point.

He pulls out his phone and starts taking pictures. I can hear the metallic little scissor-click over and over, punctuating our silence like one long ellipse.

DeVante takes the turn and pulls the car over in front of a fire hydrant. Throws the hazards on for good measure.

"Do you know how to get where you're going next?" I feel bad for leaving him alone with Robb, but what else am I supposed to do?

DeVante taps his phone, where it's resting in the cup holder. "Gonna program it now."

"Tomorrow you should leave the car and take the bus back here," I tell him. I glance in the rearview. Robb's not the public transit type, but at least I've given fair warning.

"Text to meet up," DeVante says. I close the door.

Robb and I exchange a glance through the rear window. I try not to think about the fact that this is nowhere near the end for us. I still have to live with him for another eighty-six days.

Eighty-five, if you don't count tonight.

Tonight, when I'm gambling on Vernesha's kindness. I can't go home. If my parents knew I was here, they'd light me up.

When I start walking, my jeans shift. The breeze hits and their wetness becomes uncomfortable again. Not like it ever felt great. At least my coat is long enough to somewhat cover my crotch.

All I know is I can't show up at the Johnsons' place with wet jeans. I go into Rocky's convenience store.

"Tyrell," Rocky says. "What's good?"

"Listen," I tell him. "I spilled a drink on myself in the car. I can't go walking around like this. You mind if I change up in your bathroom?" I point to my backpack, which luckily has a clean pair of jeans in it.

The bathroom is not for customers, but Rocky's known me since I was a kid. Maybe he'll do me a solid. I only hope he can't smell the pee scent wafting up from me.

Rocky starts to shake his head.

"Please?" I beg. "It's kind of an emergency. I'll buy whatever you want."

Rocky's known me since I was a kid. A good kid. Always. He hesitates. "One time only," he says. "In back on the left."

I scramble through the stockroom door before he can change his mind. I'm fast. Not taking advantage of anyone's favors. The washroom is tiny. I can elbow both walls at the same time. Not ideal, but I'm just grateful. I scrub my thighs with soap and paper towel, rinse my pants and wring them out as best I can.

Out front, I buy a soda, a sandwich, and three packs of the cookies I like. I need a treat. Rocky gives me an extra plastic bag for my wet jeans. I've always suspected he was a good person, underneath all the ways he acts like he doesn't care.

"Thanks, man. You have no idea." When I stick out my hand, it surprises him. He shakes. Then I head for the door.

"You stay out of trouble, you hear?" Rocky says.

I turn back. This, from Rocky, who prides himself on staying out of everybody's business. Underhill. It is at once home and another world.

"I'm not here to cause trouble," I assure him. "I'm just coming home."

DeVANTE

The second Tyrell is out of the car, Robb says, "Get me to some kind of car-cleaning place. Stat."

I roll my eyes. "It's not that big a deal."

"It's disgusting. What are we, seven?"

It's all I can do not to pull the car over and scream at him, like my mom used to do when my sisters and I would be fighting in the backseat. *Don't make me come back there.*

"You just don't get it," I tell him, for the thousandth time. "People die that way. You could have gotten us killed."

"We were just driving. Nothing else."

Our eyes meet in the rearview mirror. I'm driving in an unfamiliar city. I have to keep my attention on the road, but I can't let it go just yet. "All that news you watch and you still don't know that gets people like him and me killed?"

"It was never just that."

How are we even having this conversation? Robb, who always wants to hang out at the Black House, who arm-wrestled us into coming here with him to protest. I grip the wheel tight. "Just because they were black? Sure it was. Eric Garner. Philando Castile."

Robb says, "He had a gun in the car, though."

"A legal weapon, that he never pulled out," I remind him. "Sandra Bland only had a broken taillight."

"And she talked back to the cop."

Here it comes. I can feel it. I push harder, coming back at him. "She asserted her rights when they were being violated. Is that a capital crime nowadays?"

"No, but if she hadn't said anything . . ."

Fumes of rage come up my esophagus. Worse than acid reflux. I choke them down hard. We're not supposed to ever speak now? That's what they all want, isn't it? Our obedience, our deference, our silence.

"Remember those guys that got arrested while they were waiting for their friend in Starbucks?"

"That was messed up."

"Messed-up things happen. That's the point."

"Technically, they were loitering, right?"

"When's the last time a coffee place like that arrested upper-class white people for loitering? Why only the black people?"

Robb bursts out with, "They must've been doing something!"

There it is. The thing white people think that they won't say out loud. They don't believe in bias. They don't believe it happens for no reason other than racism and misplaced fear. When push comes to shove, for them, it is tragic because it was a "misunderstanding." They think that kind of "misunderstanding" could happen to a white person, that it has something to do with our actions, even though we see time and time again that it doesn't.

"But they *weren't* doing anything," I insist. "Remember the guy who was on his cell phone in his own backyard."

"Mistaken identity."

"Because he was black."

"It's—that doesn't make sense."

"When cops see a black guy, their brains kick into heightened alert. A tiny flinch is a threat. A cell phone is a threat. Standing still with your hands up is a threat. That's bias."

Robb is quiet in the backseat. He's got his head down. The rearview mirror is full of his cowlick.

"Look, if you're gonna march with us, you gotta get your head around it. I'm serious."

"Two lefts and a right," Robb says.

He's looking straight back at me in the mirror now. "What?"

"Take two lefts and then a right. There's a body shop that does upholstery."

I brake for a yellow light, and slam on the left turn signal. Goddammit. I'm speaking into a void and how can I call myself friends with someone I have to explain these things to?

And at the same time, this is Robb, the guy who was nicest to me from day one. The guy who always remembers what I like on my pizza and always invites me to do cool things around campus. My first and best friend at school, the guy I clicked hardest with when everything was new and strange. We've talked about girls and kept each other from getting too drunk, or walked each other home when we've occasionally missed the mark. He's the only one who comes close to my gaming skills.

"Whoa, this is my jam, turn it up," he says. My phone is plugged into the car. A good song is on. Upbeat. I spin the volume high, because, fuck it. I'm not getting through anyway.

We bob our heads to the beat. I rub the plush leather steering wheel, remind myself that Robb is still my ride home.

The thing is, I know that I will stay friends with him. We'll march tomorrow and wear out our lungs. And afterward, he still won't get it and I'll be more enraged than ever. The knowledge spins out in front of me. And so does the knowledge that I won't let him go because I don't know how to. And I hate myself for liking him anyway. It makes me a bad black person, doesn't it? If I'm not woke enough to walk away?

STEVE CONNERS

I can't say no to my nephew. But as soon as DeVante and his friend arrive, I know this was a terrible idea. They're college boys, roaming free. The last kind of influence we need on Will.

Over dinner, the conversation is politics, protest. DeVante is well versed in the issues. His mother, my sister, made sure of that.

Will hangs on his every word.

DeVante's friend is something else. He's that guy. The one we all know, and like, and trust, until we don't. Call me assimilationist, an oreo, whatever you want—I know who I am. There's a difference between doing what you have to do to succeed and being some kind of Uncle Tom, shucking and jiving at the knee of some master. This Robb guy is destined to be a master, whether he can see it right now or not. All the marching in the world doesn't take away the damage he'll do when he finally steps up to daddy's corporate table. And of course he will.

"Fight the power," Robb says. I wonder if he understands the irony. That's a Bulova on his wrist. He's wearing custom-tailored Diesel jeans. I know my high-end apparel.

"Right on," say Will and DeVante in unison. I wonder if someone is trying to bring back the sixties. Because that went so well for everyone.

Robb and DeVante banter back and forth, and their energy is high. My wife is laughing, delighted, and I force myself to smile when she meets my eye. She doesn't know what I know. She cut her political teeth on the streets of Underhill. It's different. Me, I remember those days. College days, the late-night talks, the vibrant debates. Safe in those ivy-covered halls, where everything is theory, you can spout off anything.

I don't know how to tell them. This is the real world. Tough talk is dangerous. Just being right, being smart, doesn't get the job done. Tomorrow, it's real.

WILL/eMZEE

Steve puts Robb in the guest room, and DeVante takes my second bed. We putter around getting ready for bed.

I like the quiet of just the two of us. There are things I want to say. But instead I hand him my toothpaste and sit on my bed to wait while he uses my bathroom.

He comes back out, puts the toothpaste back on my bookcase. I like to walk around my room while I brush, which I guess is weird or something. "Thanks."

"Yeah, of course."

We're not real cousins, we're slant cousins. DeVante's mom is Steve's sister. We were close until his grandmother died. There were Christmases, summer visits back and forth, a lot of time spent at her house. Since then, not so much. It's been a few years.

We sit around in our boxers, looking at our phones and stuff. I wonder, not for the first time, if this is what it's like to have a brother.

"How have you been?" DeVante asks. He plugs in his phone and gets under the covers.

"I'm good," I answer. "Busy. Senior year and all."

"Good times."

"For sure." I'm okay with letting him think I spend my free time partying or something, not skulking around in a hoodie with spray paint. I try not to skulk, really.

"You still painting?" he asks.

"Tagging mostly. Sometimes I mural. Wanna see my stuff?" I offer. Until Steve cracked the case, DeVante was the only one who knew about my art.

"This is killer," he says. "Really woke."

"Thanks."

"You could come for a visit, if you want a taste of college life."

"That would be fun."

"I shoulda been more in touch, with all that's going on," DeVante says.

I shrug. "No worries."

We hover in silence. After a while, I wonder if he's fallen asleep, but then he sighs.

"You worried about tomorrow?" I ask.

"Not really," he says. "If shit gets weird, we bug out, right?"

"Yeah, sure," I agree. "That's what I always do."

TINA

I watch out the window
until Tyrell is on the stoop
Then Tyrell is at the door
Mommy is the one who answers but
Tyrell is here to see me.
Hey there, Tina. How's my girl?
I pull him to the couch
I crawl into his lap
His arms are warm and safe
and strong.
Mommy says things to us
I pretend to forget how to listen
I don't want a lot of grown-up words.
It's been bad. I know, Tyrell says.
I know. It's been bad.

TYRELL

It's odd, being in Tariq's room again. The furniture is laid out the same,
but most of his personal stuff is gone. The dresser, the desk, the bed are
all as they were. The closet door looks funny to me closed. Tariq always
had a mound of clothes spilling out onto the floor. He didn't really believe
in folding or hanging anything. The bookcase is still full of his books,
although it looks like some of Tina's have taken over.

Vernesha rubs my shoulder in this way that feels nostalgic.

"Is this too hard for you?" I ask. "I can leave."

"No, baby," she says. "I like having you here." She glances around
the room, with a soft smile. "It's no harder, no matter what happens. No
easier, either."

Yeah, that. "Okay."

"Take those with you when you go?" she says, pointing to a stack of
papers on the dresser. It's the only thing cluttering the room. "I don't know
why, but I never could . . ." Her voice trails off. She shakes her head of
whatever thoughts of Tariq have just crept in.

"Sure."

Vernesha wraps her arms around me. "I'm glad you're doing well.
He'd be so proud of what you've accomplished."

"Haven't done much yet," I answer, settling into the warmth of her
affection.

"You're on your way. That's more than nothing." She kisses my cheek.
"Sleep well. If Tina comes in—"

"It's okay. I miss her, too."

Vernesha nods. "I find her sleeping in here sometimes."

"Sure, I get that."

She backs out and closes the door.

I'm alone.

First thing, check the dresser pile. Don't want to forget later.

It's mail. All of it. As I sort through the stack of fancy envelopes, my heart crumples up like a wad of paper in a fist.

Stanford. Howard. Lincoln. Northwestern. Morehouse. Penn. Hampton. Xavier. Dozens of state universities, too, from all around. I got all these same envelopes, some time ago. I loved them. Reading every one was like taking a different vacation in my brain. And all because I dragged T to some career fair and we put our names and addresses on a list. It would have been, I don't know, a week before he died? Or a month? Maybe two? When we thought we both had a hundred years ahead of us.

It never occurred to me to wonder if T was getting them, too. I never knew that his mom had to open the mailbox, every day for weeks, and . . . God.

I shovel the pile into my backpack. Maybe I'll throw them away tomorrow, but maybe I won't.

You sentimental idiot. T's voice comes crisp and clear like he's in the room with me.

"Shut up," I answer, but we both know I don't mean it.

I tug off my jeans and lie on the bed.

You miss me so much you're gonna hang on to my junk mail?

"You know I do."

You're a mess, Ty. One big hot mess, my brother.

"Fair enough."

Don't be stupid. Take care of you. Leave the rest alone.

"And Tina."

I appreciate you looking out for her. She's gonna be okay. We grow 'em tough in the Johnson family.

"Like you?"

T scoffs. *Tina's way tougher than me. That should be obvious.*

"Shae was her friend."

Yeah.

I snuggle down beneath the covers. When I close my eyes, it's easy to pretend he's mere inches away, down in his sleeping bag on the floor. We used to take turns.

Don't get too comfortable in my bed, there, you hear?

I smile. "Shut up."

Maybe, on some level, this is what I wanted all along. To sleep in his room, which I've done dozens of times. It was always the safe, happy place in my world. I don't know what it is now. Still that, sort of. But also the heart of all of this pain. The feeling of being alone in the world is both less and more all at once.

It's weird. Good weird.

To return to a part of the world we once shared, even if it's only for a little while. Even if it's only pretend.

ROBB

Will and his parents leave for school and work. We're alone in the condo, DeVante and me.

DeVante puts the breakfast plates into the dishwasher. We sip coffee and wait. There's nothing much on Twitter. No point in heading to the demonstration quite yet, either. There's nothing to do in the house, though. Will doesn't even have a video game console. How is that possible? This building is high-class. Obviously they could afford it.

Bo-ring.

"We could have driven down this morning," I say, flopping onto the living room couch.

"And gone straight to the demonstration? No bacon and grits?" DeVante grins, hauling his backpack onto the rug. He riffles through it, pulling out a notebook. "I don't know about you but I like a home-cooked meal when I can get one."

"Why'd we come so early?" I poke the remote control until the TV buzzes on.

DeVante gives me a look. "Some of us don't like driving in the dark, remember?"

Geez. They're never going to let me live it down, are they? I'm the insensitive white dude, forever.

"Anyway, getting up before dawn to start driving is no one's idea of fun."

"Whatever," I say. "I'm bored." DeVante is *studying*, which is freaky. Who brings homework on a road trip?

We're watching crap daytime TV when the front door lock snaps and someone enters the foyer. DeVante and I exchange a glance.

Will appears. "What's up?" He's wearing a hoodie over his private school vest, like he's trying to make a point.

"Coming with us?" DeVante asks.

"Of course," Will says. "Let's go."

KIMBERLY

The size of this crowd is incredible. We've filled the block and then some. From the steps of the police precinct, I can't even see the full scope of the thing past the other buildings.

The police precinct is about a third of the way down the block, which is long. The building is set back from the street far enough to allow a series of about a dozen shallow steps rising to the revolving door. The street, which is usually lined with parked police vehicles, has been cleared. The crowd presses forward, up to the barricade at the base of the steps. The series of three-foot concrete pillars has always been there, to protect the precinct from rogue vehicles, but now there are temporary construction barricades filling the gaps between the pillars.

They've set up a microphone on the fourth step. Those of us with SCORE leadership passes are allowed to be behind the barricade. Police officers in riot gear line the street. They are above us, around us, beside us, among us. A row of them hovers at the revolving door, a row stands at the bottom of the steps.

Standing on the steps, looking over it all, it is clear—there cannot be violence tonight.

This is where they want us, penned into a narrow street. Spread thin.

We've been here for several hours, awaiting the announcement. It is well past the close of business, and we are left to wonder why they're delaying their announcement. There is going to be one, we're told. The grand jury decision has come in.

If they think they can wait us out, they're wrong. It is cold, and getting dark, but we are still here, all the hundreds of us.

We're down to the last few UNARMED buttons. I've been punching them out for days and days. We had hundreds, and still there never seems to be enough. It's great, in terms of turnout. It's hard, in terms of impact.

The buttons aren't only a political statement. They might actually save people's lives.

That really was the last of them, though. None of the boxes at the base of the podium have more. There are a few more boxes on the other side of the steps. I trace the edge of the barricade, headed in search of them.

Behind me, Zeke's voice breaks out through the microphone. We've had speeches and chanting on and off through the afternoon, to keep the momentum going.

"If they're gonna make us wait, they're gonna have to listen," he shouts. "No justice, no peace!"

The crowd is primed and ready. A chorus. *No justice, no peace!*

I whirl around. NO. We agreed, no.

No justice, no peace!

Zeke stands on the steps like a rock star—arms out, palms up, pumping them like wings. Louder. Louder!

No justice, no peace!

No justice, no peace!

It goes on. And on. And on, and on, and on. Long enough for the people to have a hold of the rhythm on their own. Long enough for Zeke to notice me hovering on the steps, steeped in disappointment. He steps away from the mike and comes toward me.

No justice, no peace!

No justice, no peace!

"What are you doing?" I demand. "We talked about this."

He pulls back an inch, surprised by my fire. "I know," he says, reaching toward me. "But—"

His hands touch air. I'm not within reach anymore. I didn't plan to back away. But here we are.

Zeke comes closer again. "I'm sorry," he says.

I'm so full of other things, I don't have room to hold it. "Whatever. Do what you want," I say. "You always do."

Zeke pauses. Looks at me, really looks. "This isn't the time, or the place."

"I know. I'm sorry." I hate myself for bringing it up. I'm good at keeping a lot inside, but I've lost that skill with Zeke. And that was supposed to be a good thing. Now, I don't know. I don't know.

The stone steps feel long and high as I try to descend, away from him.

Zeke takes my arm, turns me back. "The chant was Sloan's idea. He asked for it. How am I supposed to say no?"

No one says no to the Reverend Alabaster Sloan.

"Zeke!" One of our teen volunteers, Lemanuel, bounds across the steps toward us. "The senator's asking for you."

"Okay." Zeke tosses me an apologetic glance, then follows Lemanuel back toward the microphone.

Just like that. The senator calls and he goes running. No regard for the fact that we are in the middle of something.

I knew it already, but now it settles hard in my heart: Senator Sloan is a person who takes. He takes up all the accolades, the affection, the spotlight, the light in general. Over and over.

My knees meet the concrete steps, followed by my gloved hands. The cold seeps up through me. *Just breathe.* I stare at the upside-down heart formed between my thumbs and fingers.

Upside-down broken heart, that is.

A policeman looms over me, out of nowhere. "No sitting on the steps," he orders.

My heart was already pounding and now it is bursting.

"Sorry. I know." I scramble to my feet, at once rushing to obey and trying not to make any sudden moves. I'm hot and cold, flushed with a sudden icy sweat, trapped inside my winter coat, trapped by the crowd, trapped beneath the cop's stern gaze. "I know. I know."

WILL/eMZee

It feels good to be in it. To open my lungs. I thought I liked being on the sidelines, with a can of paint, but this is a whole other level.

The four of us hang together: me, DeVante, Robb, and Tyrell. It's a little odd seeing Tyrell. It's been a long time since we were in school together, but he remembered me. Said my name when we bumped fists. Robb is mostly a white guy trying to act down, but whatever. It's kinda nice to have a posse for a minute, even if it's only temporary.

No justice, no peace! I've painted it. Shouting it is powerful in a different way.

When the chant switches, DeVante gets nervous. "If this goes bad, we can't be here," he shouts in my ear.

I nod, but in my heart, I'm thinking *Screw it. We're here.*

Tyrell, too, looks itchy. Glancing around for a way out. Itchy because he knows, like I do, we're deep in it. Way too deep.

Host: *We're awaiting the grand jury decision on Officer Darren Henderson. Joining me is attorney Christine Emory and NNN's own Bobbi Rockwell.*

Emory: *It's clear from their choice of location to announce.*

Rockwell: *What do you mean?*

Emory: *It's customary to make this sort of announcement from the courthouse, where the grand jury is actually impaneled.*

Rockwell: *Instead they're announcing from the police precinct in Underhill.*

Emory: *They know people are going to be unhappy, and they don't want it spilling over into other neighborhoods.*

Host: *We'll know soon enough. The verdict will be announced any minute. Let's review the facts of the case. The onus is on the prosecution to convince the grand jury that there is enough evidence to take Henderson to trial.*

Emory: *The district attorney's office works closely with the police. How invested are they in making that case?*

Rockwell: *No way to know.*

Host: *They have a responsibility to the citizens, as much as to the police.*

Emory: *More so. But if you look at the law, it's less clear than it seems to a layperson. A trial jury would be tasked to determine* *whether the police officer's actions were reasonable, in the moment.*

Rockwell: *Not in hindsight.*

Emory: *Exactly. Based on the information he had at the time, did he perceive a credible threat?*

Rockwell: *Obviously not. She was a small girl.*

Emory: *We know that now. Is it reasonable to expect that Henderson knew that in the moment?*

Rockwell: *Is it reasonable for anyone to mistake an unarmed child for a serious threat?*

Emory: *The issue is bias. A jury—in this country, in this time—may be operating with a similar bias to the one that led Henderson to shoot at Shae Tatum. Consider the mindset that led him to take lethal action against a child: the assumption that anything black that moves is a threat.*

Rockwell: *You think they will find it objectively reasonable that he thought she was a threat?*

Emory: *It won't be objective. Anti-black bias is part of the fabric of our culture.*

Rockwell: *How do you achieve objectivity in such a case? Isn't that a core part of the jury's charge?*

Emory: *There's the rub. What do you do when the "random" group of citizens meant to judge the case is incapable of objectivity? They're asked to imagine whether any other police officer in the same situation, given the same information, would have made the* same split-second decision. And given the nature of anti-black bias, the answer is likely yes.

Rockwell: *That's—*

Emory: *It's an indictment of something . . . but not Henderson.*

Host: *The verdict is coming in. We're going live to the Underhill police precinct for the announcement.*

JENNICA

When the verdict comes down, the diner closes early. Shades drawn, I write the sign for the window myself: *Black-Owned Business.*

Tape the corners in place. Kiss the paper with a tiny prayer: Let this building survive the night. Let my job be here in the morning.

Walk home. All is quiet, for now.

Too quiet, for me.

No Noodle. No Brick. No Kimberly.

I've never felt more alone.

OFFICER YOUNG

We are glued to the flat screen in the break room. We're on call, as second-wave support. If they need us.

The captain comes in. "Gear up. Verdict's coming down in our favor."

Boots.

Mask.

Baton.

Tear gas.

Helmet.

Shield.

Let's do this thing.

MELODY

I never felt this kinda power. Not since I can remember. We got energy.
We got rhythm. We got truth.

No justice, no peace!

No justice, no peace!

The protest is lit. It ain't even cold now. We jumping. We pumping.

No justice, no peace!

No way to get tired. No way to quit it. We screaming. We furious.

No justice, no peace!

Brick stands beside me, his fist in the air. When it was calm, for a
while, he had his arm around me, his hand in my coat pocket, keeping me
close.

It ain't calm now. I can still feel his arm, though. The little things that
show me we got something going. It's fuel. Life-giving fuel.

Zeke, at the podium, says the announcement's coming soon.

It don't matter. They gonna let us down. Again. We know it already.
Been knowing it.

We scream it, insist it: *No justice, no peace!*

High up on the steps, the line of officers parts. The revolving door
turns. White men in suits come down, followed by white men in uniform.

It's on. It's on. Brick's arm goes around me, pulling me close. The
screaming slowly settles around us as one of the suits places himself behind
the mike. He introduces himself as the district attorney.

He clears his throat. "The grand jury has determined, in its best judgment, that there is not sufficient evidence to indict Officer Darren
Henderson . . ."

The scream, it's primal. It's spontaneous. It's everyone. No leader at
the mike. We're past that.

If he has more words, we don't hear them.

No justice, no peace!

No justice, no peace!

Brick speaks softly. Am I meant to hear it? Not sure how I even do, under the shouting. "They're coming for us. We ain't going down without a fight."

That's right.

No justice, no peace!

We're energy, rhythm, truth. We're pumping, jumping. Screaming, furious.

I never felt this kinda power before. Brick by my side: all fueled up. The shield of the crowd: untouchable. The sting of injustice: no consequences.

We got nothing to lose. We gonna die anyway. Let it not be in a dark alley. Let it not go unseen. They coming for us. Let us meet them. Under the lights, in front of the cameras.

We gonna light this motherfucker up.

@KelvinX_: A grand jury will indict "a ham sandwich," but not a live squealing pig. #JusticeForShaeTatum

@TroubleInRiverCty: You indict or we ignite! #BurnItDown #Underhill

@WhitePowerCord: That's right. You niggers can't keep a good cop down. #selfdefense

@UnderhillSCORE: #UnderhillPD, you owe us answers. #TodayForShae #TomorrowForAll

@Viana_Brown: We are grief. We are rage. The flood of it is never-ending.

@KelvinX_: No justice. No peace. #burnitdown #underhillriot

PEACH STREET

The air is thick and still. Tense, like a coiled spring under pressure.

Curtains flutter, then rest. Shades are drawn. Locks clicked and double-checked. Hand-lettered signs taped to windows: *Black-Owned Business*. A thin measure of protection. Behind the glass, a feeling of held breath, of hunkering down to ride out the storm.

They march in formation. Boots, batons, rifles, shields. Riot gear. Flanked by tanks and lit by spinning cherries.

They march as a crowd. Signs waving, mouths screaming.

Water and oil, baking soda and vinegar, waves lapping up against stone. Erosion. Eruption. Natural phenomena the city is meant to hold at bay, with its brick and steel and concrete.

These walls are meant to be unmoved.

WITNESS

You've seen enough. You don't want to see more. It's inexplicable, the decision to leave home. To make your way through the heart of Underhill. Toward the action. Not away.

When tanks roll through the streets of an American city, it makes the most sense to draw the curtains. Their treads will tear up the roads. Their guns are drawn by nature. All ambiguity is lost.

Through the bullhorns, they shout for order. You don't want to be there when they start shooting for it instead.

The rage of a helpless people tastes like blood in the throat. Enough suffering to make us choke, cough, gargle our way toward breath.

One foot in front of the other. Motherfucking curfews be damned.

You have seen enough, and yet not enough. Enough to live in fear. Not enough to see Shae's killer indicted and brought to trial. You have failed.

No, the system has failed. You've studied the statistics, out of curiosity. You weren't surprised to learn how few police officers in the United States of America have ever been convicted of a wrongful shooting. Hardly any have even been indicted. Case after case: dismissed.

You walk the streets, uncomfortable. You walk the streets, with your eyes open. Someone has to be watching. Someone has to see how it all goes down.

You've seen enough, and yet not enough. Too much happens in back alleys. Too much happens in the heat of a moment. Too much goes wrong, and yet no one has seen enough to ensure justice.

The whole city's on fire. That's how it feels anyway. Underhill is a war zone. Tanks in the streets are only the beginning.

You walk, because you have the right to. You watch what they do in the name of order and law. You wonder what is the definition of freedom; you wonder what is the cost.

Shots fired. Shots fired. A symphony of sirens.

This is your neighborhood. They can't have it. This is not a peaceful protest. This is a throwdown. You will not go quietly.

It makes no sense. The urge to race toward the tanks. To run up on them, denting them with your cleats. Stabbing the metal with the spiked heels you imagine yourself to have. You would be a superhero. The picture paints itself across the back of your eyes and you emerge heroic.

There are no handcuffs. You eat no cement. The knee in your back is a badge of honor, a ghost of the hardest punch you ever threw.

TINA

I do not like the sound of tanks.
It is worse than chewing.
It is worse than the garbage disposal.
No one calls out *noise, noise*
like Mommy does before she runs the vacuum.
It is worse than sirens.
It is worse than snow shovels scraping.
Light it up! comes the shouting. *Light it up!*
I cannot plug my ears hard enough.
Mommy says *put on your headphones.*
My headphones block the outside noise.
My headphones make their own noise
inside me. I am not sure
which noise is worse.

BRICK

It's on now. Fuck all the signs, all the marching. The crowd explodes with ungodly fury, and I won't step away from the center of it.

Light it up!

They can come for me tonight, if they want to. I am one cog in the machine of the 8-5 Kings. These pigs got nothing on me. They've been trying for a decade to tear down what we've built. They haven't yet. I take pride in that. We're untouchable.

Light it up!

There is no such thing as peace tonight.

ZEKE

From the precinct steps, we have full view of the moment when the protest turns. *Light it up!* chants the crowd. *Light it up!* I did not tell them to say it. The suits moved me away from the microphone to make the official announcement. I'm no longer in control.

The district attorney drops his bomb and then retreats up the steps, flanked by his little team of men. They move like they think they're so important. It makes me want to claw at things. They move with a carelessness, too, like what happens next has nothing to do with them or what they have done.

It's impossible to see what force—save unbridled rage, save desperation—turns the tide. It seems to happen all at once, from the fringes, moving in. Down the block, a storefront goes up in flames. Across the street, the police in their helmets and shields charge forward, as one, like a wave. The shouting and chanting loosens. All rhythm is lost and chaos takes over.

The microphone is still right there, but I don't know what else to say into it. The tide has turned. What can I say to get them back? What can I say to make it all right that we are dying? There is nothing I can promise—clearly not justice. Clearly not peace.

Kimberly appears at my side. "What do we do?" she says.

I put out my hand, and she takes it. In any other light, she would run from me. Even now, probably, she is dying to run from me, but we have a job to do, and the world is falling apart around us.

The row of police officers at the barricade below us raises its shields. Their stances change in one fell swoop, as if they've been called to attention from parade rest. The people at the front of the demonstration—fists up, still chanting—sense the shift. They stare up at me, asking for guidance. I don't have any to give.

Across the street, there is fighting. The perfect picture of our crowd blurs and pixelates at the edges. We are watching something dissolve. Batons fly. A different kind of scream rises up. People down below look around, uncertain which direction to run. Among them, others move firmly, spoiling for the fight.

I'm scared. There's no other word for it. "I don't think we can hold them."

Kimberly's eyes are fire. "Can you blame them?"

My skin tingles. My limbs tremble. I don't know where to place this feeling. Somewhere between rage and despair. "We're supposed to be in charge. In control."

"We've never had control." Kimberly shakes her head. "That's the whole point."

MELODY

My gloves are green, Brick's are black.

Light it up! Light it up! Light it up! chants the crowd. We jumping. We pumping. Fists punching high.

Light it up! Light it up! Light it up!

And then someone does.

Flames burst up along the street somewhere to our left. I can't see it, past all the arms and shoulders penning me in. I only hear it. A sizzling whoosh. The crowd rocks and shimmies. Gasping, cheering.

The rhythm is broken. People move every which way. Toward the flames, away. It's hard to stay standing.

My gloves are green, his are black.

All my focus is on the place where they meet.

Brick is there, and then he's gone.

It's me. Alone, and drifting.

Shoulders, coat sleeves, elbows, fists. Tossed about in a human ocean. No shore in sight.

I never seen the ocean. Don't know what it feels like to drown. Maybe like this?

"Brick!" I shout. "Brick?"

I'm turning and turning and turning. The rock of my fist crumbles. I'm grasping for anything.

Bump. Check. Stumble.

Then, out of the ocean of sleeves, there's a face. At my level. Huge eyes. Trembling lips. Cheeks slack and shiny. We're gasping at each other. Her face, like mine, has succumbed to the water.

My gloves are green, hers are brown. We take hands. No words. Safety in numbers or something like that. We become bigger together.

KIMBERLY

"Please disperse. Please disperse." The officer's droning voice is projected from a metallic-sounding speaker. "Please disperse."

I want to find the voice. To yell STOP in his face. No one is dispersing.

Zeke hovers near the microphone. I pull his arm. "We have to get out of here."

"This is SCORE's protest," he answers.

Things are on fire. There is nothing we can do. "It stopped being ours a few minutes ago."

"I have to—" Zeke's free hand bats at the microphone stand, as if petting it will calm anything. "I have to try." There's silence for a beat, and then he leans forward. Shouts, "We are. Unarmed! We are. Unarmed!" The rhythm is decent. The crowd picks it up. *We are unarmed! We are unarmed!*

We are flanked, suddenly and dramatically, by riot-dressed cops. The line of cops at the barricade pushes forward against the crowd, while more rush forth from the precinct building, filling the steps and then some.

I let go of Zeke's arm because I have to. We put our hands in the air, because we have to. A baton passes in front of us. Terror sizzles through me. A searing streak, like lightning. My body tenses to take the blow.

What is hit instead is the microphone. It gets knocked away down the steps.

This is it. We'll be arrested.

The most terrible thought—maybe this means Zeke will get to stay. Can you work at the US Capitol if you have a record? Shame floods me. My own selfish horror breaks me harder than anything I've seen tonight. Any second now, the tears will start to fall. Any second.

I don't understand what happens next. At all. The cops flood past us. Every damn one of them. They pile on top of one another to get into the fray below. Swinging batons and knocking people to the ground.

"Please disperse. Please disperse." The drone continues unabated.

The strongest, loudest voice is still the crowd. *We are unarmed! We are unarmed!*

All but alone on the steps, Zeke and I look at each other. Are we relieved . . . or insulted? They ran past us? We are not a threat. We are two kids with our hands up, and no way left to speak.

"We have to get out of here," I say.

Zeke lowers his hands. "We can't just leave."

"We can." I shake my head, and even then the tears don't come loose. "I think we have to."

DeVANTE

I've always made fun of that thing they do in movies, that battle-scene shaky-cam effect, where everything is jostling and confused. I've always said it looks stupid. It does.

But I get it now. I mean, I get where the idea comes from.

They get it wrong, though. It's supposed to show urgency, on-screen, but that's not what it is in real life. It's terror. It's my whole body thumping because my heart is beating so hard. Every blink is like a snapshot from a slightly new angle. The whole world changes in the split second it takes my eyelids to go up and down. It's jarring as hell. My head starts to pound.

Beside me, Will jumps to the beat and pumps his fist in the air.

Light it up! Light it up!

On my other side, Tyrell doesn't even want to be here. He glances around like a scared rabbit, which is nothing new. He's been like that since we got here. Only, now it's justified.

"We gotta go," I say. "It's gonna turn."

Tyrell nods. He leans toward Robb, who's on the other side of him, bouncing and pumping as loud as anyone. I can't hear what he says, but I can see Robb shrug him off. Damn it.

"Hey, Will. Will!" I shout. "We gotta go."

"Hell no," he says. "This is my town. This is my fight. I ain't leaving."

Light it up! Light it up!

Well, crap. Tyrell is ready to go. He edges away, even as a swelling shift in the crowd strikes all of us and we're knocked slightly apart. But I can't go, not without Will. We're not so little anymore, but I'm still older. He's my responsibility. He's not even supposed to be here.

"We agreed," I shout. "Any hint of violence, we bug out. It's not safe."

Will stops bouncing. "Nowhere's safe," he answers. "Isn't that the thing?"

I don't have an answer for that, but when the storefront glass shatters behind us, when the heat of the flames rushes our backs, it no longer matters.

TYRELL

"Let's get out of here," DeVante chokes out. I don't need to do the math on this one. The crowd dissolves around us. Screaming. Coughing. Running, except we can't. We're all penned in. Smoke pours out of the building that was behind us, and is now in front of us. It turns out, you can't help but turn to look when something is burning.

Bodies slam into me, from every side at once. Smoke billows around. My feet freeze against my will. Which way to run? Which way to run?

A voice from somewhere orders us to disperse. Can't they see we are trying?

"This way!" DeVante steps behind me. His hand is on my arm. When I turn my head toward him, I can see the opening he's spotted in the crowd. People are running, shouting, railing against the night. The cluster of bodies is thinning enough to make our escape.

Time to go.

A clump of police officers with their batons up charge across the street in front of me. They begin shoving protestors aside from the edges of the crowd. They fan out, circling the scrum, as if hunting the person who threw the bottle.

DeVante moves away, toward the gap. I glance back. "Robb, come on!"

One of the officers charges toward us. Two petite young black women stumble out of the throng right in front of us—and right in front of the officer. The first woman falls to her knees. Her arm is bleeding.

"I've got you." Robb reaches down and helps her to her feet. The second woman is scared, she's trying to get out of the way of the jostling crowd. You can tell by her tears. You can tell by the way she holds her green-gloved hands up to protect her face and chest. Someone behind her knocks her forward. She staggers into the cop.

His baton, already raised and ready, comes down hard on her. Crack! She screams as the cruel metal tube strikes her shoulder. She falls to the ground. The cop spins, putting his back to us, and brings the baton down on her again.

"Oh, hell, no!" Robb exclaims. "Police brutality!"

The moment hangs above me like a cloud, even as it's happening. Robb slips around me, light on his feet, like a breeze. His hand goes out, grabs the officer by the collar with one hand. His other hand knocks the baton aside and away from the woman on the ground.

OFFICER YOUNG

I feel under attack. I feel like a monster. All at the same time. It's not so easy to breathe through a mask. We do our duty. We do the uniform proud. We stand our ground against the mob that threatens to tear everything down.

I'm not alone. But I'm at the end of the line. Exposed.

We withstand the shouting. We step strong, in formation, to drive them back.

We withstand the surge of bodies. I hold my baton down at my leg, ready, but still. Poke with it, when anyone gets too close.

The hands that shove my shoulder, jarring my helmet, knocking me off balance, are the last straw.

Whirl around, find the nearest dark, guilt-ridden face. Slam it to the ground.

ROBB

The police officer pivots away from the girl on the ground. He charges past me, slams his forearm into Tyrell.

Tyrell goes down, the cop's knee in his back. "You're under arrest," the cop shouts. "Don't move, asshole!"

Shit. Oh, fuck.

More cops.

Will kneels beside the beaten girl. I turn and there is no way out. The cops surround us with shields engaged. We put our hands up, except for the girl, who can't move her right shoulder.

Some cop grabs my hands, wrenches them behind me. It's fast and it's fierce, and we know enough to go peacefully. The plastic band tightens around my wrists.

They don't even put us in the same van.

We're split up, me and Will, DeVante and Tyrell. I don't know where DeVante even went, or if they got him. Tyrell was taken to the ground and cuffed and chained. Me, shuffled into a paddy wagon with a bunch of hissing activists, plastic zip ties around our wrists. We sit where we are told to sit.

There is energy, excitement. The worst has happened, we have done what we came here to do. Our faces will be on the news. We are willing to go down for the cause, but I can see now that we won't. That we have it easy.

STEVE CONNERS

The call you fear. When it comes, there are no words. There is no breath. There is only your wife's hand, if you can find it, and at the moment you can't.

There is the chorus in the back of your mind: *He is alive. He is alive. He is alive.*

There is, too, the extra voice. The lone gunman with his rifle cocked: *For now.*

"Steve?" Will's voice is small. "We got arrested."

ZEKE

We are smoky. We are shell-shocked. We are grateful we parked my car ten blocks away, just in case. It's barely far enough. The community has heard the news. People pour out into the streets, curious, angry.

I grip the steering wheel tight, tight. Try not to look at anything but the road in front of us. We take the long way, because we don't want to be stopped. If we see a cop . . . I no longer know if I have it in me not to strike.

I have studied these phenomena, in school. The history of so-called riots. Watts. LA. Chicago. Ferguson. Baltimore. I have wondered, time and again, what stupid, reckless forces drive people out of their homes, into the night, to wreak havoc on their own neighborhood. The buildings they pass every day on the way to work, to school. The businesses they trust. Their very homes.

I know now. Nothing is simple.

The presence of tanks is confusing. Enraging. The powers that be are ready to wage war to keep us in our place. The imbalance, the injustice, is enough to make me want to light a bottle on fire. Sure enough.

I don't have a bottle. I don't have one. I don't have one, or I might.

"Let's go inside," Kimberly says.

We're parked in front of my building. We've been sitting in the car for a while, I guess. I don't know how long. She lays her hand over mine and gently peels my fingers from the wheel.

We climb to my apartment, wash up. When we sit on the couch, it is ostensibly to snuggle, but we are too wound up to find comfort. I put my arm around her. My knuckles stroke her upper arm. She leans against my chest.

"Your heart is racing," she observes.

Don't I know it.

"Did we wimp out?" I whisper. "Did we walk away from a fight?"

"No," she says.

But we did. We did. We did, and I don't know why we did. Or how.

I unwrap my arm from her and lean forward, resting my head on my knuckles, still clenched. "I didn't think it would really happen. That we'd lose control."

"It's been happening," she says.

"I thought we could keep it peaceful." My fists sit like rocks on my knees. "I should have been able to stop it."

"Okay, Superman," Kimberly says. "Tell me another one."

The burst of my laughter is unexpected and strange. I clamp a fist to my lips. Hmm. I still can't unclench my fingers.

"It's Sloan's fault," Kimberly insists. "No justice, no peace?"

Great. She's gonna throw that back in my face right now? I glare at her. "They're just words."

"How can anything be just words?" She closes her eyes. "Most of the time words are all we have."

I don't know if I agree with that, but I also know we shouldn't be talking about this. Not tonight.

"I think he wanted a riot," Kimberly says. "I think he was hoping for one."

"That's nuts."

She shrugs. "It's better press, isn't it? You notice he didn't stay for the actual announcement. He knew what would happen."

My brain swirls and glitches over the coldness in her voice. "That's unfair."

"Whatever."

I pull out my phone. There is much still to do tonight, apart from tending our own wounds. Let us not make new ones.

"We have to work," I say. "I'll check in with legal aid, you do social media?"

Kimberly nods. We open all the tech. Between our phones, my tablet, my laptop, and the TV, we can keep tabs on the conversation across platforms.

The coverage on TV is more chilling than usual. Maybe because we were there. One shot they keep returning to is the steps where we stood, which now is lined with people seated in rows with their hands bound.

On the split screen, Senator Sloan, already back in DC somehow, sits in the studio offering commentary. I run the timeline in my mind. He spoke at our event in the late afternoon, hopped a flight home, and got himself on TV from a safe distance. All in a matter of hours.

He knew what would happen. Kimberly's words float back to me. I push them away. Our cause is being covered on national TV because of Senator Sloan. We have an advocate who people respect. Why doesn't she see that?

"He sounds good, don't you think?"

"He always sounds good," Kimberly says softly. "He seems like a good person, but he's not."

"Why are you so down on him?" My voice snaps in my throat. It hurts a little.

She glances at me. "You don't really want to hear about it," she says. "You've already accepted the job, haven't you?"

KIMBERLY

"I can't talk about this now." Zeke tips his phone toward me. "We have to work."

"You only care about the work!" I cry. "How did I not see that?"

Zeke sighs. "There's—I mean, everything is on fire right now. Can we not do this?"

Easy for him to say.

"This is my life, too."

Zeke's phone rings. "I can't hold myself back, just because . . ."

"Just because of me? I hold you back?" The knives just keep on coming.

I move to gather up my purse, except I don't have one. No bags allowed at the protest. So I grab for my coat instead.

"You can't leave," Zeke says. "It's not safe."

"I *can* leave," I thunder. "You're not from around here. I keep forgetting. But this is *my* neighborhood. I belong here."

I fling the door open so hard it smacks the wall. My body is shaking and the plan is not well thought out. I rush down the stairs and out into the cold, cold night. I zip my coat, pull on my hat, and walk to the bus stop on the corner. I want to walk it off—standing still is enough to drive me crazy—but it's far, and it's dark, and out here by myself it no longer feels like a good idea to have left.

I huddle in the corner of the bus hut with my back against the glass. The street is deserted. Zeke lives far from the action, but not far enough. Sirens wail in the distance. Smoke rises over the buildings. The acrid smell of it comes wafting through now and again.

I'm on alert—a woman alone in the dark. I sense him coming almost as soon as he steps out of the building. His shoulders are hunched, his hands tucked into his jeans. In the split second that passes before I'm sure it's him, my heart rate doubles. I pull deep breaths to calm down, but knowing it is him isn't calming at the moment.

He steps into the street lamplight. "If you won't stay, at least let me drive you home."

If I stay, won't I be holding you back? It's on the tip of my tongue, but I'm out of energy. I can only gaze at him there in the barest glow of light. His cheeks are shiny. He sounds congested. Maybe it is all too much for him, too.

"Come on, I'll drive you."

"I don't want to talk anymore," I answer. The wounds to my heart are flowing, throbbing. I wish Zeke would put his hands to them, try to stem the damage.

"Me either," he says. "Just let me drive you. Please."

JENNICA

Kimberly comes in crying so loud, I can hear it all the way in my bedroom. I throw back the covers, rush to the door. There is no sleeping on a night like this anyway.

She is on her knees on the tile, still in her coat and hat and gloves. Her pink button screams UNARMED!

"Oh, my god." I kneel in front of her. "Are you hurt? I mean, are you injured?" Obviously she is hurt. We don't know what it means to not be.

Anchor: *Kristen Blum is live in Underhill tonight. Let's return to the live feed. Kristen, how are you doing out there?*

Blum: *We've gotten clear of the tear gas cloud. It's—well, it's chaos out here. I'm with—tell me your name?*

Black Youth: *I gotta?*

Blum: *I'm here with a young man who's attending the protest. What's it about for you tonight?*

Black Youth: *We here, standing up for all the oppressed people of the world, starting right here in Underhill. We standing up for the people who can't get justice under this legal system. We standing for all of us who afraid to walk the streets. Today for Shae, Tomorrow for All.*

Blum: *What's that liquid you're pouring on your face?*

Black Youth: *It's milk. To help the stinging. We was told to bring it.*

Blum: *Protestors have been advised to carry milk?*

Black Youth: *Yeah, man. We knew we was gonna get gassed.*

Blum: *What does it feel like? How are you feeling?*

Black Youth: *It burns. My eyes are gonna be okay, right? (pounds his chest) Here, not so much. They gunning for us, man. They coming to kill us all.*

Blum: *Why are you protesting tonight?*

Black Youth: *There's only so much a guy can take, yo. Sh-*beep* like this goes down, you gotta scream out.*

Blum: *Were you surprised by the verdict?*

Black Youth: *Hell no. We knew. They always do us like this. When you live in the hood you ain't expect justice. You expect to have to fight. That's all we out here trying to—*

Black Woman: *(appears behind Blum) All you people watching! All you white suburban news junkies. You all complicit! All of you!*

Blum: *Ma'am, hello. Do you have a comment—*

Black Woman: *Every last mother-*beep*-ing one of you. Sitting at home, shaking your head. We down here getting gassed, mother-*beep*-ers! When you gonna get off your fat *beep* *beeeeeeeep*—*

Anchor: *Uh, we're gonna mute the live feed for a moment. Clearly people are extremely angry surrounding tonight's grand jury verdict. For those just tuning in, we're live with Kristen Blum in Underhill, where earlier tonight the grand jury returned no indictment for Officer Darren Henderson in the shooting death of thirteen-year-old Shae Tatum. Let's just wait until . . . okay, here we are live on scene again. Kristen?*

Blum: *Uh, sorry for the interruption, folks. We're live in Underhill, and the situation is going downhill rapidly.*

Black Youth: *She ain't wrong, yo. Tonight we speaking truth and we speaking it loud. No time for bullsh-*beep*.*

whistling sound overhead

Blum: *(looks at the sky)* Police continue to fire tear gas into the crowd, trying to get people to disperse.

Black Youth: *(pulls up bandanna over his mouth)* Gotta go.

Blum: Thank you. Good luck out there.

  We can try to get a little closer to the action . . . well, here come some more folks. Excuse me, sir. You live in this neighborhood?

Black Man: *Born and raised. We seen a lot. We can't stand for it no more.*

Blum: *What brings you out here tonight? Why was it important to be here?*

Black Man: *This is my neighborhood. I'm here for my neighbors, the Tatums. That's a good family.*

Blum: *You live near the Tatums?*

Black Man: *Same building. They ain't deserve this. Ain't nobody deserves this.*

Blum: *Sir, what can you tell me—*

Black Man: *I'm out. You be safe, white lady.*

Blum: *I will. You too.*

Black Man: *Naw. I can't. The point is, you already BE safe. You white.*

Blum: *I don't think anyone in Underhill feels particularly safe at the moment.*

whistling sound overhead

Black Man: *(smiles) You the one with the camera. You keep it rolling, you hear?*

Blum: *We will.*

Black Man: *If they take us all down, you be the one left standing. You make sure the world knows what they done to us here tonight. You stay safe, white lady.*

Blum: *Stay safe, black man.*

Black Man: *(grinning) You wanna lay odds?*

EVA

Daddy is free! The jury has decided.

"You're free," Mommy says. She throws her arms around him, squishing me in between. We are all sitting on the couch, watching the news announcement together.

Daddy holds his head in his hands. "I'll never be free of it."

@Momof6: Law and order FTW! Henderson cleared. #SupporttheBoysinBlue

@WhitePowerCord: Life and death, reward and punishment, is the purview of God Almighty. Righteousness has been on our side from day one. #HeroCop

@Viana_Brown: We need a revolution, y'all. Can't stand for this. Can't stand for it. #TodayForShae #TomorrowForAll

@WesSteeleStudio: JUSTICE PREVAILS IN UNDERHILL! But the conspiracy against Officer Darren Henderson continues. What they won't tell you about the grand jury proceedings here. #MakeItKnown #SteeleStudioExclusive

@BrownMamaBear: Have the conversation with your children: How to be safe in the world with #KillerCops on the loose.

@KelvinX_: FIGHT THE POWER #BurnItDown #ToTheGround WE WILL RISE OUT OF YOUR ASHES

THE MORNING AFTER

PEACH STREET

Blood stains the concrete. Refuse drifts. Every item a question: who was wearing this shoe? Who sipped this ginger ale?

Signs flattened by footprints, dampened by dew and human fluids. Tears, sweat, blood, urine. This night has seen it all. The dawn now bears its own witness.

The signs are strewn about the street, and trampled:

BLACK POWER TO BLACK PEOPLE

TODAY FOR SHAE, TOMORROW FOR ALL

#OFFTHEPIGS

PEACE IN OUR TIME

ALL LIVES MATTER ONLY WHEN #BLACKLIVESMATTER TOO

They have been here before. The street stands witness to the wave of rage that hits, decade after decade. Generation after generation.

They march here, they shout here, they are beaten here, they light fires here.

Then they pave over the scars to make room for new ones.

WITNESS

The holding cell is crowded but quiet. You have been to this precinct before. The air tastes different on the other side of the bars. Everything is different this time.

You can no longer say you did nothing. You can no longer say you saw nothing.

You can still never admit what you have seen.

TYRELL

The ink on my fingertips is a story I never wanted to tell. They don't let me wash my hands, so it becomes a part of me. Walls and bars and the scent of everyone's fear and rage. The salty stink of blood and tears comes at me like a wave, like an ocean.

Or, the way I imagine an ocean might wave. I've never seen that. Never walked with my toes in the surf, never felt the rocking lull of the tide. Never wanted to. We dread the ocean because they brought us over on ships, and that kind of terror goes into your bones. Into your DNA. It becomes a part of you. A part of your children and your children's children, forever and again.

The ink on my fingers feels soft as my skin after a while. Not sticky, not leaving any kind of mark on the wooden bench. My thumbs stroke circles over my finger pads until the sensation all but disappears.

My mind drifts. I think about history. About Birmingham, and courage, and what it means to win. I think about missing class on Monday, and if they'll ever let me back. If anyone will know I'm here and come for me. My mother's disappointment and my father's glaring I-told-you-so. The life cycle of a black man in America—birth, struggle, prison, struggle, death.

I wanted to be different. I wanted my life to matter. I wanted to do a different kind of math—never tick marks on a wall counting down the days. There is an ocean in me.

Can't help but wonder how Tariq would feel about what I've done. What he would say to me now. Can he hear my whispered prayer? Is he listening? Is anyone? I don't know what I believe anymore. Don't know what to make of a world without justice, of a God who turns our best intentions into the dark.

The shit of it is, I know what Tariq would have said. He woulda got me on the phone straight off. *Ty, don't even think about coming home for this mess. You got out of Underhill. Stay out. I got you.*

My eyes sting for knowing it. Sting, for not listening in the first place. Sting, for the loneliness of this ice-cold wall and the bars I can't bear to look at, let alone touch.

In all this world, the one person I could ever count on is long gone. For a minute there, I thought I was going to survive it. I thought I was strong enough to survive the world without him.

Tariq, I tried.

I tried to stand up. They shoved me back down.

Are you ashamed of me?

ROBB

"Dad, we can't leave without Tyrell and DeVante." He can afford to bail us all out. It's the least we can do. I mean, Dad's here now. He must have chartered a flight in order to pick me up from the holding cell personally.

"I've already made inquiries," he says. "Tyrell is remanded."

I'm confused. "They're keeping him in custody? No, we have to try again."

"He's being charged with assaulting a police officer."

"What?" Confusion fades and something achy takes its place. "He didn't assault anyone."

I rush over to the nearest counter, where a uniformed officer sits. "You've made a mistake. Tyrell is innocent."

The desk officer smirks. "Tell it to the judge."

Dad grips my shoulders and bustles me outside. "Don't meddle in someone else's business."

"He didn't assault anyone. It was—" I can't admit the truth. When push comes to shove, it would be a confession. What is the penalty for assaulting a police officer? Would I go to prison? "It was someone else," I finish.

"You saw it happen?" Dad says. He pulls out his phone as we stride toward wherever he parked the car. "I'll find out who Tyrell's lawyer is."

"Can you get him a good lawyer? He can't afford one."

Dad shrugs. "There are good people in the public defender's office. This is what they're there for."

I grab his arm. "No, seriously, he needs a good lawyer. The best. I—I feel responsible." I am responsible. "I mean, I was the one who wanted to go to the demonstration."

"I'm proud of you for standing up," Dad says. "Though, I wish you could find a way to do it peacefully."

Peace is for shit. Is what I want to say. What is the penalty for beating an unarmed woman? Wouldn't anyone have done what I did, seeing that?

"You've seen the footage," I remind him. "The cops are the problem."

Dad shakes his head. He steps off the curb at his parking space. "They're doing their jobs."

"Tell that to Shae Tatum."

Dad glares at me over the roof of the car. "Not what I meant."

But isn't that the heart of it, still? I glance back at the police department building. The flow of people in and out is constant, frenzied.

"I can't believe this."

"Get in the car," Dad says. "We're going back home."

Home, maybe. Back, not so much. There's no going back.

I'm not outside of it anymore. I can't pretend I'm innocent. That white privilege doesn't affect me, or that I haven't done anything to make any of it worse. I'm part of the problem. All the things I didn't understand made me part of the problem. I will always be part of the problem.

MELODY

Blinking light. Beeping sounds. A mechanical hum. Squeaking, from somewhere. Voices that sound like whispers, but not.

Ow.

Pain. Vibrating through me. My chest, my arm. My shoulder is on fire.

That miserable moaning sound . . . oh, that's me.

"Shh. Hang on. Shhh." Brick is here. "Nurse! We need a nurse in here!"

I suck my tongue, trying to get life back in it. "Brick?"

He's at my side. "Hey, there." His hand comes up, strokes my face.

"What are you doing here?" I'm in the hospital. I can tell now. I can feel the thin sheets under my heels. I grip the bed bars with the hand that can move. It's cool. Brick's fingers close over mine. They're warm.

"How come you don't have proper emergency contacts listed in your phone?" he asks. "They said they called me because I was the last number you dialed."

"You're good enough," I assure him. "You came." That means something. To rush to someone's bedside. It means something.

Ow. Breathe.

"Nurse!" Brick shouts. "Someone get in here!"

"I lost you in the crowd," I murmur. That's what comes back first, the moment when our hands slipped apart.

"I'm sorry," he says. "I don't know what happened. You were there and then you weren't." He strokes my cheek. "You're so damn tiny."

"I'm tougher than I look."

"At least you weren't arrested," he tells me. *Arrested?*

The night, the march, the melee. It all comes rushing back. The baton. Falling down. Someone knocking the cop off me. Who?

340

"Ow," I repeat. The pain is blinding, stabbing. I let my eyes close.

"Nurse!" Brick calls. "We need some pain meds in here!"

"It's not time yet," a woman's voice says. "Stop yelling, please."

"Look at her face," Brick thunders. "It's time."

Ow.

They argue. Brick is fierce. You wouldn't expect it of someone in his line of work, but he's fiercest when he's fighting for someone else. I wonder if he knows that about himself. Or if he'd want to know. It's probably not great for his street cred. I laugh to myself.

The pain is less now. I'm floating.

Brick's hands are on mine. "You're okay," he says. "You're okay."

I'm not, though, am I? My shoulder is on fire. Even as the pain dulls from the meds, it still smolders. Is it broken? Am I broken?

"How's the other girl?" I ask. The one I was running with. We tried to get away.

"What other girl?"

"I don't know. There was a girl."

Brick shakes his head. "I don't know."

Sadness floods me. I don't know who she is. I'll never know how the night turned out for her.

My hand relaxes under Brick's. It's hard to hold the bar anymore. I don't see the reason to try. He places my fingers gently on my stomach. "Rest," he says. "I'll come see you again later."

Brick's here. He's here for me. Things are okay even though they're not okay. I can sleep.

I wonder what this medicine is. I can feel it getting all up in my veins, softening my body into sleep. Whatever it is, it's the good stuff. Lucky my job comes with health insurance. This is going to be expensive.

OFFICER YOUNG

"They can't keep this up," O'Donnell says. "They're gonna wear themselves out."

"Not before we drown in paperwork," says the desk sergeant. "Christ, look at all these arrest reports."

O'Donnell throws a pen at him. "Don't take the Lord's name in vain, for God's sake." They laugh.

I laugh along with them—some things are automatic. Some things come easy. Some things, you don't think about until after.

My mind is crammed with images from last night. Adrenaline does that. Makes you remember every tiny moment of stress. Particularly the moment—*Crack!*—when my baton came down, shattering the girl's shoulder.

A girl. Small as anything. A hundred pounds soaking wet, as they say. Unarmed. In the light of day, I think, she couldn't have hurt me. There and then, I wasn't so sure.

It shakes me.

It shakes me, not being sure. You have to be sure. To lash out is a last resort. Always.

Always.

"They can't keep it up," O'Donnell says again. "Twenty bucks says it's all over after tonight."

A flare-up, we call it. A small dose of civil unrest. It never lasts. Look at the history. The worst offenders get arrested and the crowd loses momentum. Loses interest. When there's no one to follow, everybody goes home. We crack down hard, to ensure it.

Crack!

I consider the unbridled rage it must take for a girl that small to come

at a guy like me, someone armed and in uniform. She had nothing, and still she came at me. I think about how it feels to fight for your life. What it looks like when you have nothing to lose.

It isn't over. We'll be right back out there tonight. And the next night. And the next.

"I'll take that action," I tell O'Donnell. He raises his brows. I pull two tens out of my wallet, toss them on the desk. "They can keep it up at least a few more days. They don't see any other choice."

DeVANTE

"I'm sorry," I tell Uncle Steve on the drive to the precinct. "You must blame me for dragging Will into this."

Steve's hands are on the wheel, but he turns to look at me. "Not at all," he says. "Not even a little bit."

I blame me, I guess. I ran. I got out. When the ship was going down, I took the only lifeboat.

They all got arrested. Will. Robb. Even Tyrell, which seems so absurd to me that I don't even know what to do with it.

But not me. I ran.

It's not like I thought it through. I didn't make a choice. It just happened. I saw an opening and I took it. I thought they were all right behind me. Why weren't they? If I'd known they were getting caught, I would have tried to help. I think. I hope. But, I mean, what could I really have done? Get arrested alongside them? Why should I feel this bad for saving myself?

If last night proves anything, it's that there is no actual justice. There is only getting lucky, or not.

"It's not your fault," Steve says. "Try to get out from under that."

I can't. I can't. "I know. I will."

"We should blame the system," Steve says. "This broken justice system. That's the truth. But I don't. I blame myself, too."

"What? How is it your fault? You weren't even there."

Steve shakes his head. "For not stopping you from going. For not going with you. I feel like I could have stopped it."

The car rolls along through the refuse-strewn streets of Underhill. There's nothing left to say. The system is broken. The scales are tipped. No balance. All the fault slides one way. We are two black men, carrying the weight of the world.

Black men. We are always guilty. Always to blame.

STEVE CONNERS

We park in front of the precinct. "Wait here," I tell DeVante. I don't want to complicate matters inside.

My cell vibrates as I'm walking toward the door I was instructed to use. JOHN LANSBURY.

"John." I answer, against my better judgment.

"The verdict is going to complicate our lives. We expected this, but not the extent of the rioting. We need a meeting."

"I'm taking half a sick day," I tell him. "I called into the office this morning."

"Let's meet in the conference room at ten," he suggests.

"I won't be in until one," I tell him.

"Today? Why would you make a doctor's appointment today of all days? We have to turn this plan around ASAP. Anything we can do to counteract the impression that the police department is racist."

To counteract the impression . . . I stare up at the cold, grungy facade of the building in front of me. *To counteract the impression* . . .

"Steve?" John barks. "We need you."

"Take me off the account," I say. "I'm not doing it anymore."

John starts to respond but I don't know with what.

I've hung up.

ZEKE

"Get off your butt and go talk to the girl, Ezekiel!" My sister busts out my full name for emphasis. I'm curled up on the couch trying to watch reruns of *Jeopardy!* Except I'm not trying to beat them to answer. I'm not even keeping score. Monae sits in the armchair, eyeing me with annoying perception.

"Leave me alone, *Mom*," I grumble.

Monae squeals in outrage. "Oh, no, he didn't!"

My eyes are closed, but I sense her coming at me. "Oof. Monae . . ."

She's sitting on me. Her bony butt right square on top of my hip. She punches me lightly in the stomach. "You. Take. That. Back." Now she's tickling me.

"Monae!" I squirm out from under her, but she's pinned me good. "I'm not in the mood for—ahhh. Ahhh!" We scrabble for control.

"Take it back!" she shouts.

"I take it back! Uncle."

Monae smacks my butt. "Go talk to her."

"Not now." I rearrange my blanket. "I think we broke up."

"You 'think'?" Monae settles on the coffee table.

"I'm pretty sure, yeah."

"Zeke, honestly." She sips a glass of water that came from I don't know where. Tormenting me is thirsty work, apparently. "That's the kind of thing you want to be sure about before you get this committed to wallowing."

"What are you talking about?" I shift so I can see the TV past her.

Monae reaches for the remote control and powers the whole set off.

"Hey. I was watching that."

"You should be at SCORE," she says. "It's kind of a big day over there. And instead, you're here."

"Shut up." As if I don't feel guilty enough about all the ways I'm failing. I bit off more than I could chew. Everything got out of hand. My protest was a disaster. Almost a hundred people arrested. Twenty hospitalized, not even including all the folks who got gassed and showed up at the clinic. What kind of organizer am I ever going to be, with this track record? I bury my face in the throw pillows. "I screwed it all up. Kimberly hates me."

"That girl is gaga for you." Monae leans forward and squeezes my shoulder. "Did she actually say the words 'I want to break up'?"

"No," I moan. It was so much worse.

"Or, 'I don't think we should see each other anymore'?"

"No." The tiniest stirring of hope flutters inside me.

"Seriously, bro," Monae insists. "You're not being yourself. What's it going to take to get you off my couch and back to work?"

The pillow absorbs the brunt of my guttural protest. Monae yanks it out from under me. My teeth click as my face bounces off the couch cushion. "Hey."

"You need to tell me what happened. Tell me everything. You are in desperate need of a girlfriend whisperer."

KIMBERLY

Zeke texts me.

I have to be in the office all day. Can I come over later? We should talk.

My heart is exploding. Yes! Of course. I want to talk. I attempt several versions of a response. Exclamation point, or no exclamation point? Multiple exclamation points? I end up with:

Okay. Can I help at the office?

There is a pause.

Don't you have to work? I can't get into our thing yet.

I want to see him. I want to see him so bad that I'm tempted to just show up anyway. Work can just be work, right? Instead I say:

I can help from here. What do you need?

I spend the morning working on press materials and placing calls to legal aid. Zeke arrives before dinnertime. Jennica's still at work, so we have the apartment to ourselves.

"Hi." He gives me a little pecking kiss.

"Hi," I say. Then I blurt out, "We had a fight."

"Yeah." Zeke shrugs out of his coat. "Our first fight. It's kind of a landmark."

Our first fight. The way he says it makes it sound romantic. Some of the awkwardness is stripped away. Not all of it.

"Wine?" I offer. "Or tea?"

"Tea is good," he says. "Wine later?" His voice sounds hopeful, like he wants us to be talking for a while.

"That sounds good. We have all night." I set the kettle on and he hovers near the counter.

"I'm sorry, Kimberly," Zeke says, as I pull out the mugs. "I am the sort of person who gets pretty upset when I feel like I have failed at something. Sometimes I take my feelings out on other people."

The way he says it is funny. Stilted, or something. It sounds like he's repeating something someone told him about himself.

"You haven't failed," I assure him. "Why do you think you failed?"

"The protest," he says. "And then I was mean and you ran away. So, double fail." He shrugs self-deprecatingly. "I didn't handle it well."

"I didn't, either," I admit. "We were too stressed. That part was my fault. I brought up . . . things I shouldn't have."

"I'm taking the job in DC," Zeke says.

"I know," I answer. "I'm happy for you. And I don't want you to go."

"I know," he says. "I love you."

"I love you, too."

The teakettle whistles. *Zeke loves me!* I feel like we should kiss or something, but instead I fuss with the water and the tea bags. We sit on the couch.

Zeke pauses. "Kimberly, could you tell me more about your relationship with Senator Sloan?"

That stilted voice again. Is he working from a script?

"It's a little hard to talk about that." There's so much I want to tell him, and so much I'm scared to say out loud.

Zeke puts down his tea and takes mine, too. He holds my hands tightly. "You can talk to me about anything."

I stare at our hands. "I know."

"It seems like . . . maybe there's some history there?" he says. "Did he hurt you somehow?"

I can't look at Zeke. "He was nice to me in a time when a lot of people weren't. He made me believe . . ." I let my voice trail off. "I owe him a lot, I guess."

"I don't want to work for someone bad."

Oh. He *was* listening. He believed me.

"It's complicated," I admit. "The things he's famous for, I mean, he did those things. He makes a difference."

Zeke takes my hands. "Then what is it?" He's gentle. "I know you. You don't lash out at people for no reason."

"I—" I lower my head. "The truth is, I'm mad at him because he's taking you away." It is a deep truth and a huge lie all at once. It shatters the scale.

"Kimberly—"

"We just got started. I don't want to lose you." My voice gets all clogged and annoying.

Zeke frowns. "Nothing happens immediately. It's not until the summer. Not until I graduate. The job would start after that. That's a lot of time to figure out what we want to do."

We. The tiniest glimmer of hope flares, then fades. The reality of what is to come is too big, too heavy.

"In other words," Zeke says, leaning toward me. "I have four months to convince you that you should come with me."

EVA

In the end, it is just Mommy and me who get to enjoy the amenities. Daddy
has to pass a test with a doctor so that he can go back to work.

Mommy lounges in a stretchy rubber chair while I splash in the big
swimming pool until all of me is a prune. We eat fancy food that I don't
know how to say the names of. Some of it is yum. Some of it is yuck.
(Snails? Ewww.)

"We should call Daddy on the phone," I say.

"No, I don't think we should," Mommy answers.

JENNICA

Kimberly is leaving. She says she hasn't decided, but I know her. Maybe better than she knows herself.

We snuggle in my bed, for the first time in weeks, while she tells me all about it. Her body is warm against my back and she has her arms around me. It's perfect. It's lovely. I could forget all of it, I could pretend that this is how it will be forever. But she won't stop talking.

She promises to find me another roommate. One of the SCORE girls, or something. If she goes, that is.

She and Zeke will pack a U-Haul and tow his car behind it. If she goes, that is.

She says I can keep some of her furniture, partly because she doesn't want to leave me in the lurch, and partly because it will be exciting for them to pick things out together for their new place, which will be small, of course. She has been looking at DC rental listings online for days. If she goes, that is.

It is a lot of talking about "ifs" for someone who hasn't made up her mind.

I want to tell her, *Don't go*. I even know what to say to convince her. I know her better than she knows herself.

But I don't say those things. In the back of my mind, in between all the "ifs," I know what my dear friend is trying to say. She wants me to know that I am strong, that I have always been strong, that I can be strong even without her.

So I stay still, and quiet, soaking up Kimberly's smell and her touch. I remind myself that everything is fleeting. I remind myself that this place we are in, these moments together are what made me strong. I haven't always been that way.

We lie together for a long time, and eventually she does grow quiet. When all the "ifs" have been spoken, they spread over us like a blanket.

"You're going," I whisper.

"Maybe." Her voice is sleepy now. But I won't send her to her own bed. Another night or two of comfort may be all I ever get. She sighs. "It's such a big decision. Scary."

"He's so good," I remind her. "You love him. And he can take you everywhere."

For some of us, going anywhere is impossible. Kimberly is not one of those people. She never has been. Zeke knows and I know. And I love her enough to make sure she knows it, too.

WILL/eMZee

My room is too warm today, but it's where I want to be. I pace between the beds, over to the window and back. Frost has formed on the outside corners of the window, and when I press my hands to the glass it feels nicely cool.

Like every day now, I think about going out. I pack my bag and in the end it remains on my rug. Sitting ready.

When Tariq Johnson died, it was about who we are. Every black boy. Are we the faceless, hoodie-clad punks? Are we the honor students, or the gang members? Are we so flawed that we deserve this fate?

When Shae Tatum died, it was different. It was about how they treat us, no matter how good or innocent we are. It was about how a black face is a black face is a black face. A threat no matter how you slice it.

Steve knocks at my door. I can tell his knock from my mother's, because he raps, then waits. Mom raps with one hand while the other is already turning the door handle.

"What do you want?"

Steve takes that as an invitation, which it isn't. He comes in, carrying a few plastic shopping bags. He lays them on my second bed, and I can tell what they are by their shape, by the way they settle. Art supplies.

He tugs at the butts of the bags, spilling them out. Notebooks and canvases, paints and pencils and charcoal. A cornucopia.

"The woman in the shop said these were good," he says. "A variety. I didn't know what to say when she asked what medium, so . . ."

I nod. They are good. Everything an artist could want.

Almost everything.

"I don't want you to give up your art," he says. "I don't want you to be afraid out in the world."

You were right, he's saying. *Black men are in prison no matter what we do.*

BRICK

I sit at the diner counter, noshing on some pie.

Jennica says, "So, if you know anyone looking for a roommate, tell her to come by, okay?"

"Yeah, I got you," I say. "And if you ever need help with the rent, you let me know. I'll spot you."

She smiles. "The bank of Brick?"

I grin. "Interest free, for good friends like you."

Jennica glances around the diner. It's not crowded. She's not shirking, to be chatting me up. She leans across the counter. "Are you sure?" she says.

"Am I sure?"

She's close now. Her hands cover mine, then slide up my forearms to the elbow. "Are you sure that 'friends' is what you want to be? Just friends?"

Her mouth is inches from mine. My lips part of their own accord. I've dreamed of this moment. Literal actual dreams in the night. Where I woke up and thought we were together, and had to remind myself in the mirror, *She's not yours. Not yet.*

"Brick?" Jennica says. "You want me, don't you? You want more?"

We're both surprised when I lean back. "Um."

"Oh." She's startled. Her eyes go wide.

"I—" I can't believe I'm about to say this. "Jennica, I think I'm with someone."

"Oh." Jennica pulls her hands back. "Never mind. I was just messing around. I didn't mean anything by it."

It's an obvious lie, but let's go with it. "Sure," I say. "I know."

"It's Melody, right?"

"Yeah, how'd you know that?"

She shrugs. "I know you. And I know her."

Now I really wish what just happened hadn't happened, because I really want to talk to her about it. "It's weird," I tell her. "I'm not that kinda guy."

Jennica cocks her head. "What kind is that?"

I laugh. "Loyal. 'I'm with someone'? Did you ever think you'd hear me say that?"

Jennica pulls a towel from under the counter. "You've been loyal to me," she says. "I'm the one who screwed up."

"Nah."

She shakes her head. "I'm never gonna—" Her eyes well up with tears. "Everything is falling apart."

Oh, no. Shit. I don't know how to make it better. "Listen, we're gonna be friends, right? You and me forever."

"Besties," Jennica says, with a smile. She blinks hard, wipes her cheeks, and reaches for my empty plate.

"I gotta go," I tell her. "Got an errand." I toss some cash on the counter for her. Even more than usual. I'll be back, of course I will. But it might be a minute. And even when I am, it won't be the same. I know it won't. We both know.

●●●

I step to the sidewalk, and hurry on my way. It's pickup time. I've agreed to walk the girls to and from school while Melody is recovering. It's a good thing to do. I need to spend more time with Sheila anyway. I've been focused elsewhere, but losing Shae makes everything different. Guys in my line of work don't tend to live to old age. If I'm lucky, I got five, maybe ten years left, before there's a bullet with my name on it.

Can't spend it waiting. Waiting to get arrested. Waiting to do what's right. Waiting for a woman. Waiting to die.

Melody gave me this book by Huey P. Newton. It's called *Revolutionary Suicide*. I been reading it. Turns out, it's got nothing to do with killing yourself. It's about how we're all dying. Every minute. It's all about deciding how you want to go down. Or, what you're gonna go down fighting for.

Huey says guys like me can be more than the labels the world puts on us. I get to decide who I am. I'm the leader of the 8-5 Kings. That makes this my neighborhood. I can do my part to make sure people can walk the streets safe. Not shoot-'em-up style, going toe to toe with the cops, like I thought. Nothing doing. I'm gonna start me an organization.

I'm not the type to take my fortune and retire to an island. Nah, I'm going out in a blaze of glory, and I'm gonna enjoy the ride.

The sun is shining. I got a good coat. I got money. I got a good woman. I got a little girl waiting who loves me.

TINA

Sometimes
when I first wake up
I forget for a minute
that Shae is gone.
I plan out what I will say to her
when we meet
on the corner of the street.
The thing I say will be funny
and Shae will laugh and laugh.

Sometimes
when the light is right
and the world is quiet
I can squint my eyes
turn off my mind
pretend I hear Tariq's voice.
Tina, he says,
Whatchu squinting for?
When I open them
he's gone.

ACKNOWLEDGMENTS

I remain deeply grateful to my family and the many friends who support, uplift, comfort and inspire me as I work. Special thanks to Will Alexander and his entire family for keeping me company and making sure I ate meals when the deadlines were looming. Also thanks to Kobi Libii, Nicole Valentine, Emily Kokie, Cynthia Leitich Smith, Nova Ren Suma, Tirzah Price, Alice Dodge, and Kerry Land for their support, as well as all of my colleagues at Vermont College of Fine Arts. Thanks to my agent, Ginger Knowlton, and her team at Curtis Brown, Ltd., for their work in bringing my writing to the world. Thanks to Noa Wheeler for sparking the idea for *How It Went Down* and helping bring that book to life with sufficient success to support this companion book! Finally, to Kate Farrell, my editor on this book, for leaping into the existing world of these characters and patiently guiding me through the creative process.

For all the teachers, librarians, parents, and others who share this book with teens, I'm grateful for the efforts you make to bring awareness to acts of bias and violence occurring in our midst. I hope the book sparks conversation, reflection, and a desire to work for equality and justice for all.